1. 29

Ride
A
White
Dolphin

RANDOM HOUSE NEW YORK

Anne
Maybury

Ride
A
White
Dolphin

Ride
A
White
Dolphin

I

The shutters creaked as I opened them onto the fluid gold of the early Venetian morning. And as the quiet of the room met the stillness of the lagoon, I thought a voice behind me called my name.

"Leonie. Leonie . . ."

But when I looked over my shoulder, the man lying on his side in the huge, carved bed seemed asleep. I wondered what place I had in his dreams.

The mosaic floor of the room was cold, and I slid my feet into sandals, went out onto the balcony that stretched the width of the house and leaned my arms on the centuries-worn stone.

Ahead of me, the lagoon lay like a sleek and translucent mirror, broken only by the vibrating pattern of passing boats:

a skiff laden with vegetables; a milk barge piled with crated bottles; and a gondola, swan-prowed, lopsided and loaded with potted palms for someone's party that night. Away across the water, the domes and spires of the distant islands seemed separated from the earth by cushions of mist.

Venice, Europe's last fantasy; Rorke Thorburn, the man I loved and had married; the Ca' di Linas, owned by Rorke's aunt, Berenice Montegano, who was one of the kindest and most generous of women. Everything set for perfection.

Yet, wherever I went—drinking coffee at Quadri's in the morning sunlight in the Piazza San Marco; walking the twisted streets; or wandering through Berenice's vast, dim rooms—a shadow that was not my own (was not, in fact, even human) lurked by my side. I could name it. It was apprehension. But I could not begin to explain it.

On the previous night I had even spoken to Rorke about my unease.

He had said, laughing, "That's not very extraordinary. The fact that Berenice lives in this enormous house on her own puzzles a lot of people."

"It's not that. I have a feeling that something happened during the past week that I should have linked with a memory of something else. I know that sounds vague—"

"It does."

"I try to identify it, but I can't. Yet all the time it's nagging at me."

"Well, I shouldn't let it," he said easily. "It's probably just the effect Venice has on you. You can't erase a thousand years of history with a few hundred motor launches and electric light. The city is full of ancient glamour and old evil. And anyway, at every moment of the day and night, there's something wrong somewhere. You're just picking up vibrations from the atmosphere."

I said soberly, "It isn't like that at all. Whatever it is, it involves us and, I believe, this house."

"I'll diagnose your trouble," Rorke had said, and he ran his fingers through my hair so that it fell about my shoulders. "You're suffering from the anticlimax that comes to everyone after nearly a year of marriage. The excitement is over, and you're facing the thought of a lifetime with me. You're lacking stimulus, and your subconscious mind is looking for excitement. Don't worry. If the dullness of existence with me becomes unbearable, I won't hold you to any promise you don't want to keep. That's what we said in the beginning, isn't it?"

No possessiveness; no clinging to each other after the mutual need had gone . . .

I had reached up my arms to him and said, "I'll never want to leave you."

"Wild words, my darling. People change, grow up—grow apart."

⁂

Looking out over the lagoon with the early morning air soft on my face, I remembered how afraid I had been of those cool, almost impersonal words. So afraid that I had gone to sleep with my face buried in the pillow close to Rorke's head and woke after a while, nearly suffocated, fighting for breath. But I had needed the reassurance of that closeness.

As I watched Venice rising from the mist into golden life, I tried to pinpoint the person in Berenice's house from whom the sense of foreboding originated.

Berenice herself? I thought of the way she would sometimes stop what she was doing and, head tilted like an alert sparrow, eyes sharpened, would seem to listen for something or someone.

Or Willy, the little, fat, pink-faced artist who crept about the house with a naïve, smiling vacuousness. Willy Galbraith . . .

I wondered if that was his real name. All we knew was that it was the one he had given Berenice when he had been brought to her house the previous November on a freezing foggy night after being found, shivering and half-starving, in a dark corner of an alley near the Chiesa San Bartolomeo.

Berenice had not only given him food and shelter but had opened up a room on the top floor for him to use as a studio and had kept him supplied with paints and canvases. Willy, who came as a waif for one night, was now a permanent member of the household, much to the barely disguised disgust of Cèsara, Berenice's devoted maid, and Filiberto, her boatman.

Finally, there was Rorke. The necessary secrecy of his job did not worry me. Before my marriage I had also worked at Melarper's, that huge conglomeration of buildings outside London where scientific research was carried on. And although the ways of the men employed in security and the complications of countering industrial espionage were matters in which I had never been directly involved, I did not let this secret side of Rorke's life overshadow me. I looked on his job realistically and, so far as I was concerned, there was no alarming mystique about it.

The only time I protested was when my pleasant London life was ripped from under me by plans which involved me, but about which I had not been consulted.

It had happened one day during the previous April. Rorke had broken a long, easy silence between us, saying, "I'm being sent to Milan."

I was standing at the window of our London house looking out at the first slivers of rain. Opposite me, beyond the line of plane trees, were the other little houses of the square, all built for the Huguenots after their flight from France. Every house had iron trellises and bright front doors: vermilion and green and shrimp-pink.

I said, "To Milan? Oh, for how long?"

"A month, two months—perhaps more."

I shot round. "Oh, Rorke!"

He laughed at my dismayed face. "It isn't a major disaster. I'm taking you with me. It's all planned."

"Why are you—we—going?"

"Melarper's is loaning me to Ferris Caretta. There's a special job that has to be done. I'm the only man who can do it—and that's not conceit."

I knew better than to ask what that job was.

Rorke said, "The arrangements have been made. You'll be staying with Berenice in Venice, and I'll come out to you for weekends."

Suddenly I was angry. "You planned it all without consulting me."

"I had no choice. Everything had to be arranged immediately. Calls put through to Milan and Venice—"

"You could surely have put one call through," I said dryly, "and asked if I wanted to be parked in Venice when you were in Milan."

"You'll be happier with Berenice at the Ca' di Linas. You'd feel very alone in Milan."

"Alone? When you would be there?"

"The Ferris Caretta place is a good thirty miles out of the city. I could be tied up at odd times during the day and night, and you'd be very bored. You said you loved Venice when I took you there to meet Berenice."

"I know I did. But I'd have been happier if you had given me a choice. And do you realize," I added, still angry, "that I'm going to have a very bad reputation when we return to London? Ten months in my first job in Cumberland, six months with Melarper's and now just three months at the Chelsea library."

"I'll be ready to lay a bet with you that they'll have you back when we return. Good reference librarians are hard to come by." He had moved near me and drew me back against him. His hands began caressing me and his face was against my hair. I tore myself away from him.

"Rorke, I'm not a child to be told 'do this,' 'go there,' 'do that.' I need to be considered—"

"I *am* considering you. Berenice is very fond of you, and it's best that you stay there."

"Best for whom?"

"Good grief! What do you think I'm intending to do in Milan, run a brothel? At the Ca' di Linas, you'll have company all day, and anyway I'll be there at the weekends."

"Thanks for the crumbs."

His irritation fled. He burst out laughing. "Oh, Leonie, how young you are!" He pulled me down onto the settee and took my face in his hands and turned it toward the firelight. "You have a lovely mouth," he said and kissed me.

I capitulated at once. I lay with him in the soft raining twilight with the gentle thud of the fire-flames, and thought how we judged people from our own standards: I from mine, Rorke from his. Our needs were so different. If I loved him, I had to accept that not only was he a man with an important and secret job, but that his need for me was largely a physical one. If I wanted to hold him, I had to compromise, to accept him as he was, convinced that love was a one-sided thing where we were concerned—I loved him, but he merely needed me.

*   *   *

I turned away from the light shimmering across the lagoon, back into the shadowy room, impelled by a need for reassurance, wanting Rorke—the man asleep in the gilded bed.

Berenice had given us a huge room with heavy black oak furniture, luxurious old damask curtains and lovely views from the tall windows that led onto a balcony.

There was a carved pediment over the door, and the faded fresco around the walls depicted ancient myths—Jupiter and Mercury, Diana and Juno, and among them were winged horses and unicorns and a girl with streaming golden hair riding a white dolphin. I loved that girl. She was so full of laughter and rode her dolphin with a gay recklessness in defiance of the lofty, unsmiling gods and goddesses.

I crossed the room and sat down very gently on the edge of the bed and touched Rorke's hair and felt it spring back, strong and dark, under my fingers. He stirred slightly, moving his lips as if in some dreaming protest.

Sleep often irons out the lines and makes a face younger. To Rorke it gave a grave maturity. He was thirty, but he could have been older, for the contours were lean and the shadows beneath his cheekbones deep. He was not particularly good-looking, but the overall effect of his features was arresting. I liked the straightness of his nose, the curve of the nostrils reminding me of the sculptured heads of the ancient Greeks. His mouth and chin were strong; his skin clear. It was an aloof face, withdrawn—secretive almost—and slightly impatient even in sleep.

I cried his name silently. My hand went out again to touch him and immediately withdrew. He had a right to his sleep. In my mind, I said, "Is it working? *Is* it, Rorke?"

We didn't deserve failure. I became Rorke's wife knowing that although he told me he loved me—and believed what he said—his feeling at the time of our marriage was a rebound emotion from an affair which had been violent and tormented and hopeless.

Some small movement I must have made woke him and Rorke was immediately alert. It was always that way, as though he slept with half his mind awake and aware. His amazing dark blue eyes looked from me to the clock.

"Seven," he said.

"And a Saturday. No work; nothing to get up early for."

"Nothing to get up for," he repeated softly and reached for me. "But every reason to stay here . . ."

As he held me, I wanted to cry, "I love you." I didn't say it because it would have been like a plea for an answering echo from him, and I had vowed to myself when we married that I would never ask him for love, never insist on words he might use in order to please me. We had, however, a perfect physical love affair, a coming together that was utterly mutual, utterly complete.

I strung out the minutes of our closeness until I heard Berenice open the shutters of her room below us. Whenever she did this she set in motion the delicate, dancing wind bells that hung over the huge canary cage near her window.

Rorke unfolded me, kissed me and said, "Up!"

Then while I dressed, he hung about the room, listening to the complicated radio set—incredibly small, remarkably accurate—with which Melarper's had presented him and which traveled with him wherever he went.

While he listened, he went to a carved oak table and lifted some sketches that lay there, twisting the papers, frowning.

"Who is it?" he asked me.

I laughed. "Just sketches I made of bits of me by looking at my reflection in the mirror. Adrian has seen them and has let me start on a self-portrait."

Rorke said, "You aren't being very flattering to yourself. You've made your eyes too small."

"I'm not a very good artist. But taking lessons keeps me occupied while you're away."

"You should go to the Lido and get some sun and swimming. The Carters spend all their days there, and they told you you'd always be welcome to join them." He tossed the sketches back on the table. "But if working in a stuffy studio is what you prefer to do . . . well, then, of course, do it."

There was nothing stuffy about Adrian Rand's beautiful studio, but instead of protesting I went up to Rorke and folded my arms about his neck. "I'd like most of all to be in London and to see you every morning and evening."

He flicked at my nose. "The trouble with you is you're conventional. Now, go and have breakfast. We're late. I'll be down in a few minutes."

*　　*　　*

I always held onto the marble banister as I went down the staircase because, for all its graciousness of line, its curves were treacherous. Once, when I first arrived, I had nearly fallen headlong to the mosaic floor below, and now I treated every marble step, cut by masons three hundred years before, with the utmost respect.

Above me, over the well of the central hall, still hung the armorial bearings of the Parasiano family. The red, white and gold carving of crossed lances over a salamander's head had never been removed by the original family because Count Luigi Parasiano had died just after the Second World War and there was no heir to receive his insignia.

Halfway down the staircase there was, on the wall, a very large portrait of a young woman. Her features were molded in the ancient Venetian concept of beauty, the longish nose, the golden hair. She wore an embroidered dress of green velvet, and there was a black patch on her brow in the shape of a half moon, which, Berenice explained, was probably put there to hide a smallpox scar after the disease had raced rampant among the fifteenth-century Venetians. The portrait had a name, "Floriana," but nobody knew the artist.

The hall below me was very empty. It was, Berenice said, damp and impossible to keep warm in winter. The mosaic floor had been washed over by numerous floods throughout the centuries. The few pieces of old furniture, heavy and ornate, which Berenice's husband, Luigi, had bought with the house, had had to be carried to the higher floors many times. Enormous double doors flanked by Doric columns opened out onto the water steps. "Some day," Berenice had once said, "I hope long after I'm dead, this house will slip gently, with others, into the lagoon."

The dining room doors on a half landing were open, but, with the shutters closed, the room was like a forest of dark green and black polished wood, for Berenice liked dimness in her house. Outside lay the small walled garden. It had been built up so that it was many feet above the level of the adjoining streets. Like most Venetian gardens, it was hidden from the outside world, and all that could be seen from narrow streets that ran along two sides was the tip of a myrtle tree and a few plumes of wisteria.

Rorke always said that Berenice's garden had no rest about it. He was right. It poured color upon the eyes—the brilliant orange of old-English nasturtiums and marigolds, the purple of bougainvillaea. There was also a lemon tree, a medlar which clung to the south wall, and the myrtle.

I had time before Cèsara served breakfast to go to the newsstand at the top of the *calle* for an Italian fashion magazine which was so popular that it sold out quickly.

I crossed the huge, dank-smelling hall and went through the side door that led to the narrow street where the expensive shops were just being opened. Silk blouses, scarves of glorious colors, showcases of jewelry copied from Renaissance styles were displayed behind the glass windows with loving care.

There were already a number of people elbowing each other for their copies of the morning paper at the newsstand. I found the magazine I wanted, handed the money to the newswoman and received my change.

As I did so, someone jogged my elbow, and the coins scattered to the ground. I bent to pick them up and simultaneously a man dived down to help me. Our heads almost met; our hands touched.

He was a middle-aged man with a small dark beard and bright, slightly bulbous gray-green eyes. He wore the wide-brimmed hat that some artists in the Zattere quarter of Venice choose as a kind of badge of their profession.

We laughed as we jerked ourselves away from the near collision, and I took the money he had picked up. Before I could thank him, the laughter went out of his face and he drew a long breath. When he spoke, he stammered slightly over the first words as if he were afraid of saying them. "F-forgive me, s-signora, b-but please listen to me."

His voice was low and urgent, his manner almost pleading. "You may think that I'm a little mad, but I assure you I am not. There is no way, yet, that you can know it, but I must warn you. There is tragedy around you; someone near you is going to kill—" He stopped suddenly and took two jerky steps away from me. "*Dio mio!* What am I saying?"

Just for a moment, his eyes held mine in a shocked stare. Then, as he turned abruptly away, I fled. I charged into two people, apologized and slowed down, trying to look at the small scene flippantly. A silly, sadistic man with nothing better to do than to scare women, playing at seeing "auras" and pretending that his "perception" dismayed him. The whole incident was just a sick joke. I tried to brush it out of my thoughts and paused to glance in a shop window, coveting a silk scarf in colors of garnet and green. The man at the newsstand was almost out of my thoughts. Almost . . . And then something struck me. *He had been a complete stranger, and yet he had spoken to me in English.*

How could he have known that I was not Italian? I was dark; I was wearing a dress I had bought in Venice and shoes that had come from the very *calle* down which I was walking. I had bought an Italian magazine and hadn't spoken a word when I took it, because before I could thank the woman in the newsstand, she had turned to serve someone else.

The man had spoken with an accent and could have been Italian or French or German for all I knew. I had never, to my knowledge, set eyes on him before. But I told myself that there was probably something very English about me and that it was absurd to feel afraid.

What he had said could have been just a malevolent attempt to make someone unhappy on that soft Venetian morning, for I could not believe that there was any aura of tragedy around me.

The past—my past—had not held unusual sadness. My mother had died the previous year in an influenza epidemic. My father had been dead for many years, but I hadn't grieved much for him, for he had lived most of his life away from us. My mother had once made the dry comment: "Your father is always looking for adventure because he has never quite grown up." And he died fighting for some vague cause in the Near East.

I had known for a long time before I left college the kind of work I wanted to do. The huge chemical and scientific industries drew me like a magnet. I found such excitement in the experiments and discoveries that would revolutionize the world, that I knew I would be content to be just a small cog in that great wheel. That was why I wrote to the personnel manager at Melarper's, the huge research station just outside London. There was a vacancy, they said, in one of their departments, and I went for an interview. However, I came out of that huge concourse of buildings certain that I hadn't the necessary qualifications for the job. I had fought through one of the rare November fogs to get to the place, and when the interview was over, I stood disconsolately on the steps hating to go home with the knowledge of my defeat.

As I hesitated, a car drew up and a man asked if he could give me a lift. He said, "I think we met in one of the corridors here." We had. I had walked into him, a little dizzy with nerves and hope and dread at my first interview.

He asked me where I was going and offered to drop me at my door, since it was very little out of his way.

During the difficult drive through the swirling white mist, we had little chance to talk because his attention had to be fully on his driving. He told me, however, that his name was Elliot Jerome and that he worked at Melarper's.

When we arrived at my home, my mother opened the door and immediately asked Elliot Jerome in for coffee. He thanked her, but refused, saying that the fog had made him late. However, he did ask if he might telephone her sometime. My mother, a very pretty woman, nodded and smiled vaguely at what sounded like one of those casual politenesses that come to nothing. I thanked him for the lift, and he went off into the fog.

A short time later I found the kind of work I wanted to do in a large chemical laboratory in Cumberland, but after I had been there awhile I was lonely for my home and my friends. Also, I was intrigued because my mother's letters had started to mention Elliot Jerome's name. "Elliot and I went to Kew Gardens.". . . "Elliot took me to see a revival of *The Apple Cart*.". . . *We went here . . . We went there . . .*

The tone of her letters increased my longing to be home,

and after ten months in the North, I left and returned to London.

On our first evening together my mother had said, "Elliot wants to marry me, but I've been a widow too long and I enjoy my life."

She explained that he had just left for a holiday in Europe. "I'm afraid he went without me giving him any hope of marriage. Poor Elliot!"

"Elliot" to my mother, someone now familiar; but to me, a vague figure in a fog . . .

My work in Cumberland had taught me the complicated technical terms used in industrial research, and I wrote again to Melarper's telling them that I was no longer inexperienced and asking if there was now a vacancy. Three weeks later I joined the enormous staff, working as an assistant in the library.

I had been there only ten days when Mother read in a newspaper of Elliot's death in a car accident in the Pyrenees. She must have contacted Melarper's for more news because someone from the research station came to see her. Afterwards, she had refused to discuss it. "It's over. Elliot is dead. I don't ever want to talk about it."

II

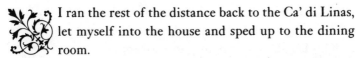 I ran the rest of the distance back to the Ca' di Linas, let myself into the house and sped up to the dining room.

Berenice was seated at her place at the head of the table. She was eating a croissant piled with too much butter and cherry jam. Her thick, coroneted hair was ash-colored, and her pale blue eyes smiled at me. Seated, she did not look particularly odd, but when Berenice stood up, her figure resembled a brandy glass, short and bulging at the hips. With her complete disregard for fashion, she innocently exaggerated her shape by wearing wide skirts. Her mouth was pretty when she laughed. In repose, it was pursed up. She explained this by saying that when she was a child she used to find the wrong things funny and was always in trouble for her misplaced laughter. It had so annoyed her parents that she used to screw up her mouth to stop herself from laughing. "And," she once said to me, "it has now got used to being that way." Her short, straight nose, though her most enchanting feature, was a permanent annoyance to her, for she suffered from a hypersensitiveness that caused her to have fits of sneezing which were small and polite like a cat's.

I reached for my coffee cup. "A man I've never seen before spoke to me at the newsstand. He warned me that either I—or someone near me—was in danger. He didn't look mad."

Berenice stopped buttering a croissant. "What was he like?"

"I was too shaken to notice much about him except that he had a beard and prominent greenish-gray eyes."

She gave a little sigh. "Well, at least he's no one I know. He must be some unfortunate who gets perverted amusement out of scaring young women. Forget it, Leonie."

"He spoke so seriously," I protested, "and he seemed troubled about it as if he really believed I would be involved in some sort of—tragedy."

"As you didn't know each other," Berenice said firmly, "the whole thing is rubbish. I've told you, dear, forget it."

"Oh, I will," I said lightly to reassure her.

Rorke broke the silence by joining us. Berenice, knowing that he listened to the English radio every morning, asked what news there was, and I sat, letting them talk, and decided to keep quiet about the bearded man's dark prophecy until Rorke and I were alone.

We had nearly finished breakfast when Willy entered, coughing softly, and took his seat next to me. He smelled of the everlasting Nazionale cigarettes he smoked. Cèsara followed him into the room and slapped a plate of eggs and tomatoes in front of him.

When he had been brought to the Ca' di Linas, wasted with

fever and starvation, Berenice had decided that he needed to be nourished and she ordered a cooked English breakfast for him every morning. Cèsara obliged with open resentment. After eight months of good living, Willy had become Berenice's fat, gentle slave. I watched him as he took a roll from the basket I passed to him. Whatever privations he had suffered before Berenice "adopted" him, his face bore no marks of it and his ginger hair had no gray in it. Once I had seen Cèsara fix her eyes on Willy and mentally cross herself because in the southern part of Italy from which she came, folk-legend interpreted red hair as belonging to an evil nature.

Berenice was saying, "I'm so grateful to you, Rorke. It will be wonderful when the whole of my plan for Eryxa is completed. It shouldn't take long, should it?"

"I should imagine it will take a very long time."

"Oh, no!" Berenice smiled at him. "I have permission from the authorities, and that is the main step. And now you're going to help me, and the rest is in the hands of God. It *will* work."

Willy asked, "What will work?" His eyes swiveled around the room with a swift defensiveness as if he suspected that we had all been holding out on him. "What's this about Eryxa?"

Berenice smiled around the table. "So far, I've told only Rorke because I felt I had to wait until I received formal permission to do what I want."

"Do what—?"

Berenice smiled at Willy. "I've bought the island."

Willy stared at her. "Eryxa? That's the deserted place beyond Burano, isn't it?"

"Yes. I have plans to build small studios there and to make the island an artists' center for those who really have talent and want to work and sell their paintings."

"You won't get any of them to move from their quarters around the Accademia."

"Oh, yes, I will." Berenice gave a small, complacent smile. "With new and clean living accommodations and publicity for their work, they'll find it a splendid proposition and far more comfortable than the unhealthy studios in which they now barely exist. Eryxa will be another island for tourists to visit, like Murano for glass and Burano for lace. They'll go there prepared to spend money and I shall charge the artists a small rent."

"Which they'll never pay," Willy retorted. "Berenice, how *could* you start such a mad scheme?"

She said quietly, "I know what I'm doing, Willy."

He went very red and his eyes bulged. "I've lived among them; you haven't. They love their squalor—it's part of their 'image'—and they won't leave their broken-down studios and their meetings in the *taverna* for some isolated, benighted island."

"Suppose you allow me to judge." Berenice spoke with unusual coldness and pushed back her chair. "I *know* it will work. And now let's stop this abortive argument."

No one spoke.

I sat and stared at my empty plate. The whole idea seemed as crazy to me as it had to Willy. The unsuccessful artists weren't going to sit on Eryxa, a lonely island far out in the lagoon, and wait for tourists, and shiver and be bored through the bitter, windy winter when no one came. They might agree to go there in summer but they wouldn't stay. They would drift back to their untidy, dilapidated places in the alleys of Venice.

Berenice was saying that she had to see Cèsara about the day's shopping. I followed her out of the room and, as she went toward the kitchen, I pushed open the garden door and walked into the sunlight.

The marigolds and nasturtiums blazed; the mist had gone and the sky was like soft blue silk. Cèsara's thin gray cat,

Angelo, came to meet me, and I picked him up and held him against my cheek. Like most Venetians, Cèsara loved cats and had refused to come and work for Berenice if she couldn't bring Angelo with her. She had argued that if she gave him to her daughter, he would probably be left to roam the alleys, grow thin and ill and linger on in misery. It was considered unlucky to put to sleep even a fatally ailing cat in Venice.

I walked with Angelo along the paths to a seat in the sun. His purring shook his sleek body, and he kept turning his emerald eyes on me.

Rorke had told me about Eryxa the previous night, so Berenice's news didn't startle me.

When I heard his plans to help Berenice, though, I had protested, "You're away in Milan all week. I thought we had planned to have Saturday and Sunday together."

"Berenice has set her heart on the Eryxa project and she is so happy about the whole thing that I must go along with her."

"Why?"

He said with a smile, "Because whether I agree to help her or not, she will go through with her plan, and she's safer having me to keep an eye on everything—at least in the beginning—than a total stranger."

"It'll take all your spare time."

"It'll take a great deal, certainly."

"But Rorke—" And then I stopped. I had been about to protest, "That means we'll scarcely ever see each other. Is that fair to me?" But I dreaded an argument that might end in bitterness. Rorke would remind me that he was now the only male in Berenice's family and that she needed him. Then I would retort that *I* needed him, too, and he might see that as the beginning of a possessiveness which I knew he would loathe. So, I had said nothing and the matter was dropped, although I had lain awake thinking about it for a long time . . .

Rorke's voice called me. I let the cat go and went into the house. Rorke was standing by the water steps.

"Filiberto is bringing the boat around. Are you ready?"

"For what?"

"Eryxa, of course."

I thought: *Darling, I could brain you! You never told me you were taking me with you to the island.* My spirits soared and I raced up the stairs, throwing back breathless words. "Of course I'm ready. But I must fetch my purse."

"You don't want any money."

"But I want my lipstick. I eat it." I laughed.

When I came into the hall again, Filiberto was saying, "Eryxa is silted up and the reeds are thick around the water banks. But do not worry. I took the Signora to see the island before, and I know a place where we can land."

He helped me into the launch that had its name, *Scaramouche*, painted in red letters along the prow. I sat outside the cabin in a place in the sun and as the launch backed, picked up speed and drew away from the steps, I looked back at the house.

From the lagoon, the Ca' di Linas was magnificent, with its carved arches over balconies which stretched the length of the building. But I knew that, seen close up, the house had a fantastic incongruity, that the dignity and elegance of its outline was at odds with the ludicrousness of its stone decoration. It was as though, after the architect had achieved his dream of design and proportion, a mad sculptor had come along and carved his nightmares on the columns that supported the balconies. Crocodiles and toads, camels and tigers crawled across the façade; a lion with a monkey on its back dominated the pediment over the great double doors that opened onto the lagoon.

I had first seen the Ca' di Linas at the time of our engagement, when Rorke had brought me to Italy to meet Berenice. I had looked on the place, then, with horror but I had grown to feel almost an affection for the time-eroded stone animals that clawed at the old pillars.

I glanced at Rorke now, squatting near the wheel with Filiberto. Rorke had never talked easily about himself, but he had told me about the chain of events that led him to work for Melarper's.

His mother had been Berenice's sister, and it was taken for granted that he would join the research station when he left the university. Rorke, however, had other plans for himself. To please his parents, he had taken a science degree. Then he announced that he had done that much for them, but that he was going to choose his own way of life. He intended to be a musician—pianist or composer, he hadn't made up his mind which. He faced the hazards of a musical career and was not daunted. He studied music in every spare moment and, after leaving the university, traveled for six months in the Far East. Then, when he returned to England, he won himself a place at the Guildhall School of Music.

Rorke was in his second year there when his father died suddenly, leaving his mother with a very small income. Immediately Rorke changed all his plans. He gave up music and, through Berenice's influence, joined Melarper's and worked his way into the Security Department.

To me, Rorke had been an employee who occasionally came to the library, borrowed a technical book, smiled his thanks and left. Then one lovely spring day when I was walking home from the station through Kensington Gardens, I saw him striding toward me. I was prepared to give him a tentative half-smile and walk on, but he stopped me.

"You're Miss Hunt, aren't you?"

"Yes."

"And my uncle knew your mother—my uncle, Elliot Jerome."

"I introduced them," I said, laughing, "by way of being given a lift from Melarper's on a foggy morning."

"Are you going anywhere special?"

"No, I'm just walking home."

He took my arm without a word and led me to a seat in the Flower Walk, lit a cigarette, stabbed it out and warned me that he was in a black mood and could I bear to cope with him for a while. He'd quite understand if I got up and walked away; in fact, he hoped I would because if he talked, he knew he would regret it later.

Intrigued, I said, "Talk. I'm a good listener."

At first he had generalized about frustrations, but after a while, his anger became a more personal thing. He had, he told me, just had a quarrel with someone. He didn't tell me her name or anything about her, nor did he tell me the reason for the quarrel. But I guessed who it was because everyone at the research station knew that Rorke Thorburn was the constant companion of Catherine Mallory, the great English opera singer. So we sat on the park bench and I listened while he blazed out at life, people, circumstances, fate . . . At the end, he had cried out, not so much to me as to the almost deserted gardens and the golden sunset: "Whatever happens in whatever place or time, she will always be in my blood. God help me, I can love her and hate her, for she has spoiled me for any other woman!" Then he had jerked around and looked at me with a kind of wonder as if he had completely forgotten my presence. "Good grief, what have I been saying to you?"

"Just letting off steam. Don't worry."

"Like hell! Of course I worry. I scarcely know you, and here I am, treating you like a sort of mother-confessor. I don't need to tell you that I've got a black temper and you're too good a listener! Forget it all. Let's go and have dinner somewhere. Or couldn't you bear it?"

"I'm hungry," I said and grinned at him. "And I love shrimps."

"You shall have a boatload of them, and we shall talk no more about my affairs."

Over dinner, he was a changed man. He made me tell him about myself, my life, my likes and dislikes. He was amused that I said I wanted to learn to pilot a plane, agreed with me that watching the sea was a magnificent pastime. The one subject we avoided was music.

For some weeks after that we saw one another often, and a month after our first meeting, he asked me to marry him.

I clung to a wild hope that what he felt for Catherine Mallory had been a violent infatuation that was now over. Certainly, he never mentioned her name to me.

*   *   *

I sat in the stern of the chugging launch, my chin on my hands, narrowing my eyes at the retreating skyline of Venice like a pale pattern on velvet. Wild hopes were usually created by wishful thinking. After months of marriage, I still had to keep telling myself that Rorke's words on that first evening, "I can love her and hate her, for she has spoiled me for any other woman," were now regretted, perhaps even forgotten. I could not ask him. That, I felt, would be an invasion of his past. But there were times when I wondered if he had married me because he needed some woman who attracted him, to be used as a buffer between himself and the vital, passionate and bitter thing he still felt for Catherine. Perhaps I would never know, for by then I understood Rorke well enough to realize that he would tell me only as much as he chose.

Because I loved him and wanted my life with him to be

permanent, I walked carefully, forcing no confidence that he did not give of his own accord. I knew by instinct that that was the only way I could hope to hold him and one day, perhaps, possess his complete love.

The launch ran between the mud banks and the palisades of sticks marking the navigable channels. An occasional solitary man waded in the green shallows looking for shell fish and, save for *Scaramouche*'s engine, the silence was intense.

Filiberto stood at the wheel, straw hat tilted over his brow, his sunburned hands light on the wheel. He was a typical Venetian, with a prominent nose like those in the old pictures of the robed and jeweled doges of the early ages. He was reserved, proud, but strongly religious and he had a crucifix on the wall of his cockpit. He kept his beloved launch *Scaramouche* beautifully polished, the velvet seats with their heavy embroidery well brushed, the awning erected as protection from the winds, stiff and laundry-clean.

Filiberto knew the lagoon as a river pilot knows the channels of his own waterway. He took us past San Michele with its dark cypresses and white walls, past Murano and beyond, turning left at last for the small remote island of Eryxa. He cut the motor and let the boat drift toward a creek where a broken-down pier stood lopsidedly in the brackish water. Then he turned to Rorke.

"Not too long, signore, or the tide will go out and we will be stuck on the mud for many hours."

"No," Rorke promised, "not too long. This is just a preliminary look around."

The boat crushed the water-reeds, and three ducks rose with heavy protesting wings into the air. The silted canal defied our approach, resenting our intrusion, and the *Scaramouche* stirred up the mud.

I had never seen Eryxa before, and my first sight of it did

not enchant me. It was an untidy island of unbroken green, from the vivid peridot of the grass through pale, sun-parched tints to the darkness of a few ragged cypresses on the near horizon. I took one look at the broken planks that were once a small pier and Rorke laughed. "I wouldn't place your trust on that. You'll have to jump to the bank. You can make it. Wait, I'll go first and catch you."

In a single leap, he landed on the bank and held out both hands to me.

I jumped and collapsed in a scrambling heap at his feet. The stiff salty reeds were scratching my bare legs, and I rubbed them and walked ahead up the slope and saw stones that still had the soft blues and greens of mosaics. Once, many centuries ago, a beautiful path must have been laid leaping to a group of storm-torn trees that formed a semi-circle around a ruined building a distance away to our left.

"There must have once been a villa over there."

"Once," Rorke said, "there were a great many villas on Eryxa. But that was hundreds of years ago."

From where I stood the lagoon looked calm, its water broken into diamond patches by the sun. A solitary boat, with a russet sail, seemed to rest on a diaphanous roll of mist in the distance; a lizard scudded across the hot stones at my feet.

"It's a sad place," I said.

"There's nothing sad about an island that's going to be reborn."

"You really think Berenice's plan will work?"

"It could. She—or rather I, it seems—will do the spade-work. And then one day when she finds it too much to cope with, she'll hand it over to the state as a nicely going concern."

"It will cost her a lot of money."

He said vaguely, "Perhaps."

I stepped over some little insect with iridescent wings, and persisted, "If you're going to turn this place into an art colony for tourists to visit, it's going to take all your spare time. But you can't work all the week *and* weekends."

"Oh, this won't be work—not, at least, my part of it. I'll just bring the experts over and then keep an eye on everything."

"For how long?"

"I have no idea. Just for as long as we are in Italy. Then I will have to hand everything over to others."

"So every weekend will be occupied by . . . *this place!*" I heard Rorke laugh as I bent down and picked a long blade of grass and bit on it angrily. "When the door of our bedroom opens at night, we'll have to have a password. Otherwise, since you could be camping on Eryxa, it might be some other man coming in to sleep with me."

He flung back his head, laughing again. "Do you imgaine I'd miss Cèsara's marvelous dinners?"

"With my company an accepted second," I murmured. "Well, I never imagined that this was the age of chivalry!"

He took my hand. "Let's go and look over that building."

"That broken-down place?" I lagged behind him. "You go. I'm staying in the sun."

He bent down and tore up a handful of grass and sprinkled it over my hair. "Now you look like a bit of the landscape."

I tried to brush the grass away. "It clings."

"Good. Then getting it out of your hair will keep you occupied."

I sat down on a huge stone, flicking grass, and watched Rorke walk away.

I saw him duck through the opening where a door should have been and disappear into the low-built house. Then I looked away across the flat land. In the Middle Ages, Eryxa had probably been one of the islands to which the rich Venetians had escaped from the terrors of the plague; built villas, laid down mosaic floors. But as I looked about me, only the parched wild grasses and the trees were living. From the human point of view, Eryxa was as dead as the old pleasure gardens of Murano that now lay beneath the glass furnaces and the showcases for tourists.

III

Gradually, however, as I sat alone in the sun, the sense of Eryxa as a depressing island left me and the peace of the place wrapped itself around me. A butterfly explored my hair. It had radiant red and mauve wings, and I watched it flutter away, a tiny jeweled ghost, toward a thin patch of flowers.

"Leonie . . ."

Rorke was calling me from inside the villa.

I got up and went toward the house. Cottage? Villa? In its present half-ruined state I had no idea of its original size or height until I saw the remains of thatched sheds and guessed that it had once been a farmhouse.

The fallen stones seemed to be alive with bright, shy lizards, and as I went through the gap where a door must once have been, I saw that the building had no roof.

"The island looks as if a tornado has swept over it."

"Age and damp and neglect . . ."

"It's cold in here, too," I said, rubbing my arms.

Rorke was looking about him, touching the walls. "I think this place could be restored and made into a kind of center. Berenice says she wants what she calls a 'group house' where someone responsible only to her can receive rents, sort out difficulties and see that the studios are kept in repair. The foundations are probably as good as any in Venice itself."

"As it is, it looks something like Stonehenge, with all those bits of masonry standing about outside . . ." I went to the gap in the wall and looked across the island. "There's nothing else to see, is there? Just grass—"

"In other words, you want to go back."

"You are staying?"

"Yes, but if you like, Filiberto can take you back to Venice."

With my finger I traced the spiders' webs of cracks along the ledge. "If you stay, I'm staying."

"It would do you far more good to join the Carters at the Lido than walk in this heat. There's precious little shade here."

"I don't care if the temperature reaches boiling point," I said extravagantly. "I'm with you and that's fine." I glanced at him. "We seem to have become like strangers since we've been in Venice."

He said quietly, "I don't share my bed with a stranger."

I bit back the protest that a man's need at night was very different from the desire for companionship by day and that I wanted the latter as deeply and desperately as I wanted the former. Instead, I took his hand. "Darling, I won't be difficult about this Eryxa project; I'll try to understand that you feel you must help Berenice. We all want to please each other. *I* want to please *you* . . ."

He said impatiently, "*Leonie, don't!* That's tantamount to being a doormat! Just be yourself." He walked away from me as he spoke.

I stayed by the gap that was once a window and looked down at the tangle of wild green weeds that reached almost to the sill. I knew I had made a mistake and I covered it up with sudden laughter, and called after him, "Oh, I won't be a doormat. They molt with age and I'm rather proud of my hair."

To my relief I saw him smile as he left me and went through an arch into an inner room. I remained where I was, and thought how quickly Rorke's moods changed. I had swung him from an absorbing interest in Eryxa to something more personal and he had reacted characteristically. He hated introspection and he hated, even more, people who became intense about the twist and turns of their own emotions.

I turned away from the window as he appeared under the broken archway. "The house has good walls," he said, "but that's about all. Come on, let's go and see if we can find a better place."

As we walked out into the sunshine, I said, "When I was at the newsstand this morning buying a magazine I dropped my change, and a man I'd never seen before helped me pick it up. Then he stared at me and—don't laugh—he warned me that I was in danger."

"From what? Losing your wallet?"

"It was rather horrible, the way his eyes looked at me . . . as if he was frightened for me."

"A crank. Forget it."

"That's what Berenice said at breakfast this morning when I told her. But the man said: 'Someone near you is going to kill . . .' and then he looked scared and walked away."

Rorke stooped to pick up an oblong of ceramic glaze, deep blue as lapis lazuli. "A piece of some old pottery," he said. "Rain and soil erosion, I suppose, have brought it to the surface." He handed it to me. "Take it as a good luck charm. It'll probably stop crazy men from uttering idiotic predictions to you."

"I don't think it was like that. He seemed . . . troubled, and although I hadn't said a word at the newsstand, he spoke to me in English."

"The magazine you bought—"

"Was an Italian one."

"Then you probably looked English to him and, as I said, he's a crackpot who goes around scaring young women." He put out a foot and brushed aside some grass, revealing another patch of flagstone path. "What did this man look like?"

"He had a brown beard and gray-green eyes. That's all I noticed."

"If he's lurking around waiting for you to offer him more money for the gruesome details of his warning," Rorke said, "just mention the word 'police.' It does wonders in any language. Or refer him to me."

The faint early mist had completely cleared and Eryxa shimmered. A sea bird flying above us uttered a sudden wild scream; tamarisk and sea lavender ringed the tiny bay around which we walked to reach another ruined building. This had quite obviously been a villa of some size. There was a beautiful old wrought-iron wellhead in the tangled garden and I traced one of its curves. "How lovely that would look in our garden in London."

(Our small garden, a world and an unnamed fear away . . .)

Rorke said, "This place is in better condition than the last." He tested the door and the single broken hinge creaked. He put his foot to it and the door broke away from the lintel and crashed to the ground. "It's safer down than up," Rorke said and walked in. I followed him. The room was large and square and there was part of a broken statue in one corner. The staircase had collapsed, and wisteria, grown wild and ragged— more brown branch than feathery green leaves—had crawled into the paneless windows and was spreading itself over the walls. In a corner was a make-shift table. It consisted of a few rotting planks laid across two pieces of old discolored marble; another stone had obviously served as a seat. On the table was a wine bottle, lying on its side and empty; part of a loaf of bread and some olives. The bread wasn't moldering and the olives weren't wrinkled.

I said, "Someone has been here recently."

Rorke picked up an olive and ate it. "Probably someone from the mainland who came over here to get away from the summer crowds." He threw the olive stone out into the long grass.

"Or he might be homeless."

"In which case he wouldn't be able to afford to hire a boat to get here; and anyway, I doubt if there are many homeless in Venice."

A newspaper, the *Gazzetino*, lay on a mound of rubble. It was turned neatly to an inside page. I picked it up and saw that it was only a day old, and at the top, staring at me, was a name.

Catherine Mallory.

My heart turned over. I wanted to throw the newspaper to the back of the stone seat; I wanted to walk away without reading what was said about her. But that was asking too much of me.

Rorke had wandered away and was poking into corners, tearing away the undergrowth just outside the door, looking at the foundations. I bent over the paper without touching it and almost wished that I could not read Italian.

Catherine Mallory was in Milan. Short strings of words

stood out from the rest. Catherine Mallory, sweeping the sophisticated Milanese into ecstasies with the concert she had given. *"Divina"* . . . *"Superba"* . . . *"Bellissima."* And Catherine looking straight at me from the photograph, her classical face crowned by hair that I knew was the color of copper, her large, sensuous mouth faintly smiling. Power emanated even from the reproduced photograph.

I had to swallow twice before I could find my voice and call to Rorke. "Did you know?"

"What?"

"That Catherine Mallory is in Milan."

"Yes."

"You didn't tell me . . ."

"My dear child, why should I? Of what interest would it have been to you? You aren't musical."

"You knew her very well . . . once . . ." I broke off and dropped the newspaper. "Whoever was here was reading about her."

"Well, newspapers are for the public." He kept moving out of my sight behind corners, through alcoves, inspecting the ruin with apparent absorption.

If I asked him, "Have you seen Catherine?" and he said that he had, I would ask why, since she was so famous, he had not told me. And Rorke would then close in on himself, hating what would probably seem to him like the questioning of a suspicious wife. If he had seen her it might merely have been that he was present at the concert in Milan and had gone round to her dressing room afterwards to congratulate her. Old friends . . . But why should I assume that they had met?

I wandered through the open doorway and sat on a block of stone that could once have been a plinth for a statue. Tamarisk brushed my arm, and I turned and saw Rorke some distance away, looking out to sea. I wondered if the newspaper lying on the mound of rubble so coincidentally folded to the page that featured Catherine Mallory had destroyed his interest in Eryxa.

A whisper of music ran through my mind; I knew its title; I knew the words. It was one of the songs Rorke had composed and Catherine had sung at the Festival Hall in London. I hadn't, at that time, known Rorke well, but the newspapers had seized on the story. Catherine Mallory had sung two songs by an unknown musician. The compositions had "promise" but the singer had lifted them, by reason of her glorious voice, out of amateurism and into splendor.

Soon after I had met Rorke, I had gone alone to hear Catherine sing at the Queen Elizabeth Hall. Again, she had sung one of Rorke's songs, and the music had haunted me because it was his; the words I scarcely remembered.

Once, I had come in from some Saturday morning shopping to find him listening to a record of Mallory singing *"Vissi D'arte"* from *Tosca*. When we married, Rorke's fine antique furniture, his few pictures and his records had been moved into our small house. The records had been put up in the attic, but while I had been out shopping that day, he must have gone up there and brought this one down to play.

He hadn't heard me come in, and I saw a look on his face I had never seen before. Longing, anger, joy—a curious paradox of emotions that seemed to isolate him from me so much that I backed from the room and crept to the kitchen hoping that he didn't know I had seen him. I wondered whether it was Catherine or his love for music that was tearing at him.

Later, I asked him if he wanted to take up music again. I said, "If you'd like to leave Melarper's and get established in music, I'd be perfectly happy, whatever the initial financial difficulties."

His answer had been brief. "I shall never do that. And, if you don't mind, the subject is closed."

I never referred to it again, and he never played the record again, to my knowledge.

❆

      I got up from the stone where I had been sitting and joined Rorke. A slight breeze, soft as muted woodwinds, stirred a group of trees and was gone.

"Did you feel that odd little wind?" I asked.

He did not answer me and, turning to look at him, I knew that he hadn't heard what I had said. We walked on in silence.

Ridiculous as it might seem, after a year of marriage, I still could not force a way through his reserve. If the barrier between us was Catherine Mallory, then the practical part of me argued that it would do no good to talk about it. My reticence was not shyness but, I hoped, common sense. I must wait for an obsession to die, and when it did, I would have a complete Rorke . . . *if* it did . . .

We continued on our way, encircling Eryxa, finding piles of crumbled stone, overgrown paths and broken statues that nobody wanted in a country which was a vast treasure-house of such things.

Suddenly Rorke stopped and looked about him. "Dear God, what dereliction."

"It's going to be an enormous task to make it habitable. And when it's done, it may not work."

"That's true."

"Then tell Berenice so. Now that you've seen Eryxa for yourself, it's only honest to warn her."

"And disappoint her?"

"It's better than letting her pour money into something that will probably be a failure."

"You must let people indulge themselves in their own way, Leonie."

"Look at it," I cried. "Just *look* at the place! You can't go back and feed Berenice with assurances of a wild success. Can you imagine what it is like in winter with the fogs and the winds? The artists will never stay."

"This part of Italy is Berenice's home, and she's perfectly aware of the hazards. I shall play along with her for as long as she thinks the idea can be made to work. Perhaps it will. How do *I* know? How do *you*?" He noticed my set expression and laughed and touched my cheek. "All right, you don't approve. You want everything brought out into the open, analyzed and mulled over. You tackle your problems your way, my darling, I'll tackle mine my way." He looked across the island to the lagoon. "Come on, or *Scaramouche* will be mud-bound with the receding tide."

A question kept nagging at me as we made our tour of the island. Who had left the newspaper in the ruined villa? Had someone folded it, inside page out, so that I would see the notice about Catherine Mallory's visit to Milan? I was quite certain that it was no coincidence. It must, then, be a piece of deliberate malice—or a warning. But by whom on this seemingly deserted island?

It was another twenty minutes before we eventually reached the broken landing stage where *Scaramouche* lay, with Filiberto sprawled, sleeping, on one of the velvet seats.

He leapt to his feet as soon as Rorke called him, started up, stretched and grinned at us. "Sleep on a boat is beautiful, signora," he said and reached out and helped me jump onto the deck.

I went through the little cabin to my favorite place in the stern. The engine sprang to life and the launch scraped the water-weeds and fought the clinging mud. Filiberto was asking Rorke what he thought of the island, but I stopped listening to them.

IV

I slept quite well for the early part of that night. At three o'clock, something woke me. I lay for a few moments, willing sleep, but my mind was too active and I supposed that I must have had some violent nightmare which I had forgotten on waking but which left my heart thudding like a train over a railway track.

The Venetian bed was huge, and I stretched cautiously, not wanting to touch Rorke and wake him and yet needing to feel some of the warmth that emanated from him. He wasn't there and the sheets on his side of the bed were cold, so that I knew he had been gone for some time. Rorke often slept badly and sometimes had a drink and a cigarette in the middle of the night. Occasionally he went downstairs and raided the icebox, for he ate small meals for a man and sometimes became hungry in the early hours of the morning.

I sat up and decided that I, too, felt hungry and slid my arms into my robe. Tying the sash, I had a deliciously childish picture of Rorke and myself sitting at the kitchen table enjoying a night's feast. We had done it before and had eaten chicken legs with our fingers and drunk milk.

I went out into the corridor. The moon, through a tall Gothic window at the far end, lit up the carved frames of the paintings so that they were square empty outlines, their sitters dimmed by shadows. There was a sound near my feet and I stopped, momentarily rigid, and looked down. A mouse was scuttling away from me. I would have to tell Cèsara about that at breakfast, and Filiberto would come and find the hole and fill it in with cement. That was how Venice existed in spite of erosion by water. Cement, carefully hidden from view, strengthened the weaknesses, buttressed the crumbling palaces, filled the rat holes.

From behind Willy's door I heard clear, rhythmic snores; outside in the narrow *calle*, a man laughed and someone began to run. The Venetians never seemed to sleep, but I was used to the all-night voices and footsteps and had steeled myself to sleep through them.

I went down the staircase without turning on the light, holding onto the marble banister. The *salone* and the dining room were in darkness; the passages stretched away to the kitchens where Rorke must be.

A light suddenly flashed on behind me. I wheeled around and could see nothing but the yellow beam of a flashlight from Berenice's private sitting room. I stopped, standing rigid, listening. Whoever was in the room either moved with the stealth of a cat or had heard me and was waiting, very still and very alert, for me to go nearer.

"Who—?" My voice came in a harsh croak.

No one answered and the light went out.

It would be useless to shout a warning, because there was so much distance between the bedrooms on the upper floor and where I stood that nobody would hear me. Rorke must be even further away, probably stretched in Cèsara's big wooden kitchen chair eating biscuits.

I went cautiously through the thick darkness toward the open door of Berenice's room and pressed myself hard against the wall outside. I had an absurd idea that if the light went on again, I would be invisible and that, anyway, it would be safer to stay still than race back up the staircase where I would be a target for whoever heard me.

Suddenly the flashlight blazed onto my face. Rorke was standing by Berenice's desk.

"Go back to bed, Leonie."

I walked into the room, letting out the breath I had been holding. "You scared me. Turn on the lamp and switch that thing off."

"I told you to go back to bed." He held the flashlight in one hand. In the palm of the other was a ring. I leaned over and looked at it. The gold was curiously carved and there was an intaglio that looked like a tiger's head cut into a vivid purple amethyst.

I put out my hand to touch it, but Rorke drew away. The desk by which he stood was a beautiful Sheraton which Berenice had brought from England when married. Like so many examples of that craftsman's work, it possessed a number of fascinating small secret compartments. There was one drawer that lay behind a larger one set between two little columns. This was open and Rorke dropped the ring into it and closed both drawers.

"I've seen that ring before." I said. "Berenice must have

worn it sometime, I suppose. But why were you looking at it?"

I waited and he did not answer.

"Rorke, someone was here! You heard a noise and came to see and found the drawer open. That's it, isn't it?"

He replaced the ring. "There is no one in the house but the people who live here."

I breathed a sigh of relief. Rorke too must have wondered about the noise. Old houses were always full of strange sounds and, like me, Rorke was not used to them.

"It's odd," I said, "that Berenice keeps that ring in the desk drawer instead of in her jewel case, isn't it?"

"People keep odd things in odd places. Now I'm going to make some tea. Would you like a cup?"

"Please."

He closed the door softly behind us. "And next time you wander about the house, put some slippers on. These mosaic floors are chipped in places."

In the bedroom, I plumped up the pillows and sat against them. I had supplied the obvious explanation for finding Rorke in Berenice's room, but why had her desk drawer been open? She could, of course, have forgotten to close it sometime that day.

I couldn't stop myself asking, when Rorke entered the room carrying two green kitchen mugs of tea, "Did you check the doors? Were any of them forced?"

"No."

"Then you possibly heard mice playing around. Or even a water rat."

"Forget water rats and drink your tea," he said softly.

As we dressed the next morning, I asked Rorke if he was going to Eryxa.

"Yes, with Carlo Pallamundi, the architect."

"Working on a Sunday? I wonder how he likes that?"

"Berenice is anxious to get started so the place will be ready—we hope—by next summer."

"Do I come with you?"

"As you like. Only you'll be bored. We'll be talking technicalities and, as you've already seen, there is nothing of interest on the island."

(Except the remains of someone's meal and a newspaper folded to Catherine Mallory's name.)

Rorke said, "Why don't you go to the Lido with the Carters?"

"I might do that. There's no painting lesson today." I picked up a comb and drew it slowly through my hair. "You don't mind me taking lessons from Adrian, do you?"

"Why on earth should I, if it amuses you?"

❦

Carlo Pallamundi, lean and thin and semi-bald, called for Rorke soon after breakfast. While the two men were with Berenice, I sat in the garden waiting to tell her that I was going over to the Lido for the day and would not be in for lunch.

Willy came, nursing Angelo, and sat beside me on the swing seat.

"So Rorke's going to Eryxa again?"

"The sooner the architect and surveyors get to work, the better Berenice will like it."

"It's all crazy." He glared into the distance as though Berenice's plan was a personal affront to him. "I know these people she thinks she can help. They will just make use of her. They'll go over to the island when they want a good time with their wine and their girls—"

"They'd get those more easily here in Venice," I said dryly.

He ignored my comment. "And Rorke will go out of his way to help Berenice. You see! He'll do everything he can to please her."

"I expect he will; he's fond of her."

"And she is rich."

The implication was too obvious. I could have put Willy in his place with a sharp retort that it was, after all, Berenice's affair. But I said nothing. Willy could no more help being malicious than he could help breathing. Perhaps his past had made him bitter; perhaps he saw, in this Eryxa plan, a threat to his own easy existence at the Ca' di Linas. I was quite certain that Berenice would never turn him away to live on the island; he was too established as part of the household.

He was watching me and obviously waiting for me to speak. At last, he said, "I made a disparaging remark about Rorke, didn't I? Most married women would rush to their husband's defense, if only to bolster their own sense of importance as wives. You didn't. Why?"

"I don't need to."

"Oh, Leonie, that's just shutting your eyes to the truth! Rorke neglects you disgustingly, and you know it." His hand went out to touch mine but I leaned away from him.

"I don't need sympathy. What Rorke is doing for Berenice is only a temporary thing. Once the work gets going on Eryxa he'll have nothing more to do with it. He's only 'putting the first spade into the soil' as it were."

"And after that?"

"We'll have our weekends to ourselves—that is, if we don't return to London soon. I doubt if we will be here much longer."

He had not taken his eyes off me. "You're here for just as long as Rorke thinks it expedient."

"That's where you're wrong. We shan't stay in Venice after he has finished the job he is doing for Ferris Caretta."

Willy tipped Angelo off his lap and sat forward, elbows on his knees, examining his broad hands. "You've never been to Rorke's old room in the wing, have you?"

"Oh, yes."

"When?"

"He showed it to me when he brought me to Venice to meet Berenice soon after we were engaged."

I sat staring ahead of me, remembering. He had taken me through the garden door to the wing over the boathouse, up the stairs past Filiberto's quarters, and then we had branched off up another little flight of stairs and stopped at a door. He had turned a key and said, "This was my special room when I came to spend my holidays here. I used to call it my hideout."

I had lingered, wanting to push back the shutters and see the room clearly, to touch the things that had been Rorke's as a boy. But Berenice had called us from the garden and Rorke said: "Tea. Berenice's sacred British custom. There's nothing of interest to you here, anyway." And he closed the door.

I had never seen the room again.

I was suddenly aware of Willy's unblinking stare. "Rorke still uses that room."

I shook my head. "You're wrong. He never goes there these days. I doubt if he ever thinks about it. It belongs to his boyhood and he's not given to nostalgia."

"That's what *you* think!"

My patience with Willy was becoming ragged. "It's what I *know*."

"I'm afraid you don't, Leonie. You're married to Rorke, but I'm the outsider who sees so much more. There is a light in that room sometimes on Friday nights."

"I see," I mocked. "He slips out of bed when I'm asleep and goes and sits there and sentimentalizes about the past. Well! Well! How little I know my husband."

"And how little you realize the truth of that!" There was

a sudden note of sadness in Willy's voice that stopped my anger. Our eyes met—his pale, bulging a little and troubled; mine defiant. He looked away first, bent down and picked off a dead marigold head, crumbling it between his fingers. "There are times when Rorke apparently doesn't return from Milan until Saturday, aren't there? Suppose he *does*, though? Suppose he sometimes comes on Fridays, but goes straight to that room? How would you know? The way into the wing is through the garden door, so unless you were looking out of the side window late at night, you would never know."

The silence between us seemed to shudder and settle. I knew I had to have the final word and I got up so abruptly that the swing seat rocked.

"The room is nothing to Rorke now, so let's drop the subject, shall we?" I walked a few steps and said, "The Carters have asked me to join them at the Lido."

Willy smiled. "And Adrian?"

"Oh, he sometimes goes, too, on a Sunday. But I've no idea whether he'll be there today, or not."

He gave me a small, knowing nod. "He will. And Rorke will be too busy at Eryxa to be around. Make the most of it, Leonie." He padded quickly from me before I could think of a sharp retort.

I wished him a thousand miles away and, more practically, I wished that Berenice was more perceptive. But she seemed blind to his little troublemaking probes, and I doubted whether it occurred to her that he listened at half-open doors and heard and saw too much. Saw, for instance, a light in Rorke's old room.

Unfortunately, I believed Willy's story although I was quite certain that it wasn't Rorke who used that room. There was a piano there, and music still had the power to hurt. Rorke's rejection of the thing he loved had nothing to do with blind obstinacy, which is the defense of the weak. On the contrary, it was part of Rorke's strength, of a resolve to change the pattern of his life—to close a door, both metaphorically and realistically, and never open it again.

The light? Could it be Filiberto who turned it on? He was the sole inhabitant of the wing over the boathouse and could have had a key made for Rorke's unused room without anyone knowing. He could be entertaining his friends there when no one was around to hear him. The unused room probably was bigger and more comfortable than his own quarters.

The idea comforted me. I went into the bedroom and stood at the mirror, pinning my hair up so that my neck would feel cooler. Over my shoulder I saw the reflection of the fresco, and the sun through the half-open shutters beamed on the girl on the dolphin, giving her face such light and vitality that my sense of everything being right with my world returned. She was like my mascot, pale and painted yet radiant; and suddenly Willy's ridiculous hints that Rorke crept back, unknown to me, to spend nights in his old room in the wing were just poor attempts at troublemaking.

I turned away from the mirror and picked up my purse. But as I closed the shutters and left the room, I found myself humming a song. It was one for which Rorke had composed the music:

"The hours blow down the wind
I heard them sighing . . ."

It was a sad song that was full of a nostalgia for something gone. Something lost . . .

V

Inez and Richard Carter owned an apartment in Venice and a villa on the Lido. Their three small children, Jason, Hester and Marian, were healthy, rather plain and tremendously good fun. They swam like wriggling fish, all arms and legs and splashes, and whenever I appeared they pounced on me as if I were an outsize Christmas present they had all wanted. Inez scolded them for their complete takeover of me, but I enjoyed it.

When I telephoned to ask if I might join them at the Lido, Inez poured welcome over me. "You don't ever have to ask. Just say you're coming and at what time and someone will pick you up at the ferry."

The Carters' villa was on the lagoon side of the Lido—a long, low, wisteria-covered house. But I knew from experience that the car which would collect me would take me straight to the beach, for the family almost camped there during the hot weather.

To my surprise, it was Adrian Rand who stood waiting for me by the Carters' white Mercedes at the boat station.

I usually saw him wearing old, paint-stained clothes, but wherever he was, he never lost his aura of casual sophistication. A tall, fair man, he walked gracefully toward me, smiling.

"I'm selfish," he said. "I wouldn't let Richard come and fetch you." He took my beach bag and flung it into the open back of the car. "I like looking at you."

"You won't have much chance while you're driving if you keep your eyes on the road."

He laughed. "Then I'll feel you next to me." His tone had the softness of a lover, and though it meant nothing, it was flattering and warm. As the car began to move forward, I felt suddenly light-hearted. Nothing mattered but the sun and the sea and charming company.

"Where's Rorke?"

"He had to go to Eryxa with an architect."

"Oh, that island Berenice Montegano is making over for the artist squatters of Venice? I'm surprised Rorke hasn't talked her out of it."

"You don't know Berenice. Nothing moves her when she has set her mind to a thing."

We spent the morning swimming, idling under gaudy umbrellas; we raced each other into the sea and lay sunning our dripping bodies on a raft.

Halfway through the morning, Inez said, "There are iced drinks here, but if anyone wants coffee, Rosetta will make it for you up at the house . . . No, not you"—she reached for Jason. "You're staying here. Richard, your son and heir is a pest." She ran after him, caught him and hugged him.

Adrian said, "Come on, Leonie. Coffee for us."

"How do you know I want any?"

"A walk will do you good."

We uncurled ourselves, slid our feet into sandals and padded through the sand, across the road and past the luxury hotels to the Carters' villa.

The house looked a little unreal in its setting of palms and with its sun terraces, like something out of a glamour advertisement. Inside, however, it was comfortably furnished, homely and cluttered with the possessions of an extrovert family. The Carters' maid, Rosetta, greeted us and asked, "*Caffelatte*, signora, signore?"

Adrian answered for us both, told her she looked prettier than ever, gave her a mock-lustful grin and led me out to the loggia. He said as we sank into the long chairs and swung our feet up, "I didn't really want coffee. I just wanted to get away from the others."

I watched an outsize bee trying to crawl into a flower that was so small it looked like a pink thimble on its tawny head.

Beside me, Adrian began in a singsong voice:

> "*The lion and the unicorn*
> *Were fighting for the crown,*
> *The lion beat the unicorn*
> *All round about the town.*"

The pause was long. I asked, "So—what?"

"I wish Rorke were the unicorn."

"And you the lion?"

He laughed. "Of course."

"And the crown?"

"*You.*"

Just a light flirtation in words, harmless if I kept it so. I said, "But, Adrian, since unicorns are never-never animals, you don't exist."

"Oh, I exist and so do you. And what's more hellish, so does Rorke."

"That bee," I said, "will get its nose stuck in that flower. Look."

"What's wrong between you and Rorke?"

I was careful not to let him see that his question startled me. "Don't be idiotic. Nothing's wrong. No quarrels, no regrets. And why on earth should you think there is?"

"One hears things—"

"Small cities . . . large rumors," I murmured and turned my head, saying gratefully, "Ah, here's Rosetta with the coffee."

She had come on cue, as if I'd rehearsed her, and smiled broadly at us, her big body wobbling in her striped dress. The coffee was perfect. We drank it out of porcelain-thin mugs and Adrian began to sing again, softly: " 'The lion and the unicorn' . . . What's wrong between you and Rorke."

"You nag," I said. "And, as I've told you, nothing is wrong."

"Then you could have fooled me. He works in Milan all week; he fills his weekends with some damned silly idea his aunt has got into her head about turning Eryxa into some place for displaced artists who'll get bored with the whole thing when winter comes . . . Why don't you start a family?"

"That's not your question to ask, is it?"

"You'd make an enchanting mother. But I can see Rorke as the kind of father who'd flip a smile at his son or drop a vague kiss on his daughter's dark hair—she'd have to be dark, like you—and then off he'd go, out to whatever it is keeps him so busy."

The tone of his voice was light, as if everything he were saying were part of a game. Adrian looked on the people he met with bright, amused eyes; he treated life as fun and, for everyone, he turned the world into a gayer place. But his mood as we sat in the rose-showered loggia had an underlying seriousness. For the very first time, I was uncomfortable with him and I knew that I had to break the growing intimacy that he was deliberately creating between us.

I fidgeted with my sandal, slipped it off my foot and shook sand out of it; I retied the sash of my beach robe and said, "I bought this in the Merceria."

"If you're trying to change the subject, that's a pretty poor line."

"I *am* trying to change the subject. I don't want to talk about my life."

"All right, then, let's talk about mine."

"Go on." I waited.

"Three years at art school, then commissions for portraits. Once married to a wife who liked some South American beef millionaire better than me—or perhaps did her running away out of bravado, just to see if I'd fight to get her back, which I didn't. Me! Adrian Rand . . . Have money, will travel."

"I know all that about you already."

"What else do you want to know? That I'm in love with you?" He put down the delicate blue mug and watched me.

"I'd be happy knowing that, if I were in love with you, but I'm not. We only met a week ago and—"

"And what?"'

"I think I'm just someone you can't have, and you're one of those people who always finds the other man's grass is greener than his own."

Adrian flicked a small insect from his arm. "Have you finished your coffee?"

"Yes."

"Then let's go back to the sea."

"That's fine. Come on."

He got up and followed me through the garden. The way

to the beach had been carefully cultivated by the Carters and was a long cascade of color, of bougainvillaea and oleander and yellow cactus flowers. Where the path narrowed, the hem of my beach robe caught on a spiky leaf. I stopped and bent to release it and found myself in Adrian's arms.

"Oh no!" I held my face away from him. "You'd better stop before you spoil everything."

He held me with strong fingers. "Who do you really think is spoiling your life?"

"*You* are at this moment."

He said in a low, angry voice, "What are you doing? Hiding your head under your wing, like a sleeping bird?"

"I don't know what you mean."

"Like hell you don't! Venice is a small city, and I've heard—" He stopped.

I turned my head, stretching it back, away from him. "What have you heard?"

"About Rorke."

"What—about—him?"

"Oh no, I don't repeat tales."

"You've done the next best thing," I flashed back at him. "Having hinted, you'd better explain."

He took my face forcibly between his hands and his fingers were so strong that I couldn't move. "I asked you a few minutes ago what was wrong between you and Rorke. I'm serious, Leonie. I've heard rumors and I'm damned if I'm going to stop listening to them when I like the girl who is involved—*you!* 'Thorburn,' they say, 'and the Mallory.' "

"Just—let—me—alone—" I twisted out of his grasp.

"Good God, girl, do you have to waste your life?" he shouted.

I heard the last words as I ran down the path between the flowering bushes. A piece of broken stone tripped me and I fell flat. A bird sang madly on two notes . . . *Rorke and Catherine* . . . *Rorke and Catherine* . . . My shock and anger supplied the vocalism.

Adrian reached me and put his arms around me to help me up. Was I hurt? Could I stand?

"Thank you," I said crossly, "and without your help."

He stood away from me and I got to my feet. For a moment we faced one another and I said, "Get this quite clear. I love Rorke. It's as simple as that." I started to walk on and Adrian caught my arm. I wrenched myself away. "Oh, not again!"

"No, not again. Just that I'm sorry. I'm not given to being brash, and that's what I was. All right. Your life is your own, and you can be quite sure I won't try anything like that again, but if you should ever need me, I'll help you in any way I can—and without strings attached." He relaxed suddenly and his eyes danced. "Though I'd better not make rash promises. Small dark girls with green eyes and long hair have always been my downfall. Now, come on, let's get to the sea and I'll race you to the raft."

It was he who set the mood as we sped to the beach and down to the sea. We plunged together into the blue water and turned wet, laughing faces toward one another. I had no intention of letting the brief scene at the villa spoil my friendship with Adrian, for I knew too few people in Venice and I needed his painting lessons to occupy my time.

After another spell of sunbathing, we all went up to the house for lunch. While we sat over drinks, the conversation turned to the changes that might come to the city. Inez and Richard argued without rancor, Richard wanting to sell the Venice apartment; Inez wanting to stay. "However much they up-build, the city will never change. How can it?"

"Unless it sinks."

We all turned at the voice. It was Rorke. He had walked in upon us with laughing suddenness.

"Filiberto brought me over," he explained.

"You see—" Inez turned to the group. "He can't let us have Leonie for more than a morning without coming after her."

Richard asked what Rorke would drink. He chose a martini, and Inez removed a clutter of things from the only vacant rattan chair. The family was intrigued by Berenice's plan to make Eryxa into an artists' island, and I sat quietly, watching and listening to the conversation, very aware of the easy dominance of Rorke's personality.

Having him there with me made all the difference. I no longer felt that I was only half a person, that I was "tagging along" with a happy family. We stayed together, idling the afternoon away, and at half past six piled into Richard's launch and went to Adrian's for a drink.

His elegant Venetian home, the Palazzo Kronos, was a tall, narrow house looking onto the Campo San Geralimo and a distant half-view of the Accademia Bridge. It was much smaller than the Ca' di Linas and less rambling, but I always felt that people had laughed and danced and been gaily wicked in Kronos.

The *palazzo* was approached from the Campo up a flight of marble steps. Four Doric columns supported the upper floors and the back looked onto a *rio* with a view of peeling houses and wash hanging on ropes from balcony rails.

I heard Inez talking about the Fenice Theatre. It was, she said, being redecorated. "I wish there was something playing there at the moment. I'd love you to see the inside. It *should* be opened," she added, "even for one night—for Catherine Mallory. She's coming to Venice, did you know?"

I stayed where I was, half turned toward a window, but I was sharply alert to the quickening of the atmosphere. Inez and Richard were part of the Venetian scene; they probably heard all the rumors that circulated, and although Richard might dismiss them, Inez loved gossip and would make it her business to know as much as she possibly could of Venetian hints and rumors and scandals. She was not vicious, but small talk was the breath of life to her.

"Catherine Mallory is coming for a short holiday," Richard said with exaggerated disinterest. "And I suppose she'll stay at Danieli's."

"Oh no," Inez said. "She detests hotels. I heard them talking about it when I was at the Conservatoire the other day. She's looking for a really glamorous apartment." She paused for one of those dramatic moments she loved. "Adrian, what about yours? It's empty, isn't it?"

"Yes."

"And what have you done about trying to let it?"

"Nothing much. It's in the hands of an agent."

"After that expensive conversion," Richard said lazily, "I would have thought you'd want to try and get your money back with interest."

"If anyone wants to pay my price, they can have the apartment."

I decided that I must have imagined the awkward silence after Inez's announcement that Catherine would be coming to Venice, for now the whole family joined in the discussion. The Palazzo Kronos was far too large for one man and everyone knew that Venice was choked with summer visitors. Catherine Mallory must have decided on an impulse to give herself a holiday in the city and she would have a hard time finding somewhere to stay. So? . . . Each left it to the others to answer the question.

Inez, who took over the problems of everyone within her reach if they seemed to her unable to cope, said briskly, "If you like, Adrian, I'll go to the agents tomorrow and jog their memories. If you haven't kept in contact with them, they've probably forgotten all about your apartment. I suppose the letting is in the hands of Bartolomeo Asponi?"

Adrian said that it was but added that he wasn't at all certain he wanted someone living above him who might raise the roof with her voice. "I'm not musical," he said, and added wickedly, "Ask Leonie. She has heard me sing 'The Lion and the—' "

"Once was enough," I said firmly. Everyone laughed.

As I half-listened to the rest of the conversation, I recalled that Adrian had told me that after having had the Palazzo Kronos converted in order to let the upper part furnished, he had regretted what he had done. But I knew, too, that half a house lived in, even for part of the year, was preferable to emptiness in a city like Venice where dampness and neglect could soon destroy even the finest of furniture and loveliest of materials. And, with Adrian's characteristic dislike of anything cheap or makeshift, the two floors above where we sat were ideal for a rich and selective visitor. Yet I wished someone would veto the idea of Catherine being told about the apartment. No one did.

Adrian said, "Of course, if the great Mallory is stranded in Venice—which I very much doubt—let her rent my apartment. But at a price." He whistled softly and looked at everyone except me. "I'll take her lovely lire. How long is she staying?"

"I think someone said until the season opens at La Scala. She's singing Desdemona in *Otello*, I believe, and some other big role. But that's in the autumn."

So, she would be in Venice for some time—certainly as long as Rorke and I were there.

". . . don't expect me to do anything for her," Adrian was saying. "I'm not running errands for a prima donna. She's got to live entirely her own life, *if* she comes. We share one thing, the main staircase—and that I can't divide."

I said from my place alone by the window, "But her husband is partly paralyzed, he can't even walk, so she couldn't possibly take your top apartment. No one could get a wheel-chair up and down those stairs every time they took him out for air."

"Oh, didn't you know?" Inez said. "Her husband died while she was in New York."

A stab of news at a party . . . Catherine Mallory was free. And coming to Venice . . . I turned back to the window. The sky was full of amber light and the scene was like a Canaletto painting.

Richard said, "Your glass is empty, Leonie."

"I don't want—" I began and then changed my mind. "Thank you."

They began to talk about music. I was out of my depth, so I remained where I was, like a deliberate outsider. Perhaps, I decided, I was left alone by the window because the family felt that the enchanter's touch had rooted me to the radiant sunset scene outside; perhaps they thought I was quietly composing immortal poetry to commemorate Venice.

Then Richard came and laid an arm across my shoulder, and my last thought before I was drawn into their circle was that if I wanted to hold Rorke, I had to give him his freedom to find, not himself, but his real relationship with me. And if there was no longer anything that held him to me, then I had to let him go. The thought was a physical pain running through my body.

VI

 On the night of the Gala Regatta, the people of Venice poured out of their homes to watch the spectacle on the Grand Canal.

Willy and I had dined with the Carters and afterwards all of us were going to the Ca' di Linas to watch the grand fireworks display from the roof of Berenice's house.

We made our way through the Camp to the Accademia, walking to the place where Filiberto would be waiting for us with *Scaramouche*. The people and the boats on the Grand Canal looked like a stage-set for a ballet—glowing, weaving and glittering where the lights caught the black water. I watched a yellow balloon float under a bridge. Just as it reached the far side, something struck it and it exploded with a bang. I jumped like a startled cat and just behind me, Inez laughed. Gondolas and launches and the more humble little boats were decked out in the finery of Chinese lanterns and streamers. An illuminated barge carried an orchestra toward the lagoon; cornice lamps lit up the dark angles of the *calli*, and the trees were strung with fairy lights. The windows and doorways of many of the palaces were usually plunged into darkness as if each housed a recluse, but on the night of the Regatta many of them were lit up.

While the Venetians and the tourists streamed toward the Giudecca Canal to watch the fireworks, we were trying to make our way to the steps where Filiberto waited for us. Inez, by my side, put an arm around me, laughing. "You're so little, you need protection in this mob. What a pity Rorke couldn't be here."

A group of people pushed us from behind, and Inez and I became separated. They pressed on past me, shouting at one another in a language I couldn't recognize. I looked around for Inez and, in spite of the lights, was unable to see her because everyone around me was taller than I and blocked my view. It didn't worry me. I knew where Filiberto would be waiting and all I had to do was to get there.

Below me, three little boats full of young men began tossing streamers up to the crowds on the bank. Someone from further down the Canal was singing something that was obviously opera. A woman pushed me aside, shouting to someone ahead of us, "Giovanni . . . Giovanni . . ." and gave me a final nudge that sent me side-stepping to the edge of the Canal. I paused to let her pass. Then, quite suddenly, I felt such a violent jerk from behind that the woman's sharp elbow in my side had been gentle by comparison.

For one frightening moment I swayed; then I managed to brace my feet and grab a bystander while I got my balance. But a hand clamped down on my shoulder and again I felt myself being powerfully jerked forward toward the Canal. The black waters with their dancing lights seemed to rise up, and I screamed. I put up my hand and tried to wrench the steely fingers from my shoulder, leaning back onto whoever stood behind me. I also tried to turn my head but another hand gripped my neck in a vise. I shouted, and as the hold tightened on me, I gave such a tremendous kick backwards that I lost my balance. But I fell the right way, back into the crowd.

A voice said, clearly and angrily, in English with a faint accent, "What the hell are you playing at?"

Hands helped me up off the ground and steadied me while I fought for the breath that fear had almost pumped out of me. I looked at the face of the man whose arms held me safe. He wore a broad-brimmed hat and had a beard—and his eyes were full of recognition. He said sadly, "I warned you, didn't I?— that morning at the newsstand."

"Someone—pushed—me—"

"I know. Don't bother to talk. Just calm down. You're quite safe now. He won't try again tonight. He'll be too afraid of being watched."

"You must have seen who . . ."

"I saw a man grip you from behind. As I shouted at him he turned and disappeared in the crowd. The lamps shone onto him. All that was significant about him was that he had very blue eyes."

"That . . . that doesn't help much, does it?"

"I don't know. But I thought it might."

Just a man with very blue eyes . . . I shivered.

The crowds had thinned out, pouring toward the place where they would wait and watch for the first firework to cut the air. But a woman with a red shawl round her shoulders paused, looked at me and said, "The signora feels faint?"

"Only for a moment," I said in my halting Italian. "But I'm all right now." I thanked her. She walked past and then seemed to stumble over something. She bent and picked it up.

I raised my empty hands and looked at them and cried, "My purse—" The woman held the small black bag by its strap. "Is this it? Then it is good that I find it on such a night. It could have been kicked into the Canal—or stolen. I hope that nothing inside has been broken. Perhaps someone stepped on it?"

I took it from her, thanking her, and flipped the catch and glanced inside. Everything seemed intact. She wished me a happy evening and walked on.

The man was still by my side. "Are you now all right?"

"Quite, thank you." I glanced over my shoulder, saw Inez, who had come back to look for me, and said to her, "I would like to introduce you to someone who saved my life just now —at least saved me from falling into the Canal. But I don't know his name. Signor—?"

I turned back. He had vanished.

I said, puzzled, "I don't think he's real. . . . I've met him once before and he did the same disappearing act."

"If you mean the man you were talking to as I came up, he has gone down that *calle*. Who is he?"

"I don't know. I wish I did." I was still shaking. "I must have met him somewhere because he knows I'm English. He wears one of those artist's hats they wore in Edwardian times and he has a beard, but then you saw—"

Inez said, "I noticed that you were talking to someone, but he's a stranger to me." She took my arm. "We'll describe him to Adrian. He knows every artist of any quality in Venice."

We had reached the place where Filiberto waited for us and went down the slippery steps and into the boat. We were being shouted at to hurry because, by waiting for me, *Scaramouche* was causing a holdup. The children were already in the boat, winding colored streamers round each other and shouting, "Got you; got you; got you . . ." with interminable repetition.

We slid down the light-strewn waters of the Grand Canal,

past floating streamers and bright balloons. A fine fat cabbage bobbed near the steps of a *palazzo* and in the glowing lamps at the water steps, it looked like a gigantic yellow rose.

I sat inwardly shaking and Inez, who was next to me, was telling Richard and Willy what had so nearly happened to me.

Richard said, "A drunken joker. There'll be plenty around tonight."

"I don't think so," I said. "The hands were too strong and too firm. Whoever he was, he was sober."

Willy, sitting opposite, leaned forward, saying, gently, "You'd never have drowned. You can swim and there are all those boats around."

Oh surely! All those boats around . . . But the idea worked two ways. It could have saved me or, equally, it could have caused my death. My hands were gripped so tightly in my lap that I hurt my palms. *It's easier to drown among a crowd than alone in the quiet where screams can be heard.* Again, the wash from motorboats could have dragged me under and how many people celebrating at a carnival would have noticed me? People drown off crowded beaches . . . People drown . . . I shut my eyes.

When we reached the Ca' di Linas, Inez told Berenice of my near-accident. She stood by the window in the *salone*, her tubby little body in an elaborate dark blue gown. There were emeralds in her ears and on her fingers, and she carried a beautiful lace handkerchief, for she was having one of her sneezing fits. Three times . . . stop. Three times . . . delicate sounds such as Angelo, the little gray cat, made when pollen from some flower he was sniffing got up his nose.

I said, when Berenice was over her spasm, "Who could have done it? Who wants to harm me?"

"Darling Leonie, no one. Such an idea is too absurd. Some man wined too well."

"It was odd. The man I told you about at the newsstand,

the one who warned me of danger, was there and saved my life. But he wouldn't tell me his name or where he came from. When I wanted to introduce him to Inez, he just vanished. It's like being watched over by a shadow-man who knows something about me, something *I* don't know and *he* doesn't dare to tell."

Berenice said softly, "I wonder who your particular saint is?"

We knew the sign. Berenice adored talking about saints. Richard smiled. "Well, I doubt if the man who saved Leonie was a saint in your meaning of the word."

I said, "He saw the man who pushed me. He said he had very blue eyes . . ."

"I'm afraid that doesn't narrow the field much," Berenice said sadly, yielding to our refusal to accept a materialized saint. "There are so many blue-eyed people in Venice." She made an odd little gesture with her hand as if dismissing my terrifying experience. "If only Rorke were here! Such a pity Milan is so far from Venice."

Willy, picking a purple grape from a bunch on a side table, said softly, "But he likes it that way, doesn't he?"

Berenice heard him and swung around. "Why do you say that?"

She was so seldom moved to anger that Willy wasn't quick enough to see its stirrings. He said brightly, "Well, Rorke is your nephew, you should know his character. It suits some types of men to have an excuse for being free to come and go and—"

"And—*what?*"

Willy gave a little gasp and tore his eyes from Berenice's indignant stare. "Well, I just mean that Rorke puts his work before everything . . . He's utterly single-minded about it . . . We know that . . . don't we?" He spoke in such a lame, hesitant voice that I knew he hadn't meant to say what he had, but had swiftly seized on a fairly harmless alternative as soon as he realized that he had angered Berenice.

Her expression remained dark with disapproval. "I don't like your hints, Willy, and I won't have idle gossip in this house. Rorke brought Leonie here, not to suit some free-living plan of his own, but because she would be lonely in Milan while he was working."

I sat feeling invisible—an eavesdropper among friends.

Like so many fat people Berenice moved lightly. "You will never again utter malicious hints in my house. Is that understood, Willy? Good!" She went to the door. "Now let's go and watch the fireworks."

We climbed together, passing empty rooms on the top floor, to the *altana*, the flat roof terrace. In medieval times, Rorke had told me, the Venetian women would sit there wearing open-crowned hats, with their hair spilled out over the brims so that the sun would bleach it. I thought of all the portraits of golden-haired women I had seen in the city.

These days, the *altana* was used by Cèsara to hang out the family washing. It was not a very prepossessing roof, just flat stone and chimneys, but a number of wicker chairs had been placed against the parapet and as we sat down, the first crack of a firework split the sky and fell in a crimson cascade.

I leaned with the rest on the low stone wall and watched without really seeing or caring about the display. I was well aware that had someone else told me the story I had told the Carters about being nearly flung into the Canal, my reaction would have been the same as theirs. "Someone wine-drunk . . ." Only I knew it wasn't so. And so did the man with the beard.

Someone in Venice must surely know him; he would have a wife, a family, or a mistress. Or he would live alone and go to the *trattoria* for his meals, buy his wine and his pasta locally, comment on the weather with his landlady. And he probably lived near the Ca' di Linas or he would not have been buying newspapers at the newsstand at the top of the *calle. Unless his one reason for being there was to speak to me.*

He was my benevolent ghost although he was a living, breathing man. . . . But he needed a clearer identity. If I ever came across him again—if this was the beginning of a pattern—then until I found out his real name, I must give him one.

A great burst of color splashed into the sky and Inez cried to the chiidren, "Oh, look at those two rockets with a long space in the middle, like a dark river."

With those words, "a dark river," a name came to my mind. As a child I had loved the ancient myths of Greece, and I remembered the legend of Charon, the ferryman who took souls safely across the River Styx. A man of darkness. And this strange man was just that, both warning me and then saving me from disaster. It was possible that I would never see him again, that his presence at the Accademia was by chance. Possible, probable . . . But I didn't wholly believe it. I named him Charon.

Cèsara brought coffee up to us. We drank it sitting under the stars, watching the fireworks and the lanterned boats and listening to the music from the illuminated barge.

At half past twelve we went down to the water-gate to see the Carters off. Filiberto was waiting with *Scaramouche*, and we watched his expert maneuvering and called "Goodnight" until we could no longer see the wildly wheeling arms of the children.

"They keep those young people up far too late," Berenice said.

"A Venetian habit. It won't hurt them for once," I answered.

Berenice yawned. "I'm getting too old for fireworks. I suppose I've seen them so many times." She climbed the stairs a little wearily and I wondered why she hadn't had a lift put in. The Ca' di Linas had such ample space for one.

As we walked behind her, Willy drew me into the alcove with the long narrow window that looked onto the *calle*. He held my arm, detaining me without a word until Berenice had disappeared up the second staircase to the *salone*. Then he said, "Do you know that Rorke is in Venice?"

"Of course he's not. He's in Milan."

"I saw him as we passed under the Accademia Bridge. Someone swung an outsize torch up onto it and there, right in the center, was Rorke. But I think he saw me and turned away quickly and I lost him in the crowd."

I said easily, "It was probably a trick of light and shadow —or perhaps it was Rorke's double."

Willy shook his head. "It wasn't. Leonie, I'm not trying to be funny or mysterious. I really did see—"

I interrupted him. "Then he's here on orders from Ferris Caretta. He doesn't spend his days sitting at an office desk, you know. And if he really *is* in Venice—which I still don't believe —then whatever he's doing is between the head of his department and himself. It could be that something very secret has to be passed on to someone working here, or there's a leakage in an important new project."

"In Venice?" Willy gave me a look of cool disbelief.

"Strange things happen in small, seemingly innocent places," I said vaguely.

"That's right, they do. These industrial security people, it seems, don't have to give explanations for being in a certain place at a certain time."

"And if Rorke is in Venice, he'll either come here later and hammer on the door to be let in, or he'll have to report back to Milan tonight. I'm not worried." I walked with a firm, defiant tread up the next flight of stairs to the *salone*, aware that Willy was pattering behind me.

Berenice looked up from unclasping her diamond watch. She smiled tiredly at me and then looked over her shoulder. "Go to bed, Willy, the party is over." She treated him like her child, gently but firmly.

He hovered at the door. "I thought I'd just go out for a while."

"And leave doors unbarred from the inside? Oh no. It's after twelve-thirty and I don't trust anyone who has had too much wine not to be up to some mischief. I don't want young invaders, however gay and apparently harmless they may be, swarming over my garden, nor do I want drunken singers at my windows."

"But that seldom happens in Venice."

"There's always a first time. Now go to bed."

He went like an obedient child, and I said, "Willy thinks he saw Rorke this evening. He could possibly have been sent on some job or other, which will mean that he might come here for the night. If you lock the doors—"

"Of course Rorke isn't in Venice," she said firmly. "If he had been, he would have called us. Willy has an overactive imagination and, I'm afraid, a liking for intrigue. It's harmless enough so long as one takes no notice of it. Now"—her voice became softer and she stifled a yawn—"Cèsara has locked up and we can all go to bed."

Berenice went to the shutters and closed them. I walked out of the room and saw Willy sidling toward the stairs. I guessed, by the guilty look he gave me, that he had been listening. He joined me as I went up to the next floor. "I *did* see Rorke," he protested plaintively.

I quickened my pace, but he came panting behind me. "It's true, Leonie."

"I must tell him that he has a double." My hand was on the handle of the bedroom door, turning it.

"You don't believe me."

"No."

"You're so trusting!"

"I'm trying to be practical," I said, as patiently as I could. "Rorke's job is security. I can't ask questions. I don't even know why we're in Italy, but I refuse to mistrust him, so you're wasting your time trying to make me. I'm going to bed. Goodnight, Willy."

I pushed open the door of my room, closed it and was mercifully alone. I stood with my back to the cool wood and closed my eyes, realizing just how badly my head was aching. I put my fingers to my temples—the throbbing was like two small drums.

Rorke was in Venice. Did I believe it? If I did, then the explanation I had given Willy was the obvious one. Yet, alone in our room with the sounds of the dying carnival coming muted through the shutters, I felt uneasy.

I went onto the terrace and looked out at the dwindling number of boats on the lagoon and the lights being extinguished in the houses. The music and the laughter and the shouting were dying down to distant bursts at the steps where the gondoliers were gathered, after mooring their boats, to talk and drink the last of the wine.

Of course Rorke was not in Venice that night . . .

Before I went to bed, I changed the things in my evening bag to the one I used during the day. Money, compact, lipstick. A piece of white paper fell out. I unfolded it and read the words written there.

Have patience, Catherine.
No happiness is achieved by rushing.
It is too dangerous. I will see you tonight.

There was no signature, but I knew the handwriting. It was Rorke's.

The note I was gripping gave an unreality to everything that had happeneed. My purse hadn't been out of my possession, so none of this could be really happening; the note was part of some nightmare. Then I remembered the woman with the red shawl handing my purse back to me down by the Accademia Bridge. Had I dropped it? Or had someone very cleverly taken it from me in order to slip in the note? Had that, then, been the real reason for the seeming attack? Did someone want me to know the truth, to be warned that I was in the way of a violent obsession between two people? The note could have been stolen from Catherine or intercepted on its way to her.

I went to the dressing table and stared at myself in the mirror. Long dark hair; eyes mauve-shadowed; lightly tanned face; wide mouth with the not-too-red lipstick still intact . . . Leonie Thorburn—known enemy to no one, yet someone's deadly target. Oh dear God, not Rorke . . .

I went to the telephone, lifted the receiver and then put it back on its cradle. I did that twice before I managed to find the courage to ring Rorke's hotel in Milan and ask for his suite.

I sat on the side of the bed and waited for an unendurably long time. The ticking of the clock standing by the telephone seemed to quicken its pace. Somewhere in the distance a guitar was being played, the sound of the plucked strings seeming to swell in my ears so that, listening to it and the footsteps going up and down the *calle*, I was terrified that I wouldn't hear Rorke's voice from Milan. And he had to be there in his room . . . he must hear the telephone and answer . . .

But he didn't.

The night telephone operator told me that there was no reply from the signore's suite.

At one o'clock in the morning, Rorke was out. With friends,

talking the night away; arguing about politics; reminiscing; sitting with their drinks in someone's apartment? *Or here in Venice?*

I clung to the receiver for a few moments. Rorke could, of course, be sleeping heavily. But that wasn't his way. He slept lightly, like an alert animal.

Fear crawled through me as I lay sleepless, not even bothering to close my eyes, but watching an occasional light from a boat on the lagoon streak through the shutters and fall in thin strips across the ceiling. I heard the dying sounds of the end of the Gala night and knew that when next I saw Rorke I must show him the note to Catherine and demand the truth. He knew he need have no fear either of hysterics or martyred protests. Whatever I felt inside would be my own affair.

It seemed that I had two problems. One, my danger from someone unknown; the other, Rorke's love for Catherine. The two must be quite separate, for men did not harm the women they made love to unless they were mad. And Rorke was not that.

VII

He arrived on Friday evening a good two hours before dinner. I had kept his note to Catherine in my purse, pushed out of sight under the paraphernalia of money and cosmetics.

Rorke found me in the garden and sat down by my side. I was fully aware that Willy was the only one who might join us, for Berenice had her regular beloved visitor, Father Ignatius, with her in her sitting room. Even so, the garden was not the place where I could talk to Rorke about Catherine.

He was asking me how I had enjoyed the Regatta. It was a perfect opening for what I had to say to him, yet I merely answered briefly that it had been interesting.

Rorke was leaning forward, looking at me over his shoulder,

laughing. "You look like a sleepy tabby cat in that brown and white dress."

I said mechanically, "Oh, do I? If you hate it, I'll go and change."

"Don't be silly, of course I don't hate it. But I've seen you in ones I like better."

"The yellow, for instance," I said vaguely, staring at the marigolds until their color hurt my eyes. "Rorke—someone tried to kill me last night." I kept my eyes on the flowers, sensing the slight withdrawal of Rorke's arm that had been touching mine.

"What did he do? Point a bullet at you? Or did he poison the wine?"

"I'm serious."

"Then you'd better tell me about it, hadn't you?"

Rorke was always a good listener. When I had finished, he said, "That's the sort of thing that can happen anywhere in the world where crowds collect. There are youths hell-bent for mischief."

"It wasn't mischief, it was a deliberate attack. A simple and obvious way of getting rid of me—the easiest way of all—in a crowd."

"Some drunk steadying himself with a hand on your shoulder. Then seeing what he had nearly done, staggering away. It was a nasty moment for you, but obviously no one was deliberately trying to throw you into the Canal, if that's what you think."

"That's what I think."

"How could you have drowned with all those people looking on?" he demanded and ruffled my hair as if I were a rather likeable but tiresome child.

"It was *because* there were so many people milling around, so many boats, so many things happening that I probably wouldn't have been seen—or heard."

He said calmly, "You would have made a pretty good splash if you'd fallen in. Someone would have heard—"

"Above all that din and the hilarious boatloads of people and the wash of the motorboats? Anyway, I'd probably have been tipped in in such a way that I would have hit my head before I fell and just slithered into the water without resistance. . . . I could have been stunned. Killed . . . *Rorke, I was there* . . . You weren't, so—" I stopped. *You weren't there, were you?* I tried to say it aloud and couldn't. My lips stiffened; my voice was silent.

He put a hand on my shoulder. "You're all right, Leonie. You're safe. Forget what happened. Don't dwell on it, it's wrong to—"

"It's wrong to try to kill," I snapped back and slid shuddering away from his hold. It reminded me too vividly of the hand at the Canal side. I said, loudly, "Someone thought they saw you on the night of the Regatta near the Accademia."

I did not only sense the overlong pause, I felt it and it filled me with a mounting terror. I swung around and my eyes met Rorke's.

"Saw me?" he asked lightly. "Well, I never did think my looks were unique. One of these days it'll be my turn. I'll see your double walking up Regent Street or along the road home. And then I'll probably be arrested for stopping to kiss a strange woman."

"Willy saw you."

"Oh, *Willy!*" There was the faintest breath of relief. "He'd probably see leprechauns in Ireland or werewolves in Bulgaria." He touched my cheek. "And next time you go among a crowd of revelers, keep hold of someone all the time. Then you won't get caught up in trouble."

"I wasn't caught up in any trouble; I was the object of it. And while you're about it, why don't you suggest that a label be put around my neck in case I get lost?" I added. "I'm not so much younger than you, Rorke. I'm not a child."

He smiled. "Of course you aren't, but you're not particularly tough, either. I'm glad. Shrewd, overcivilized women bore me. They're as indigestible as hard-boiled eggs." He tilted my chin, and for the first time, the shadow of gravity took the place of light-heartedness. "All right, so some reveler tries to tip you into the Canal. And fails. If I had any idea who it was, I'd go and beat hell out of him, but I haven't, darling, and the Regatta is over and you are safe."

"There are other ways of killing—"

He slid his hands under my hair and turned my head so that I was looking directly up at him. "Don't let this fear of persecution get hold of you. No one wants to harm you. You're living safely with Berenice, and I'm here, too."

I shut my eyes in sheer self-defense against my love for him that could weaken me. I had to go through with what I had started. "Come upstairs. I have found something I have to show you."

"Very well." He spoke with amused resignation and took my hand.

The sunlight made a thin gap in the barely opened shutters so that the bedroom was full of shadows. I, too, was in the shadow as I snapped open my purse, but I couldn't feel, inside, the smooth surface of paper. I tilted the purse up to the thin light and peered in. Rorke's note to Catherine was gone.

No one had been in the room but Rorke and myself—I to change my dress for dinner, Rorke a little later to tidy up after the long drive from Milan.

"What is it you want to show me?"

"A . . . a letter. A note."

He held out his hand for it.

"Rorke, it's—gone."

The heavy flap of pigeons' wings outside the window and the engine of a vaporetto were the only sounds that broke the room's silence.

I said, "When I was attacked down at the Accademia, I dropped my purse. Someone picked it up and gave it back to me. It was only out of my hands for a few minutes, but in that time someone had opened it and slipped a note inside."

He asked quietly, "What did it say?"

Something strange happened to my eyes. I seemed to have become physically blinded so that I would not have to watch Rorke's face. To the blackness in front of me, I said in a voice that jerked every word, "It was a note written by you to Catherine Mallory."

Rorke's silence was almost unbearable. Then the blackness cleared and I saw him move away toward the half-shuttered window and stand facing me, his back to the light.

"Something I am supposed to have written to Catherine found its way into your purse?"

"Yes." I saw his hand go to his pocket for a cigarette. He smoked only under stress. "Catherine is in Milan," I said.

"I know."

"You've seen her? You've written to her?" As soon as the words were out, I knew I was that all too common phenomenon: a suspicious wife confronting her husband.

Before I could think of a way to soften the harsh note that had crept into my voice, Rorke spoke. "Yes, I've seen Catherine. This is a civilized age, Leonie. I didn't promise, when I married you, to renounce my—friends."

The pause before the last word was barely perceptible but, highly sensitive as I was to every light and shade that emanated from Rorke, I caught the hesitation. It was a devil's temptation to continue the argument, to say, "Any other woman you know, yes. But not Catherine," and to remind him of his violent outburst at our first meeting. Yet, once the forces of recrimination were released, I knew nothing would be the same again between us. So I stood, my hands folded in front of me, and waited for him to speak again.

He said, "I want to see that note. Try to remember what you've done with it."

"I've done nothing. Someone has taken it."

"Why?"

"How do I know? Perhaps because it had . . . it had achieved its purpose."

"What purpose?"

"Rorke, you aren't in a court of law, so don't snap questions at me."

"I'm sorry." His voice was gentle, but his eyes were watchful and his brow was deeply furrowed. "But I must know, Leonie. What purpose are you talking about?"

I cried inside myself. *Suspicion . . . my suspicion of you . . .* and I knew in that terrible moment that one could love and mistrust at the same time. "I've got to know the truth, Rorke."

"What truth are you talking about?"

"You . . . and Catherine . . ."

"For sweet heaven's sake why continually bring her into the conversation? I've known her for many years—you're perfectly aware of that." He walked away from me. "I still don't understand what all this is about; what is this note you had and which has disappeared?"

"It said that she was to be patient and that you would see her that night." I watched him, wanting to believe that it was my imagination that read relief on his face.

"So that's all?" he exclaimed. "How much more harmless could it be? I often saw her after concerts—her dressing room was always full of people. And as for patience, she loves singing so much that she can scarcely wait to get on the stage."

"But whoever put the note in my purse didn't think I would read it that way. Who was in Milan when Catherine gave her concert and is now in Venice?"

"A great many people, I fancy," he said indifferently. "How should I know? She probably threw the note away when she left La Scala and someone picked it up—"

"And used it against you—against us. Rorke, don't you see? Whoever put that note in my purse wanted to hurt me." I thought, *Or warn me*, and with an involuntary shudder of fear, covered my face with my hands. Rorke reached toward me and pulled them down, gripping them hard. His voice, when he spoke, was low and shaken. "Leonie, there's one more question that's got to be asked. And for God's sake answer me truthfully. Are all these things real—the attack on you, the note? Or are they—"

"Make-believe? Fun and games I'm playing because I'm perhaps bored?" I cut in roughly.

He dropped my hands. "There's nothing more we can say until I see that note. Try to find it, darling. Search the room —you may have put it somewhere and forgotten the place; or it could have dropped out of your purse."

"It didn't. And I know I shall never find it."

He stubbed out his cigarette, only a quarter smoked, in the glass ashtray. "Why are you so sure?"

"Because it must be obvious that whoever took it from my purse has destroyed it. He . . . or she . . . wanted me to see it but was careful that I didn't have it to show you."

"You talk of a near-accident at the Accademia and the only witness vanishes; you tell me a note was written by me to Catherine and put in your handbag, but that can't be found and there is no one to prove you had it. What am I to make of it all, Leonie?"

"The truth," I said. "But you only half believe any of it,

don't you? What do you think I'm doing? Inventing some drama just for the fun of it?"

"You said that before, but I didn't accuse you of such a thing then, and I'm not now. Unless—" He stopped abruptly.

"Unless you decide, on thinking it over, that I'm living in a fantasy world—a black fantasy." I turned away from him and went onto the balcony and stood holding onto the warm stone. It was all so inconclusive, so overladen with questions that could not be answered and evasions that I wanted to hammer into some shape.

A harmless note from a friend to a friend. Nothing more.

There was a sound behind me and I knew that Rorke was near me. A wave of emotion swept over me so strong that for a moment I felt faint. Then, when it passed it was as if it had taken all fears, all suspicions with it. I had such a sudden sense of well-being that I wanted to laugh aloud at myself.

Something sang inside me. *Nothing is wrong except in your imagination.* I saw the sense of what other people had told me. The things that had happened had logical and unfrightening explanations. The note to Catherine could have some entirely different meaning than the one that had leapt to my mind. Someone was trying to make mischief and I would not let it tarnish my love . . . to hell with the note! Rorke's closeness made me tremble. I narrowed my eyes against the dazzling sky, and it was as if he were deliberately imposing his will on me, magnetizing me, willing me toward trust and malleability. Or perhaps it was my own love for him overriding what I had thought was reason. I did not know, nor did I care.

I turned from the window, put up my arms and drew his head down, pressing my mouth against his. It was I who demanded him; who held him tightly against me. I said his name. "Rorke!"

"Take that dress off."

As he closed the shutters, I slid the sheath of silk over my head. Rorke turned, lifted me up and laid me on the bed. I put my arm over my eyes and waited with my heart thudding, strangely excited and with no thought in my mind, only an overwhelming physical longing. I felt the weight of his body and then he took my arm down from my face and said, "You are smiling, Leonie."

Without a word I pulled him more closely to me and wept with sheer emotion. At last we were ourselves again, and when the pitch of excitement was over, I lay with my head against his, my hair tossed across his face. He put up a hand and held the long strands there, imprisoning me, sighing with sudden peace. I, too, was filled with peace.

Nothing in the room stirred. I thought that the ormolu clock must have stopped or that time itself had been brought magically to a standstill. Then, through the silence, came the jangle of the telephone bell.

Rorke turned from me and slid off the bed. "I suppose I have to answer it."

"Why bother? Cèsara can take a message."

I heard him lift the receiver, listen a moment and then say: "Why, hello. Welcome to Venice . . ." A long pause while he listened, then, "Yes, thank you, we'd both like to come. It's an occasion . . . You're pleased with the apartment? . . . Fine." Again, a silence while the person at the other end talked. Then Rorke said very quickly, without comment on what had been said at the other end of the telephone, "Good-bye, Catherine."

He turned away, draped himself in his navy blue dressing gown and came and sat on the edge of the bed.

"That, as you heard, was Catherine. She has now settled in Adrian's top apartment and is giving a housewarming party next Friday and wants us to go."

"Did *you* arrange that she should take the apartment?"

"I? Good heavens no. Apparently Inez got the agent to contact Catherine and offer it. And anyway, who can ever find a place to stay in Venice at the very last moment in summer? She's lucky to have found Adrian's house."

"Why did she suddenly decide to come here?"

"How should I know? Maybe she likes Venice."

I began to laugh.

"What's funny?"

I turned over and hid my face in the pillow. "Nothing is funny."

"Leonie—"

I said furiously, "You had no right to accept for me."

"Why not? You like parties."

I lifted my head. "When that telephone rang, Catherine came into this room."

"She merely called to invite us both to her housewarming. And if you don't want to go, then you must stay at home. I shall be going."

"Suppose I asked you not to . . ."

"I'd go just the same." He bent over the bed and kissed me. "Stop being a little ass and get up."

Rorke was dressed first. He closed the door behind him as I was coming from the bathroom, rubbing my face dry. I dragged on my clothes and sat at the dressing table and combed my hair.

Rorke had said, "Find that note." But did he already know that it would never be found? The magic of our coming together on the balcony was gone.

I dropped the comb and put my face in my hands. What had happened? I had brought Rorke up to the seclusion of our bedroom in order to force the truth from him and even found the courage to begin to question. Then, suddenly, the stage changed and I had moved out of drama into elation. Had it been my own weakness, my own desperate longing to bury the truth, that had made me turn to Rorke as I had? Or had he exerted a curious power over me? Whatever it was, he had wanted to silence my suspicions as deeply as I had, and accepting Catherine's invitation and taking me to her party was to allay suspicion and silence gossip, to say to Venetian society, "You see? We are all three friends . . ."

Oh, dear heaven, how could love and suspicion be such close companions? But I already knew. Love was a far deeper thing than any assessment of character. . . . I fled from the mirror and dressed quickly, wanting to escape from the room.

When I came out onto the landing, Willy was at the top of the stairs. He said, "Come and see my new picture."

It was a diversion and I welcomed it. I went up to the next floor and into his studio. It was packed with canvases, some turned to the wall, some facing me. I liked none of them.

The one on the easel was a painting of a part of a dilapidated corner of Venice with peeling pink plaster, clothes hanging on lines strung from crooked balconies, and a boat high and dry in a yard. It was so elaborately constructed that it was only by careful scrutiny that I managed to recognize these things because of the way their shapes merged into one another. The colors, also, were too brilliant. Venice was not garish; it was muted and opalescent.

I had to say something. "You enjoyed painting it?"

"I'm always happiest when I'm working."

I laughed. "*Are* you, Willy?"

He went as pink as an adolescent boy. "All right, so I would give up my painting rather than my comfort. You would, too, if you had known what it was like to spend a winter in Venice almost at starvation point."

"I'm sorry, but you could have gone back to England."

"I've always felt that Venice is my home."

"Even on the cold stones on a foggy winter's night?" I asked.

He sighed. "Even then."

"Why don't you paint Berenice's portrait?"

"I will one day."

"I'm sure she'd be very happy if you suggested it."

"Oh, I have already, but I've told her she must wait till I've improved."

"You're very modest."

He said, with a sudden burst of real sadness, "That's my trouble. Humility. Don't ever think of it as a virtue, Leonie."

I put my hand on his arm and pressed it. "Then snap out of *your* humility," I said.

To my amazement he swung around, took my hands in his and gripped them hard. His eyes were moist. "I like you. I've liked you from the moment you came here."

"Thank you, but don't look so sad about it."

"I'm scared to death for you," he whispered.

I dragged my hands out of his. "Let's not get dramatic. Just because I nearly fell into the Canal, I'm not doomed."

He shook his head and said miserably, "I see so much. Heaven help me, I see so much!"

"So much—what?"

"Of the truth."

"What—is the truth?"

I was aware of the brilliance in the room—of the outflung shutters, the low sun blazing straight onto the violent colors of the oil paintings. A wildly colored room for a seemingly gentle, timid man whose face had suddenly lost its pink glow and was pale.

"The truth is—"

"Go on. *Do go on.*"

"Do you love Rorke?"

"Yes."

He passed his hand over his face. "Oh God, how hard it is to tell things."

"I'll make it easier for you. You wish I didn't love him quite so much. Why?"

He took a deep breath. "Because I don't believe you really know him . . . as he really is, I mean." The words were strung together as though he knew he had to get them out quickly or not at all.

"I've been married to Rorke for nearly a year."

"Knowing is altogether different. Do you realize, Leonie, that when Berenice dies, you and Rorke will be rich?"

"I suppose so. Yes. Unless she leaves her money to the penniless artists on Eryxa." I tried to hold the conversation on a light note.

"She's quite determined not to do that. She'll establish Eryxa and that will be that. The artists who live there will have to prove themselves and earn their living. She told me she's just giving them the initial chance. But you and Rorke—"

"All right. So Rorke will inherit from his aunt. What's at the back of your mind? That I married him for that?"

"You? Oh Lord, no!" His distress would have been comical if it hadn't been for his genuine misery. "It's just that—well, you know, don't you, that—that Berenice—that she—"

"That she *what*?"

He said desperately, "That she is a very, very devoted Catholic. That she would never accept divorce in the family. Or rather, if there were a divorce, Rorke's divorce I mean, she would disinherit him."

For a moment the full impact of what he meant did not occur to me. I said, "Oh, these days, if two people aren't happy together, then they separate. Life is a precious thing—it isn't meant to be lived in martyrdom."

"*I* know that and so do you. But Berenice doesn't. What the Church taught her in her youth is law to her for the rest of her life. And she has so much for someone to inherit—or lose. Her vast shares in Melarper's, her jewels, this house . . .

There's no Montegano heir, so a Thorburn will one day own it all . . . Rorke."

"I don't see the connection between that and your fears for me—"

"It's obvious, isn't it? Rorke won't dare let you divorce him."

I stepped back from that desperate pale-pink moon face. I said, icily, hating him, "There is no question of that. So you can save your warnings and your pity. I—"

"Catherine Mallory," he said.

I stared at him for one ghastly moment and then I walked out of the room. I went slowly down the stairs, past the brooding portrait of Floriana, and into the *salone*.

Rorke was mixing martinis.

"Darling Leonie," said Berenice. "Where *have* you been?"

"Willy was showing me his latest painting."

"And did you like it?"

I said, cruelly, too shocked for kindness, "As much as I enjoy a nightmare." Then I asked, "May I take my drink into the garden?"

"Of course, dear." But she looked a little hurt.

I said quickly, "I've got a headache—I think I need air."

Berenice . . . Rorke . . . I saw them watching me, each concerned in his and her own way. For what? For my supposed headache? I took my martini glass from Rorke and escaped, walking to the seat under the vine.

Think . . . Think . . . Think . . . That is, if you aren't too blindly in love with Rorke to dare the truth.

I sipped my drink and watched wisps of vermilion cloud tease the low sun. I could not go to Catherine's party at the Palazzo Kronos. I could not bear what I might discover. Yet, just because of that, I knew that I would go.

VIII

All that week I thought about Catherine's house-warming party, and by Friday the dread built up to a wild hope that something would happen to prevent me from going, but my imagination could think of nothing more drastic than pleading a headache, and that would fool no one.

On the morning of the party, the clocks of Venice were striking eleven when I arrived for my painting lesson. Adrian himself opened the door to me and explained that he had sent his man, Nicolo, on an errand of mercy to cook a meal for a fellow artist who had been rather roughly handled the previous night by someone who disagreed with his views on Italian foreign policy.

The studio was on the ground floor and as we turned off the

marble hall, I glanced toward the staircase which swept up past the next floor, where Adrian had his living quarters, to the two floors above.

I knew that he had a large double door built to shut off the top apartment, but nothing could divide the staircase which rose to the molded roof where a chandelier hung, which, while magnificently lighting the two upper floors, sent only a glimmer far down to the floors below. That was why along the walls of the hall were lamps set in gilded torchères. Between them hung the favorites among Adrian's own paintings, mostly portraits, which were what he liked doing best.

The studio was enormous, jutting out slightly over the *rio* so that from some angles, if I looked out of the windows, I seemed to be standing miraculously on the water.

Adrian uncovered the self-portrait I had begun and set the tall mirror at the right angle for me to see myself as I painted without having to change the position of my head.

I picked up the turpentine, uncorked it and then put the bottle back. I said, "I don't seem to be in the mood."

"You're paying for painting lessons, not moods."

"And a lot it worries you whether you get my few thousand lire or not."

"It is useful for my needy friends."

"Whom Berenice will soon be promoting on Eryxa."

"Oh, Eryxa!" he said, and we laughed.

I tried again to take an interest in painting, but after a few rather bad daubs, I put down my brush and palette and went over to where Adrian was working.

"May I look?"

"Of course."

He was painting shadows into the copy he was making of some soft blue silk material draped over a chair. He often worked in this way, painting the background before the sitter. He had once explained that to reproduce lovely materials was joy to him and he liked to indulge himself without the distraction of the sitter. So far, there was just a vague outline of a woman's head and shoulders.

"Who is the girl?"

"Isobel Mallory."

Catherine's young daughter. "You already know them?" I asked in surprise.

"When La Mallory came to look over the apartment, she saw some of my work and wanted a portrait of her daughter and I named a price so phenomenal that I thought she would walk out. Instead, she agreed to it. Isobel Mallory isn't my idea of an attractive sitter, but I've made preliminary sketches of her and so I know the pose. I've told her that she needn't come for a day or two while I work on the background."

"Blue," I said, "a gentle color—"

"To soften the harshness of her face. That's what her mother wanted. She said, 'I want her to look back on this portrait of herself in adolescence and not be ashamed of her sullen expression, so please paint in a smile.' She is a sullen child; spoiled probably, being taken round the world with a famous mother; indulged, spotlighted, bowed and scraped to—"

"Or perhaps," I said, "she's sullen because she hates it. Perhaps she doesn't want to be everlastingly in the shadow of a famous mother and would rather spend her holidays with girls of her own age."

"Perhaps." He wasn't interested.

We worked for nearly two hours, and Adrian came over occasionally to criticize and correct what I had done.

When I had to leave, he came to see me off. The great double doors of the *palazzo* opened and the sun streamed in. A boy, carrying a huge cellophane-wrapped bouquet of yellow roses, dashed up the steps.

"For Signora Mallory," he said and, by-passing Adrian, pushed the star-quality bouquet at me.

"I'm not—"

"For *you*, signora," the boy said in Italian.

Very quietly Adrian intercepted, taking the flowers and thanking the boy. "Signora Mallory is out and so is her maid. I'll put them in water for her."

The boy fidgeted; his thin dark little face went very red. "Signore, somewhere I . . . I have lost the card that was pinned to the flowers. I am sorry."

"Then I suggest you run back to the shop and find out who has sent them," Adrian said.

"Oh, but I know. You see, signore, *I* took the message for them. The flowers were ordered by a gentleman in Milan."

"Perhaps you can remember enough to tell me the name and I'll write it down."

His face was still suffused with the dark red of embarrassment. "Signore, the message said . . . it said . . ."

"Go on," Adrian urged.

"The gentleman made me write it down: 'The hardest thing in the world is to wait for great happiness. But it will come.' " He rushed the words out as if hating to have to say them and then took a gulp of air. "The signore who gave me the message had a funny name. He spelt it, but I do not remember. It sounded like Teerburno."

Teerburno. Thorburn . . .

Dear God, why did I have to understand Italian? I turned blindly, without knowing where I was going, knowing only that I had to escape from the tormenting beauty of the sunlight on the yellow roses, and found myself in the kitchen. I looked about me, my mind registering unimportant things, seizing on them as if I were drowning and they were my anchor.

The room was large, tidy and rather dark. The walls were

scrubbed white and there was every possible modern gadget. Adrian was very nearly a gourmet. An electric coffeepot was hubble-bubbling on a white stove.

Adrian entered, saying, "Signor Teerburno isn't the first to send flowers. They've been pouring in for La Mallory all day. I suppose he is famous like the rest, but I have never heard of him. Have you?"

"Yes," I said. "Oh yes. It's the best the boy could do with 'Thorburn' . . . my husband."

Adrian unwrapped the flowers and put them in a pitcher of water. "If you can make 'Thorburn' out of 'Teerburno'—"

"A small Italian boy would, especially if he were told to when he saw me."

"Oh come! How could the kid arrive at the precise moment when you were leaving?"

"Because someone knew I was here, and told the boy to hang around and wait until he saw me."

"And the flowers—*are* they from Rorke?"

Adrian served coffee from the bubbling pot.

"How do I know? All I *do* know is that someone made very sure I would be around when the flowers arrived. Perhaps the boy was bribed to tell someone . . . someone if an order for flowers was telephoned through in the name of Thorburn and report to him. Perhaps Rorke's message was deliberately destroyed so that the boy had to give it verbally."

"What an imagination you've got!"

"It's developing with experience," I said, and drank my coffee scalding hot.

"What you say is quite outrageous—"

"Not if you knew what I know," I said shakily, and told him about the meeting at the newsstand and also what had happened at the Accademia Bridge. I said, "Adrian, someone is watching me; he is like a kind of guardian and he knows all the moves made by the people involved." I finished my coffee and it tasted bitter. "You once asked me what was wrong between Rorke and myself, so obviously you heard rumors. Someone, who has also heard them, is using any method —even what happened just now with the flowers—to warn me."

"Of some affair that probably won't last if you let time take care of it." `

"Of tragedy," I said, "and don't ask me how it can happen or what it will be, because—I don't—know."

"I wish I could understand . . ."

"I only hope to heaven that I don't!" I said.

"Do you want me to give you some advice?" He didn't wait for me to answer. "Men stray and wives only have to play dumb and blind and deaf and it all blows over. Nothing is as daunting to a woman having an affair as dinners that have to be eaten in out-of-the-way places and rushed love on crumpled beds. And hell!"—he moved away from me—"why am I giving you advice like that? I should be saying 'Leave Rorke, divorce him and then you can come here with me. There's room for a woman about the house.' "

"Adrian, please, I'm serious."

"So am I."

The telephone began to ring.

"Answer it," I said. "I'll see myself out."

"No, don't go yet."

But I was already running down the hall.

I left the Palazzo Kronos and walked through the narrow *calli* and along the Frezzeria, making my way to the Merceria. I had seen the florist's name on the paper that had wrapped the flowers and remembered Iolanda Corvo's beautiful little shop where I had sometimes bought roses for Berenice.

I knew exactly what I was going to ask the signora and as I entered the shop, she came toward me between the banks of carnations and Madonna lilies. I greeted her and asked, too abruptly because I was nervous, "Would you please tell me if an order for flowers for Signora Mallory was telephoned through this morning from Milan? Your boy has just delivered them at the Palazzo Kronos."

The expression in the small black eyes sharpened. "Why do you ask me such a question, signora?"

"I have a reason."

"Doubtless. Just as I have a reason for not answering you. Details of our orders are private; we do not discuss them with strangers." Her voice and her manner were cold, and as she spoke she edged me toward the door.

I said, "I'm sorry, but can't you just—?"

She interrupted. "I am very busy. If that was all you came for, perhaps you will be kind enough to let me get on with my work."

I left the shop aware that I should have thought up some better way of finding out about the flowers. Signora Corvo had probably thought that I was a newspaper reporter probing into the affairs of the great Catherine Mallory.

I walked back through the Piazza; the old knife-grinder smiled at me and I smiled back. The woman at the kiosk had the current English edition of *Vogue*, and I bought it and carried it with me to the unprepossessing side door of the Ca' di Linas.

IX

For Catherine's housewarming party the apartment at the top of the Palazzo Kronos was full of people and flowers and among them, in the glamorous bewilderment of urns and vases of living color, were the yellow roses.

Catherine was tall, elegant, without beauty but possessing a kind of timeless magnetism that was far more dangerous.

The *salone* in which she received us was filled with carved and gilded furniture and bronzes. A chandelier illumined Catherine's chestnut hair as she stood greeting her guests, her face alight with pleasure as she touched the hands of each one and occasionally leaned forward to kiss a cheek.

Then my turn came. Her hand went out, her smile was charming, but I guessed what she must be thinking: "Rorke's little dark wife . . . my lover's cute little handicap . . ."

I wanted to leave almost as soon as I arrived. Instead, I joined in the party talk, tried to look intelligent when someone mentioned *Thaïs* or *Dido and Aeneas*, knowing them only vaguely as operas. I skated through the superficialities of conversation with what I hoped was a bright, intelligent face.

There were about thirty people in the room that ran the length of the house, but the mirrors that were hung between the tall pointed windows reflected the flow and movement of the guests, giving the impression of a great crowd.

I caught sight of myself many times in those mirrors—a girl in a chiffon dress the color of green water and wearing a pendant of moonstones interspersed with tiny diamonds, Rorke's gift at our wedding. I thought, "I should have worn dark red or a richer green—something that did not merge into the pale tints of the walls." I tried not to move around in Rorke's shadow and to mix independently of him, but it was not easy. Music was the accepted topic of conversation. I nodded knowingly when the guests discussed how Catherine had had the audience on their feet at the end of *Manon*, her dignity and pathos as Desdemona in *Otello*. When a woman in white turned and said that of course my husband and I had heard Catherine sing the part in London, I murmured something that could have been "Yes" or "No." Alarmed at the danger I could be in of betraying my ignorance, I turned my head and saw Catherine's daughter, Isobel, sitting alone on a red brocade settee. In her dead black dress, with a desperate, rather silly-looking magnolia stuck in her hair just above her ear, she looked solitary, defiant and a little tragic; a thin girl so sullen with loneliness that she defeated her own longings.

I made a quick excuse to the group who were discussing the Leonora costumes in the last production of *Fidelio* in Paris, and joined Isobel. Her eyes lit up as she sensed the shadow of someone near her, then dulled when she turned and saw me.

I had a feeling that it was a man she wanted as companion, but since no male guest was taking the slightest notice of her, I felt that talking to me would be better than this dumb aloneness to which she was being subjected.

I began by asking the usual questions. Had she been around and seen all the fascinating places in Venice? "There's something for everyone here," I said. "Paintings, architecture, the Piazza in the evenings and the Lido for sunbathing—"

Isobel's hands were clawing at her dress. "I hate the place. I hate all these people. I hate the whole world. I even hate— Oh—" She stopped and put her hand over her mouth like a child scared of saying something she would be punished for.

I said easily, "Well, you'll probably be back in England soon. You're only here for a short time, aren't you?" I watched her.

"I don't know. Mother has no engagements for six weeks and I suppose we'll stay here all that time. I wish she'd let me go!"

"Back to London?"

She nodded. "For a while, and then to the school in Switzerland where I'm supposed to be learning languages."

In the difficult silence that hung between us, and above the murmur and thrust of voices, I heard someone call to Catherine to sing. The request was taken up until the room was filled with it.

"A song, Catherine" . . . "Just one" . . .

She had been talking to Adrian and she looked around, laughing. A man called, "Sing 'The Willows Are Young.' "

I saw Catherine hesitate and look quickly across at Rorke. I kept my head turned stiffly toward the grand piano, away from the sight of Rorke's face, for the song was one for which he had composed the music during the height of their love for one another.

I had no idea whether Rorke made the slightest gesture, but Catherine walked to the piano and a man, who I was told was her accompanist, sat down and played a few soft chords.

I remained on the hard Recamier settee next to Isobel. And when Catherine began to sing, I shut my eyes and clasped my hands, digging my fingers into my palms.

> *"The willows yet are young beside the river*
> *Oh Youth of me,*
> *What love, what calm, what dreams have rolled forever*
> *Songless to the sea . . ."*

It was a gentle night, warm and calm, and yet I was frozen inside. The lovely cadences rose and fell; the voice was controlled and exquisite and full of poignancy.

This was their song—Catherine's and Rorke's. How many times had she sung it in her Mayfair drawing room or his Chelsea apartment? And when the song was over, had they come together as lovers? If they had, it was nothing to do with me. What had happened to Rorke—how he had lived, the women he had thought to love before he met me—was all in the past. Our lives were here and now.

But this love affair wasn't dead. I felt it pulsating in the song, in the room, in my very bones, as Catherine sang.

There was sudden silence; the singing had stopped and as the applause began, I looked across at Rorke. His face was very still and he wasn't applauding. It was as if he were still listening, as if he possessed some strange superauditory power that enabled him to hear the song's echo long after the singing was over. There were only two people in that room and the rest of us were interlopers.

When the calls came for an encore, Catherine shook her head and turned away and walked quickly onto the terrace. As if by some common consent, no one joined her. I could see her, outlined in moonlight, in her smooth silk dress and high-piled bronze hair. I had one fear. *Will Rorke leave the party and go out to her? If he does . . .*

If he did, what would I do? I knew the answer. Exactly nothing. And Rorke remained in the room.

Catherine didn't stay long on the terrace and I wondered, when she returned, if she had been expecting him to join her and if he had not done so because the whispers would continue more blatantly. And that could mean that the caution was for my benefit.

The clocks everywhere struck midnight and Catherine walked up to the man she called Maestro, and spoke to him. I saw him nod, and then she kissed him on the cheek and moved away. I recognized the gesture as a signal that the party was ended when people immediately began to move toward her and say goodnight. Her gesture had been a royal dismissal.

"Up you get, Leonie. The evening's over."

I started as Rorke held out a hand to pull me from the uncomfortable sofa. I looked at my watch and said unnecessarily, "It's midnight."

Filiberto was waiting for us with the launch, and we gave a lift to two of Catherine's guests who were staying at the Bauer Grünwald.

※

Back at the Ca' di Linas, I undressed while Rorke had his customary quick shower. When he came to bed, he switched out the light and lay beside me, his body cool. I turned immediately to him, my hands moving lightly over his face, feeling, like someone blind, the faint furrows of the brow, the high cheekbones with the firm skin over them. I laid my lips on his and spoke into his mouth softly, "I love you so much."

Immediately his hands tightened around me and he moved, burying his head against my hair, saying something that I couldn't hear. I had to know what it was. I said, "Tell me again . . ." But he didn't answer and we lay for a long time clinging to one another as if we had both been lost and had come together out of some unbearable need.

When, at last, sheer muscular exhaustion made me relax my hold, I lay with my head against the strong bones of his shoulder, my terrible suspicions dissolved by intimacy, as if by an enchanter's wand. I had never yet turned away from Rorke. Yet I knew that this ready giving of myself was no slavish capitulation, nor was it unselfishness. I wanted to please him in order to hold him; I was indulging myself in indulging him, but I faced the fact once again that physical passion was all I had from Rorke—and that was not love.

X

Early the following morning, Signor Lorenzo, the surveyor, arrived, looking martyred and politely resigned to the demands of a rich woman who desired him to work on Saturday. He and Rorke then left to pick up the architect, Carlo Pallamundi, who lived near the Rialto, and the three of them would go in his launch to Eryxa.

After breakfast, Berenice called me into her small sitting room. She was at her desk, riffling through an untidy pile of papers.

"Tell me about your party, Leonie. I'm afraid Rorke and I were so busy talking about Eryxa over breakfast that I forgot to ask you."

"It was a very glamorous affair."

She nodded. "I once heard Catherine Mallory sing at Covent

Garden, but I'm afraid I'm not very opera-minded. What is she like off-stage?"

"Oh, tall, impressive and . . . so marvelously sure of herself."

Berenice laughed. "When you enjoy adulation as she has, I suppose you can't help seeing yourself as someone special. Did you like her?"

"I didn't talk to Catherine enough to know whether I liked her or not," I said. "There were so many people there. But I talked to her daughter, Isobel. She made me feel sad."

Berenice raised her eyebrows, smiling at me. "At a party, my dear, you shouldn't let anyone make you feel that way!"

I said dryly, "Nothing there made me want to dance a fandango."

Berenice picked up some typewritten sheets and sorted them out. "I'm sorry the girl spoiled your evening."

Not Isobel, but Catherine . . .

I tried to think what else I could tell her about the party, as Berenice leaned over and pressed one of the small fluted columns at the back of her desk; the drawer opened and she pulled it out and then pressed the spring which opened the small second drawer hidden behind it.

"*Leonie!*"

I went quickly to her side. "What is it?"

Her fingers gripped the desk. "Someone has been through my private papers." She began scrabbling with both hands through the drawer in what seemed to me unnecessary frenzy. I held my breath, watching her. Her fingers flicked through folded parchment and printed slips clipped together. The gold ring I had seen in Rorke's hand glinted in the half-light of the room. Her voice rose in agitation.

"I *know* that my papers have been touched; I always keep them in a certain order."

The alarming picture of Rorke the other night standing by

the open drawer made a strange and ghostly third in the room.

I said, weakly, "Someone must have broken into the house and searched your desk for jewelry."

She shook her head. "There's nothing in this drawer of value to a thief. And I doubt if that type would understand how to open the secret compartments Sheraton made." She sat biting her lip and frowning.

I thought, my heart beating with horrible doubt: *But Rorke would not pry into Berenice's affairs.* And even if by some outrageous possibility he had, he was too highly trained to leave evidence that papers had been disturbed. He must have found the drawer open the other night simply because ntrenice had forgotten to close it. I willed myself to believe that was so and said, "I think you must have moved the papers yourself—perhaps Cèsara came into the room or you were called to the telephone."

"Oh, no!"

As I bent to put my arm around her, she reached out and closed the drawer, and I heard the click of the lock.

"Hadn't you better see if your jewel case is intact?"

"I opened it this morning to get out my sapphire brooch. I don't think the clasp is very safe and I'm taking it to the jeweler. Nothing was missing there."

"But you do keep valuables in that drawer." I nodded toward the desk. "I once saw something gold—"

"Just a trinket," she said lightly, "which has sentimental value to me. That's all." Her eyes closed momentarily and there was a pause, then in a changed voice, she said, "Perhaps you are right, my dear. Perhaps, after all, I disturbed the papers myself. I'm getting absent-minded." She glanced up at me—her eyes bright, her mouth stiff with her forced smile —and changed the subject. "What are you going to do with yourself today?"

I told her that I was due at Adrian's studio at eleven o'clock.

She was watching me anxiously. "I've grown very fond of you, Leonie. I hope and pray that you will always be happy with Rorke."

Her conversation seemed to change its direction so rapidly, I suspected that either she wanted me to forget her agitation over the disturbed papers or that there was some connection I hadn't grasped between the seeming odd tangent of her thoughts.

She was still watching me closely. "You and Rorke *are* happy, aren't you?"

"I love him. Doesn't it show, rather?"

She smiled with relief. "Love *should* show."

I wondered how she would react if I suddenly broke the reassuring silence by announcing, "One day Rorke might leave me. There is someone he has never stopped loving. Or perhaps 'love' isn't the right word. Perhaps it's an obsession." Instead I said, "I think I'll go for a walk before the sun becomes too hot."

"Yes, do that, dear child. Get some exercise. But mind you put on comfortable shoes."

"My sandals," I murmured and as I left her I had the feeling that she wanted to be alone.

When I was leaving the house, she came running down the stairs. "As you are early for your painting lesson, why don't you look in at some of our marvelous churches?" She went to the refectory table standing along a side wall of the hall, opened a drawer and took out a small square mirror bound around the edges with black tape. "Take this with you. Some of our churches have glorious ceilings, but you can see them much better by their reflections. Just hold the mirror flat, like this, and then look into it. You'll be surprised how it draws the beauty closer to you."

I managed to fit the mirror into my handbag, and felt that from her point of view—although she was far too kind to say it to me—I deserved reproach for not having already made a pilgrimage to the splendid Venetian churches.

The morning sun shone onto Quadri's side of the Piazza and I saw Isobel Mallory sitting at a table watching a muzzled Alsatian slink into the shadows.

I didn't stop to wonder whether she would welcome my company, but crossed to her. "Hello. May I join you?"

She moved her purse from the second chair and I hesitated. "If you want to be alone, do say. I won't be in the least offended."

"I hate being alone, but I had to get away from Mother and her string of serfs."

I laughed at the word. "It's possible that she gets a little tired, too, of being always in the limelight."

Isobel turned and her dark gray eyes mocked me. "Mother tired of being a prima donna? When that day comes, she'll be dead. She loves every bit of her life." She waved away a newsseller who was dangling *Paris Soir* in front of us. "And even somewhere in *that*"—she glowered at the newspaper—"you'll find a reference to my wonderful mother spending a holiday in Venice."

A waiter came and we asked for *caffelatte*. The silence between Isobel and me wasn't an easy one. I tried to think of something to say that would interest her and asked her about the school she went to.

"It's very smart and I can't wait for term to start again, though I don't enjoy it there. The girls are mostly from France and Scandinavia and they don't seem to like me much. But it's better than—*this*—" She flicked her hand at the vivid, weaving crowd before us.

I said, "Oh, I don't mind the tourists. Venice is meant to be looked at, like a great painting. I think if you tried, you could have a lovely time here."

"You don't understand," Isobel said angrily. "You think I

103

have so much, don't you? But do you imagine anything I have is given to me because my mother loves me?" She threw back her head in mock amusement. "I'm part of her shop window. If I wore cheap clothes, people would criticize her; if I didn't go to some expensive foreign school, they'd think she was neglecting me. She doesn't do anything for love of me. Mother loves one thing: being a public figure."

"I wonder how well you know her?"

In the moment's silence, I was shaken by my own defense of a woman I distrusted and should be detesting. But something in Isobel Mallory's attitude irritated me. She was like an angry little cat and I was her scratching post.

I was wondering how quickly I could escape when she said, "Mother is having an affair."

My impulse was to remember an urgent appointment and rush away. Instead I sat and stared at the sun gilding the bronze lions over St. Mark's, and made no comment.

"That's what makes it all the more horrible being here," she continued. "I'm out of everything; out of her life. I'm a kind of third, unwanted party."

"If she didn't want you, she would probably send you away to stay with friends."

"But I've told you, I'm part of the picture. Though she doesn't want me, I've got to stay so that people will say how wonderful she is, what a good mother, having her daughter with her—and a dull daughter at that. It's a charming picture she makes for herself, isn't it? But all the time, there she is, looking on me as a nuisance, itching to go to this man, yet knowing that she'd lose face if she sent me away so that she could be more free." She drew in a sharp breath. "It's awful, isn't it? *But I hate her.*"

"I don't believe that." Yet I did. Unless she was a consummate actress, she could not have said it with that desperate passion unless she had meant it.

I watched the toy-seller near the Doges Palace lift one thing after another from his tray and show them to a couple of interested tourists.

Isobel picked up her purse, pulled out a mirror and looked at herself. She said, "When I was very young, I was taken to hear Mother in *Manon*. I didn't understand the music or the story and it bored me. Afterwards, they showered her with flowers and I saw her standing on the stage looking as if she'd conquered the world. It was like looking at someone you'd never known before; she was so powerful, she terrified me. People like Mother should never have children." She picked up her coffee cup and crashed it down again. "And now there's this—this man. I know by the look in her eyes and her secretiveness that she's planning something—and it's to do with him."

"It could be all in your imagination. It may be that she is excited because of some new opera—"

"Oh, she's not excited. She's calm and yet on fire inside herself. I know Mother, and I wish the man, whoever he is, were dead."

I let her rave in her low, furious voice. But while I could not help listening, I felt fear creep through me. Catherine's strength was in her daughter, too, although in Isobel's case it was channeled into bitterness. I wanted to change the subject, but I couldn't. A devil rode my mind and I had to say, "If there was a man your mother was in love with, you would obviously know him. He would be around."

"Not if he were married, and I'm sure he is. Oh, Mother is so cautious. She would never be part of something which tarnished her reputation. Whoever the man is, I'm certain he has a wife. In the end, however hard she tries, this wife will be the loser. That is why it's all so secretive." She pushed away her cup and lit a cigarette with a little gold lighter, smoking in short, nervy puffs. "I've thought it all out. I know why she chooses a married man. It's because there is so much more thrill in taking from someone else. It's like winning wars. There's a lot more excitement in grabbing from an enemy than taking land you could have because it doesn't belong to anyone." She shuddered and plunged her quarter-smoked cigarette into the huge white ashtray. "Mother frightens me."

She frightened me, too.

"I even know where Mother meets this man. I followed her one evening, and she went throught a gate in a high wall."

I managed to jerk out one word. "Where?"

She said vaguely, "Oh, somewhere near the Chiesa San Moisé."

And that was the church at the far corner of the *calle* along which ran the garden of the Ca' di Linas. But that couldn't be a meeting place, not where one of us might see her. Not with Berenice wandering through her dim, shadowed rooms; Willy padding around in his slippers; and I, knowing exactly when Rorke came home, sometimes on Friday nights or sometimes, if work held him up, on Saturday mornings. I knew his movements during the weekends, and at night he was with me.

I sat tensely in my chair, willing the truth to be that Catherine had no important place in Rorke's present world. My mind swung so wildly between hope and self-mockery that the Piazza and its vivid life receded in a mist that was not caused by tears but by panic. I wanted the name of Catherine's lover to be utterly strange to me; I wanted to be able to laugh aloud . . .

Isobel was saying, "I'm going to find out who the man is if I have to follow Mother right into whatever house it is and up to the bedroom. I'm going to see—"

Someone swung into my misty, emotional vision. Willy was coming toward us, walking lightly between the strutting pigeons and the people, his baby-soft ginger hair catching the sunlight. He reached our table, shot a quick look at Isobel and, drawing out a chair, asked, "May I?" His overwhelming feminine curiosity could not resist finding out who my companion was.

I introduced them and Willy said, thoughtfully, "Mallory . . . Mallory? You couldn't possibly be the daughter of the singer, could you?"

"It so happens"—she scowled at him—"that I am."

"But that's wonderful!" His radiant smile was intended to bring Isobel back to good humor. "I've often seen your photographs in the papers."

"My mother's, you mean."

"And yours." He made the words a compliment and wriggled in his chair, settling for a pleasant coffee session with us. "I've just bought a little present for Berenice"—he turned to Isobel—"Signora Montegano, my dear hostess," he explained. "It's a fan." He unwrapped the parcel carefully and spread the fan for us to see. It was of black lace, charming and inexpensive.

Isobel took it and her face brightened. "It is so pretty! Where did you get it?"

"They're all over the place here, but that shop across the Piazza"—he pointed—"has some rather nice ones. I'll take you to look at them if you like."

Animation lit up her face. I doubted if Isobel wanted a fan, but for all Willy's odd little womanly ways, he was a man to her starved emotions.

As I ordered coffee for him, I heard him say longingly, "You must meet such interesting people. I've always admired your mother as an artist . . . her voice—" He waved his hands expressively but avoided my disbelieving eyes—Willy had probably never been to the opera in his life. "It would be marvelous to meet her."

"I'll introduce you if you like," Isobel said disinterestedly.

"You really mean that?"

"Why not? I don't see why *I* shouldn't bring a friend to her parties."

"You're sweet."

Isobel gave him a startled look. "That's the last thing I am."

They weighed each other, intrigued, each wanting something from the other—Isobel a man's interest in her, Willy to touch the fringes of a world that was only a dream to him. As real people, with minds and hearts, neither existed for the other.

It was still too early for me to go for my painting lesson, but I wanted to be free of them both. "I'm off to do some sightseeing before I go to Adrian's," I said. "You two wallow in coffee and then go to look at fans." I called for the bill, paid it and left them.

But as I walked under the arcade toward the Grand Canal, I felt a vague concern. I wondered whether I had done Isobel a favor or whether I had tossed her to unknown wolves. A man like Willy, with a doubtful background, a waif from the back streets, his integrity never really proven, was not a companion for a young girl who had lived in protected luxury.

Nevertheless, the small, lurking fear that it had been an unlucky meeting for Isobel was banished by the thought that any possible friendship was better than none at all for Catherine Mallory's bitter daughter.

XI

I took a vaporetto to the Zattere and, walking up a *calle* lined with ancient, pale golden houses leaning on one another, I found a church. It was empty except for one shawled woman. The smell of incense lingered; the altar glowed in the twilit darkness and I wandered into a small side chapel with an ornate altar, a large wrought-iron candelabra bright with votive candles, and a painted ceiling. I took out the mirror Berenice had given me and turned it so the ceiling was reflected perfectly.

The painting was, however, too large for the whole of it to be seen at once. I had no idea who the artist was and I remembered, without any sense of guilt, how Adrian had once accused me of being abysmally ignorant of the great masters. I'd retorted that at twenty-five I had plenty of time to learn.

I bent my head, looking in the mirror at the reflection of the central characters of what was obviously a religious masterpiece. The blue had the soft depth of an English spring sky; the gold glowed; the crimson had a sheen like velvet.

Around me was the typical hush of an empty church. I felt its peace stealing over me, sweeping away all tensions, and gave a thought to Rorke, wondering if he would be interested in this lovely quiet place. We had visited so few of Venice's marvelous interiors together because we had had so little time in each other's company.

I looked down into the mirror again, adjusting it to another part of the ceiling painting. As I did so, I saw the reflection in the mirror of a movement behind me. It was just the shadow of something too near, like the swift sweep of an arm.

My reaction was entirely involuntary. I leapt to one side with such force that I overbalanced and fell sprawling onto the stone floor. At the same moment the heavy wrought-iron stand that held the lighted candles came crashing down onto the place where I had stood. The sound reverberated through the hushed church; the candles flickered and some broke, some were snuffed out; the smell of burning wax drifted in my direction. The mirror had slid from my grasp but miraculously had not broken.

For a moment that seemed endless, there was silence and utter stillness as though the noise of the crash had shocked even the old stones. Then I sprang to my feet and whipped round, alert, furious, ready to hit out at whoever was behind me.

I was alone in the chapel.

I picked up the mirror and, shaken, went to the archway that led into the body of the church. The praying woman had lifted her shawled head and was looking my way; a priest was hurrying toward me. There was no one else in sight.

But someone had been there, someone whose movement I

had seen in the mirror just that moment before the crash; someone who had followed me, perhaps all the way from the Piazza.

The old priest said gently, "You tripped, signora?"

"No. I wasn't even touching the stand." I stared down at it and its sputtering candles as if it were a monster.

"I was in the sacristy when I heard the crash. I understand what happened." He smiled. "You stepped back to look at the reflection of part of the painting—a lot of people look at it in mirrors—and your foot caught the stand. You tripped and fell and it came down with you. It is very heavy—"

Heavy enough to have crushed or even killed me with its weight. . . . I said, "I didn't trip against it. There was someone behind me who reached out . . ."

"But there is no one else here, signora."

"*I saw*—" I broke off. What was the use? He believed I was lying so that I would not be reprimanded for what was my clumsiness.

He bent to lift the stand and I saw that he could not do it alone; he was too small and too old. Trembling, I helped him and together we got it upright while some of the candles which were still alight streamed in the draught our movements made. When the stand was in its place again, the old priest shook it and said, "You see, it is very firm. So, without knowing it, you must have knocked against it. But do not worry; you are unhurt. I will light the candles again. Perhaps you would like me to leave you to give thanks quietly for your escape from what could have been a nasty accident."

For my second escape . . . I said, "I have to go, Father. I have a painting lesson. But thank you for coming so quickly."

Someone had followed me to an almost deserted church. How easy, after the attempt, to walk quietly away and not disturb the praying woman who would be slow to come out of her religious absorption. How easy to slip from pillar-

shadow to pillar-shadow until at last he reached the doorway
of the church and could escape, mingling with the crowds,
turning into the narrow streets and disappearing.

The priest was carefully straightening a few bent candles,
relighting them and setting them more firmly in their iron
holders. I crept out of the side chapel and, because my legs
were so weak, sat down in a chair near the door to collect what
little courage was left me in order to walk out into the street.

A few more people had drifted into the church and I eyed
them with suspicion. Had one of the three women and two
men who came to kneel so devoutly been my attacker? Perhaps
he—or she—had been curious to know what had happened to
me and had crept back to find out. I leaned back and closed
my eyes, trying to clarify the shadow of movement I had seen
behind me just before the crash. Had I seen a man's dark
sleeve? . . . a woman's hand? . . . a ring? . . . a bracelet? I
could recall nothing save that I had seen a moving shadow and
that some inner warning had sent me leaping to safety.

I glanced at my watch and saw that, unless I hurried, I was
going to be late for Adrian's lesson and, although never punc-
tual himself, it infuriated him when other people were not on
time. I got up quickly, made my way to the door and looked
down at the steps, treading each one carefully as if afraid they
would dissolve under me. I trusted nothing to be solid and
safe. People wandered past me, all seemingly quite indifferent
to a dark girl in a yellow dress.

According to the little map of Venice which I always carried
with me, I was only a short distance from the Accademia and
Adrian's house. And I went quickly through the narrow
streets, out of sunlight into sharp shadow, into sunlight again.
Canaries sang from half-shuttered windows; there was a tiny
shop displaying a single golden dress, and windows full of
sandals.

I tried to tell myself that what had happened could have

been an accident; that the dark moving reflection I had seen behind me in my mirror could have been a shadow across the sun that had dimmed, for a moment, the light streaming through a window. The stand in which the candles burned could have had a weak joint; or the floor could have been uneven and a stone become loosened by age so that my footstep on the adjoining slab could have tipped it and sent the stand and guttering candles crashing. I argued every possibility—and dismissed them all.

More than once, I looked back and tried to memorize the people following me. At no time did I see the same face and that gave me a brief confidence; the danger was momentarily over. All the same, I began to run and, turning the last corner, flung myself at the heavy door of the Palazzo Kronos.

Nicolo let me in and gave me his broad, beaming smile just to show me once again what beautiful teeth he had. The signore was in his studio. I would like coffee, yes?

"Please," I said and paused in front of a heavily gilded mirror, doing the best I could with my hair, which was limp from the heat of the blazing morning and my panic run. My skin was the color of a grubby tennis ball and when I took out my lipstick Nicolo, who had seen so many women come and go at the Palazzo, turned away tactfully and pretended to sort out some papers on a table. But he must have been watching me out of the corner of one eye, for when I moved away from the mirror, he also turned and very politely and gravely led me to the studio.

Adrian was sitting cross-legged on the floor studying some canvases piled against the wall. He turned, said, "Hi, there!" and then, with a single fluid movement, rose and came toward me. He looked me up and down and said in a startled voice, "What's happened to you?"

I looked down at myself. "Grubby dress—"

"No, frightened eyes. Why?"

I dropped onto the long settee and said, "I was too early for my painting lesson, so I went to look at a church near the Zattere."

"And you thought you saw someone's ghost. Titian? Veronese?"

I lifted my eyes to his face. "It happened again, Adrian. Someone tried to kill me."

For a moment I thought he was going to burst into laughter but the expression flashed swiftly across his face and was gone. I must have been sending out black rays of fear which Adrian, always sensitive to atmosphere, picked up, for he said very gently, "Suppose you tell me what happened this time, and let me give you my opinion?"

I brushed my hand over my hot face. "I'm a sight, aren't I? My hands—" I held them out, grazed and scratched and rather horrid with little pinpoints of congealed blood.

"To me," Adrian said, "you look rather fetching in that dress. Like a water nymph who has dried off. But . . . Here, my girl—" He dragged me to my feet and pushed me toward the small cloakroom that led off his studio. "I'll talk to you when you have cleaned up those hands." He shut the door and left me.

When I came out again, he took my fingers in his. "They are only scratches after all. They looked a mess before. Nicolo"—he raised his voice to a bellow—"caffè."

It came almost immediately, and Adrian handed me a cup and sat down by my side. "Now tell me what happened."

I left out nothing, from the time I had met Isobel in the Piazza to the moment when I tilted the mirror and saw the moving shadow right behind me. "If I hadn't been trying to focus the mirror properly onto the corner of the painting I would never have seen the lifted arm," I said.

"Was it a woman's hand? Or a man's?"

"I don't know. It was very dim in the chapel; there were

only the candles. And it all happened in a flash—the move-ment, my leap away. It's odd, isn't it, how quickly one's re-flexes work?"

"I don't think the stand would have killed you. Given you a concussion; even broken a limb. It would have had to be a very powerful and accurate aim at your head to have killed you." He ran a finger lightly along my cheek.

"I can't demonstrate the force that was used on that stand," I said. "But it was a powerful, incredibly swift movement."

"Drink your coffee while it's hot."

"You don't believe me, do you? Well, I don't blame you. I don't think I look like someone's mortal enemy . . . Oh, Adrian—" I leaned against him. "It's all true!"

"Darling girl, tell me which church it was and I'll go myself and test the thing that holds the candles. I'll bet it's so old that its joints are cracked."

"I don't know the name of the church. I didn't look but it's on that narrow *rio* that leads off the Zattere—"

He nodded and began to play with my hair. "I know the one. The whole place is crumbling with age."

"Isn't it odd," I said, "that whenever anything unusual hap-pens, people think you've made a good story out of nothing very much! *You* do, don't you?"

"I don't know what to think. Two near-accidents in such a short space of time seems to me a pretty poor joke fate is playing on you."

"And that's all?"

"What else could it be? Dear Leonie, you enchant me, but I can't go along with some secret intrigue against your life."

"That's what Rorke will say, too!"

"Ah yes, Rorke . . ." Adrian stood up abruptly and crossed to the canvases lying about on the floor.

"What did you mean by, 'Ah yes, Rorke'?" I demanded.

"I've learned never to discuss a woman's husband with her."

"You don't like him, do you?"

"I would dislike any man who is married to you. Now, suppose we forget rickety church furnishings and get on with painting."

It was the last thing I wanted but Adrian saw that I was about to protest and crossed over and adjusted my easel. "It's therapeutic," he said.

I looked at the beginnings of my self-portrait and capitulated. It was useless to fight unimaginative logic. I said, "Awful, isn't it?"

"For a first effort at portraiture, it's not bad at all. The trouble with you is that you want to walk before you can crawl. You really needed a good many more basic lessons before you tried portraits."

"I haven't time." My quick retort took on another, more sinister meaning. I shook the morbid thought away and said with a poor effort at a laugh, "I shouldn't be here at all, should I?"

"Why do you say that?" He folded his arms about me and I leaned against him, glad of his support.

"Because I'll never be an artist, and all I'm really doing is finding something to occupy me."

"An escape."

"Yes." I closed my eyes and felt his hand smooth my cheek. Inside myself I was trembling with gratitude at his gentleness.

There was a small rustle of sound.

"*Escape? From what?*"

The voice cut clearly across the quiet of the room. Startled, I opened my eyes and saw Isobel in the doorway.

Her face was tight with anger, and she gave me a glare that should have withered me. I tried to move out of Adrian's arms, but he held me as if it were the most natural thing in the world.

116

"Hello, Happiness," he said. "What are you doing here?"

"I thought you wanted to get on with my portrait. But I can see you're otherwise engaged."

"That's right, I am. I don't work weekends."

"Only when Leonie is around. And of course, you couldn't call *that* work, could you?"

Adrian released me, took a cigarette from a shagreen box and lit it. "No one invited you here today, so I suggest you go upstairs to your own apartment and play with your dolls."

Her face twisted. "How cruel you are."

"My dear child, you don't know what cruelty is. All I'm trying to convey is that I don't much like little girls who walk into my private apartments uninvited."

"I live here."

"Upstairs."

She walked to the center of the room, and the eyes which I had thought to be dull, dead gray blazed as they turned to me. "Why don't you watch your own husband instead of coming here pretending you want to paint?"

"I may be very bad at it," I said steadily, "but I happen to like daubing color about."

"But *here*," she snapped, "with Adrian. Why don't you go away and leave him to get on with my portrait? Or are you jealous? After all, it's *me* he wants to paint, not you."

I found myself laughing. "I don't want to be painted. I couldn't afford Adrian's prices, and for another thing, I hate to have to sit still so long!"

Her eyes flew to Adrian's face. He said, "If you persist in being such a little bore, I won't finish your portrait—"

"Oh, but you will. Mother's paying you a high price—"

"I don't give a damn for the price," he retorted, "and if you want to know the truth, your mother wore me down with her requests for me to paint you. You don't think I find your face particularly interesting, do you? You've got a bad-tempered mouth and as yet the only bit of character that's formed on your face is sullenness. Now, skip off."

Isobel looked stricken. For a moment I thought she was going to burst into tears. Then, she controlled herself. "I'm sorry you find me so detestable," and turned away.

I said quickly, "Isobel, listen. I'll tell you what led up to what you think you saw—and didn't. I'm not having an affair with Adrian. I came here a while ago straight from looking at a church where I had a very near accident. It frightened me and I told Adrian all about it." I held out my scratched hands. "Look, there's proof. I fell—"

"And I'm sure you ran all the way here to get sympathy and kisses."

My sudden rush of pity for her exploded, but before I could speak, Adrian said, "That's one way in which you differ from your mother. She's never cheap!"

"Ha! She doesn't need to be. The men do the groveling."

In a single movement, Adrian was across the room and shaking her violently. "Come to your senses, you little brat, and go! This is my house and you'll come to my studio when you're invited. And even then, you'll only stay if you behave yourself. Thank God you're not my daughter."

Hands on her shoulders, he walked her to the door and opened it for her. She stood for a moment and all the anger went out of her. Everything about her—her eyes, her mouth, the droop of her shoulders—had a wounded and infinitely lonely look. Then her glance rested on me again and her eyes flashed. I saw her hands working, tensing and pulling at her skirt.

"Do you really think I don't know who my mother's lover is? Do you think I'm *that* blind? I thought you'd jump to it without my telling you. And I'm not saying his name now because you *do* know, don't you? When did it first dawn on you? Soon after your marriage—?" She broke off, choking and weeping, her hand across her eyes.

We watched her rush up the staircase, her blue skirt swinging, one hand on the gilded banister.

Adrian closed the double doors. "And you can wipe *that* speech off the agenda! Of all the little bitches—"

For the first time, I saw Adrian look embarrassed and I guessed why. All Venice knew—whispered about in the drawing rooms; tossed laughing across café tables; bandied around the Conservatoire of Music . . . La Mallory and Rorke Thorburn . . .

I felt a blind fury sweep over me that was a mixture of pain and pride.

"It's an extraordinary thing about people," Adrian said. "If there's no great crisis to talk about, they manufacture juicy bits of gossip and with each telling it becomes magnified. Now, about this—" He picked up a brush and reached over to the canvas and drew it across my painted shoulder. "It's all wrong. The line from the neck to the left arm should be here."

I took the brush from him and returned it to the turpentine pot. "I can't paint this morning. Please understand."

"I do. You've had a horrible morning, so go home and forget about it. Come on Tuesday. And see that you don't fall over a step on the way home or that somebody doesn't drop a pot of geraniums onto your head from an upstairs window."

At the door, the sunlight shafted onto his face and turned his hair to corn-gold. He stood looking down at me, smiling. "If you were free, I think I would marry you."

"Oh no," I tried to make my voice light. "If I were free, you wouldn't be interested. You've probably forgotten, but you once told me that, for you, the unattainable has charm."

I smiled and left him. At the corner of the Campo where an old tree stood surrounded by a wooden seat, I turned. Adrian was still watching me from the doorway.

XII

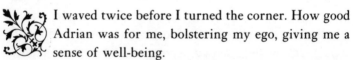 I waved twice before I turned the corner. How good Adrian was for me, bolstering my ego, giving me a sense of well-being.

A vaporetto had just pulled into the pier as I reached the Accademia. I bought my ticket, went on board and made my way up to the front of the boat. When I looked back, I could just see a corner of the Palazzo Kronos. At one of the tall, pointed windows of the upstairs apartment, a woman stood looking out. Standing or sitting, Isobel slouched, so I knew from the erect, imperious line of the head and shoulders framed in the window, that it was Catherine. From this distance, I knew she could not possibly recognize me in the crowd on the boat, but I could not help feeling that that was exactly what she was doing.

I had nothing to fear from her. If Isobel ran to her with the news that she had found me in Adrian's arms and if Catherine told Rorke, I had a perfectly reasonable explanation. I had escaped there from a near-accident; I was frightened. Arms had comforted me. Yet, words could be added, hints and implications that could distort the truth. But Rorke would believe me. He had said, soon after we were married, "You never prevaricate, do you, Leonie? However unpalatable the truth might be, you give it."

And so he would know that if Isobel spread a rumor that I was having an affair with Adrian, he need only ask me and I would tell him that I was not, and he would believe me. I had not the courage to ask him the same question about Catherine.

*   *   *   *

For all his Italian name, Luigi Montegano, Berenice's husband, had been British. The wealth he had passed on to Berenice was from Melarper's and, under British law, she was free to dispose of her fortune as she wished. I faced the fact, as we cut through the smooth Venetian waters, that Willy had been right when he said Berenice would never accept divorce in her family.

If Catherine and Rorke shared an obsessive love, then they did not dare make it public. For, standing between them was a very ordinary girl with her own great obsessive love. Leonie Thorburn, who was awakening to her own expendability.

The Canal widened into the lagoon. I looked for the first time without pleasure at the Byzantine and Gothic palaces, at the arches and pinnacles, the marble water-steps. A wedding gondola, decked out in white flowers, passed at a cautious distance from our churning waters. The bride sat shyly aware of her importance. Among the mound of white flowers and silk, she looked like a little figure sinking into the melted icing of a wedding cake. The gondolier smiled up at us; the crowd on the vaporetto waved to her. We wished her well, we smiled down at the child's face above its white enmeshment.

*   *   *

When I reached the Ca' di Linas, Rorke was there. I saw him sitting in the garden, poring over some plans that were pinned to a board on his knees, and I watched him as he marked certain spots on the paper. He was so absorbed that he obviously didn't hear me come through the high gate.

I made my way slowly along the path toward him, noticing the way his dark hair shone in the light as he bent forward out of the shadow of the vine. I thought: "How much longer have we got together?"

I loved him and I fought to keep my trust in him. The circle of danger in which I was caught had nothing to do with Rorke. He would never harm me. Somewhere, for some reason heaven alone knew, I had an enemy. Not Rorke . . . I clung to that as I moved close to him and saw my shadow fall across the paper that he was marking with little crosses.

He looked up, screwing up his eyes against the light. "So there you are. How did the painting lesson go?"

"It didn't." I sat down beside him. "How did the session go with the surveyor?"

"Well enough. He thinks the whole plan a little mad. Eryxa might have been a fine and noble island in the sixteenth century, but the soil is now thin, the clay underneath soaked by the rising lagoon waters. It can't be otherwise, with the increasing flow of traffic and the high tides of 1966 which flooded the island and which no one bothered to do anything about because it was uninhabited." He laid the paper on the table by his side.

I sat next to him, staring ahead of me at the morning-glory already wilting against the wall. "Have you been on the island all the morning?"

"Typical of Pallamundi, when we went to fetch him, he hadn't even had breakfast."

"So you waited."

"Not in his apartment with that raucous-voiced wife of his. Lorenzo stayed but I went for a walk."

"So did I. First I went to Quadri's for coffee because I was too early—Adrian doesn't like to be disturbed before eleven. I met Isobel in the Piazza."

"That maladjusted child."

"I think she's just wildly unhappy—and lonely."

"Lonely? With all Venice at her mother's feet?"

"Perhaps that's why."

He said impatiently, "She should have a taste of what it's like to be poor and deprived."

"Perhaps she is deprived . . . and needs friends."

"You earn your friends," he said. "Come on, let's go in and find a drink."

"There's something I want to tell you first and I'd rather Berenice didn't know. I don't want to worry her."

He reached up and pulled off an earring. "You've lost the other," he said. "I'm glad. I don't like you wearing them. They don't suit you; you're not the exotic type." He tossed the little garnet and pearl earring up and caught it. "Come on, what do you want to tell me that Berenice mustn't hear? Have you broken one of her special Venetian vases?" He spoke with the kind of light indulgence of an adult for an immature girl's confession.

"I went to look at a church near the Zattere and had an accident. One of those stands that holds the votive candles fell and I only just managed to dodge it."

"They're usually firm and very heavy."

"But it fell. I jumped in time and went flat on my face on the ground. Look at my dress."

"It's a bit dirty. You'll have to give it to Cèsara to wash or clean or whatever you women do with your dresses." He spoke lightly, turning away from me.

I said violently, "Rorke, listen. I was nearly killed in that church and though I said it was, it *wasn't* an accident!"

He had been leaning forward. As I spoke, he flicked aside a tendril of the vine and looked back at me, his eyes wary—as if he were wondering if I had developed a paranoia, *or as if he knew what I was about to tell him.* It was a terrible and outrageous thought.

I sat back, hunched in my corner deep in the shadow of the vine, and told him exactly what had happened. I spoke without looking at him, fixing my eyes on the vivid patch of flowers immediately in front of me.

When I stopped speaking, Rorke said, "You saw a shadow in the mirror. And that's all?"

"And the corner of a hand . . ."

"Reaching out for a candle to light."

"It wasn't. The hand was near my head, cutting the air, chopping . . . I didn't have time even to turn around. The hand was coming *at me*. I just leapt to one side."

"And the priest who heard the noise and came to the chapel saw no one?"

"No one. But"—my voice was tight because I was holding my breath—"this is the second attempt." I let the breath out. "The *second!* The first was at the Accademia. I told you about that and you thought, like everyone else, that a drunk had pushed me. This time—" I stopped, rigid with fear.

He laid a hand over mine and spoke gently. "A lot of us go through phases of being accident prone. One thing and then another happens. But it passes. And it probably has with you. You're safe and well—"

"*It wasn't an accident.* Someone was there; someone who had followed me into the church."

"Leonie—don't!" His fingers gripped my wrist. "Don't let your imagination play sinister games with you. Listen—darling. No one was following you; no one wanted to harm you."

"How do you know? You weren't there." I remembered that that was exactly what I had said after I had told him about the attack at the Accademia.

Rorke got up and walked, head down, as if studying the flowers. The sun was in my eyes but instead of moving to another seat under the awning, I bent and picked up Angelo and held him purring against me.

I had a sudden fear that Rorke was going indoors, and I raised my voice in panic defiance: "Whether you believe me or not, it really happened, just as I told you. Someone is either trying to frighten me away from Venice or else wants me dead."

He stopped and turned, holding out both hands to me.

I put Angelo down and went to where Rorke stood. He drew me to him and his face was grave. "Let's put it this way, shall we? I'm quite certain that *you* believe it happened. Does that satisfy you?"

"No."

"Then I believe that someone entered the chapel behind you, was careless and knocked against the stand, saw it fall and was scared at what he had done and fled."

"Oh no, if you knock something over, you stop and pick it up. This man disappeared, so you are not even being logical."

"I'm facing the fact that there is nobody in Venice or any-where else who wants to harm you." His voice was gentle, anxious—he who by nature was impatient. "You have no enemies. Leonie, listen to me. You must stop this persistent suspicion. You're a perfectly normal young woman, you know; there's no cloak-and-dagger mystery surrounding you."

We stood in silence, looking at one another as though a sudden huge gap had come between us, then I shivered in the hot sun and turned abruptly and walked into the house. I met no one in the vast dark hall, nor on the stairs. In the bedroom, I pushed open the shutters, and the light surged in. I looked at the shining world outside and then, as I turned, caught sight of the fresco around the walls. The light I had released would fade it just a fraction more, but I looked at the girl on the dolphin. The artist must have painted her there among the Olympian gods for a purpose. Perhaps she was a symbol. Of what? I could imagine the white dolphin plunging suddenly into the water, taking the high waves with the same abandoned joy that was on the girl's face. But she was not a mermaid, so the dolphin's heady dive into the wild dark sea might be the end of her. And perhaps, like the girl on the dolphin, I was riding the unridable . . .

I closed the shutters and went to the bathroom, washed and then put on a fresh dress. Rorke came in as I was combing my hair. He perched on the dressing table and watched me.

"I've hurt you, haven't I? I'm sorry. I suppose I'm too trained by my job in questioning and in doubting."

I went on combing my hair. "You don't believe me. Let's leave it at that."

"God knows what I believe! But there's one question you've got to answer. Do you want to go back to London?"

I wheeled around. "With you?"

"No. I have to stay for a while."

"But you'd like me to go back?"

"I didn't say that. I just felt that you'd feel safer in your own mind, perhaps, in London."

126

"In—my—own—mind . . ." I cried out again in protest. "*You want me to go!*"

"What I want isn't entering into the argument. It's what would be best for your happiness—your health, even. Leonie, please try to understand—"

"I do. I *do*! You think I haven't enough to do here and I'm creating drama to thrill—and scare—myself."

He said quietly, watching me, "All I think, darling, is that you can't go on like this, continually on the edge of fear."

"That's a neat turn of phrase!" My voice was so high, so mocking that it could have been a stranger's. I flung down my comb and watched it slither across the polished wood. "Isobel told me that her mother is having an affair."

"Why are you changing the subject?"

"I don't think I am. I think it's all tied up." I swiveled around and faced him. "Rorke, about Catherine—"

"We were talking about *us*. What Catherine does is her own affair."

And mine . . . I said aloud, "Can't we be honest with one another?"

His expression sharpened. "Why do you think we aren't?"

"Catherine."

"We'll leave her out of the conversation." He spoke quite quietly, yet I sensed a sudden widening of the void between us. I wanted to shout: "Is she your mistress? Isobel thinks so." But I could not get the words out. And, anyway, questions were useless unless one could believe the answers.

An immense despair swept over me, sapping my energy. In Rorke, I was up against a will stronger than my own and I was tired and frightened. I sank onto the bed and Rorke came and took me in his arms. "Suppose we stop this conversation; it's leading nowhere. Berenice will be waiting for us, so I'll go down and mix you a long, cool drink." He kissed me and let me go.

"Rorke, we must talk this thing out . . ."

But I was pleading to an empty room. He had left me so swiftly that I doubted if he had heard me. His quick footsteps died away down the stairs.

XIII

The house was busy with the morning's activities. Berenice had gone to church to ask a blessing for the success of her Eryxa plan, then she was going on to see the *dottore* who was treating her for slight hypertension. Willy was out, probably in some café with friends somewhere near the Rialto. Cèsara was sweeping the top balcony. The maid who came daily was cleaning the hall and her singing joined with the scraping of Filiberto's knife as he cleared the moss that fought a battle for survival on the water-steps.

When the telephone rang, I answered it.

The voice asked in English, "Signora Thorburn?"

"Yes."

"Are you alone?"

"I am. Why—?"

"I want to help you."

I said quickly, angrily, "Thank you. But who are you and why should you think I need help?"

"I am someone who cares about your—survival."

The hesitation before the last word was so melodramatic that I laughed. "Oh, I'm surviving."

"Please believe I'm serious."

"You may be, but I'm not. I don't like anonymous callers."

"You must believe me when I tell you that I dare not give my name. And don't replace the receiver. Please, please listen . . . Are you still there?"

"Yes."

"You know that your husband is seeing the singer, Catherine Mallory."

"They're old friends."

"You misuse the word 'friends,' signora, and you know it. Why not say 'lovers'?"

"I won't listen—"

"You will, because you have already had two very near misses—"

"Misses . . . ?"

"From death."

"That's rubbish," I said angrily. "I had two near-accidents. There are times in some people's lives when they're accident prone." I added glibly, "I refuse—"

"Do you know why your husband is in Venice, Mrs. Thorburn?"

Mrs. Thorburn this time, not signora . . . I said, "To do a job for his firm."

"To kill . . ." The line went dead.

I sat by the telephone in the little room off the *salone* and stared at the wall. I was neither stunned nor shocked. I was beyond all the superficial feelings, plunged into the limbo where the body remains living and breathing but the spirit feels the touch of death.

I had no doubt at all in my mind that the man who had telephoned me was the man I called Charon. I had two things to go on. One was that he seemed the only man in Venice to admit that I was in danger; the other was that he spoke English with a faint accent, but whether that was faked or natural, I did not know.

I pushed the telephone aside and put my head on my hands. "To kill . . ." But kill whom? Not me . . . Men didn't harm the women they made love to. Or was I being naïve? What had my body and Rorke's desire for it to do with the consuming flame that tied him so inexorably to Catherine Mallory? Perhaps, when he made love to me, he closed his eyes and saw Catherine; perhaps, if I listened hard, I would hear him whisper her name in those moments of high passion in the dark. "Catherine . . . Catherine . . ."

I flung back the chair on which I sat with such force that it overturned with a crash. As I picked it up, I burst into tears. People ask, "What are you crying for?" And you answer, "Because I'm lonely". . ."disappointed". . ."in pain". . . My weeping came from a dreadful mixture of fear and despair.

I went into the *salone* and sat down on the settee, enveloped in the soft yellow cushions. I had to find out the identity of this man who knew the truth about Catherine and Rorke. Venice was not a large city. Somewhere, at some time, I would see him again and I would make certain that he did not escape me before he had answered some questions. I would ask, "Who hates me so much?" And I would anticipate the answer, "Catherine Mallory." He might ask me again, "Do you know why your husband is in Italy?" and I would say, "You told me on the telephone that he is here to kill. But whom?" And if he said, "You," I would laugh at him. I'd say, "You've got your facts twisted somehow, Signor Shadow Charon. However strong my husband's feelings are for Catherine, however powerful and terrible the thing that draws them together, he would never harm me. He would tell me the truth and I would free him."

But there was Berenice . . .

I said aloud to the quiet room, "*Rorke wouldn't give a damn for his inheritance.*" And my devil answered me, "How do you know? What has Rorke ever said or done to give you that lofty idea of him? Money is power.". . ."*I love Rorke and I trust him*". . . My devil laughed at me. "Then ask him and see if he will deny Catherine. But perhaps he would lie to you and that would be almost as unbearable, because in your heart you know the truth, don't you?"

I turned my face into the silk cushion.

"Why, Leonie—!"

I lifted a startled face and saw Berenice enter the room. She threw off the chiffon scarf she wore over her hair, tossed her purse onto a chair and came to sit down by my side. Her dress fanned out as if she wore a black crinoline. Her cheeks were pink with the effort of walking in the heat from her favorite church; the hands that gripped mine were moist and strong.

"You are crying!"

"It's nothing . . ."

"You're not the type to cry over nothing."

I broke away from her. "I've got to get a handkerchief."

"Don't go all the way upstairs. There are tissues in that table drawer."

I found some, wiped my eyes and blew my nose. I wept so seldom that I had not learned to do it prettily.

"What is it?"

"Rorke."

Berenice asked gently. "What has he done?"

It was useless to dissemble. "I think our marriage has been a mistake." My words sounded formal and hideously restrained.

The silence was a long one. Then I heard Berenice's voice,

unusually firm, a little hard, saying, "Leonie, come here."

I went to her and she pulled me down again onto the settee. "What is all this?"

"I believe Rorke is still in love with Catherine Mallory."

"The singer?" She gave a small relieved laugh. "But my dear child, what nonsense! They live in entirely different worlds."

"They didn't once, before I met Rorke."

"I know all about that. But it has been over a long time. Rorke was younger then, and impressionable."

I doubted if he had ever been that. Impressions were superficial; Rorke was deep.

Berenice asked, "What has happened to make you think such a thing?"

"So much," I said. "Rumors, for one thing."

"What—*rumors*?"

With my face half turned away I told her about the telephone call ten minutes earlier.

She sat very straight, her eyes staring at me, looking huge and angry. "Who? Who would dare to accuse Rorke of that? Leonie, the voice . . . did you recognize it?"

"It could have been the man who spoke to me at the newsstand."

"That crazed creature, some stranger—"

"Who knows my name."

"There's very little that goes on in Venice that isn't common knowledge. I should imagine everyone has heard that I have my nephew and his wife staying with me." She got up and began to pace the room. "We must report this man, whoever he is, to the police. These people are wicked, or sick, and they should either be in prison or in a doctor's care."

"Crazed or not, he knows about us . . . about Rorke and me. And about Catherine." I gripped my hands in my lap. "I can't . . . Berenice, I *can't* go on living with Rorke—"

Before I could add that I also had to make some move to

safeguard my own life, Berenice, who had been half-heartedly rearranging a bowl of flowers, swung round on me.

"My dear child, what can you be thinking of to say such a thing? You're overwrought—"

"I'm not, and I won't cling to a failed marriage."

She said stiffly, "I can only think that this horrible business with a lunatic has totally upset you. You and Rorke are married; you went through a ceremony in a church; you made a vow and you must keep it. Whatever happens, you must never break your word to God."

"I won't live with a man who loves another woman."

Berenice's face went pink. "I'd have thought you had more sense than to let a stranger's malicious words affect you. I really cannot take this conversation seriously. You and Rorke—" She checked her anger, leaned over the coffee table and picked out a marzipan from a Sèvres dish full of candies. The action seemed to ease her tension and when she finished eating, she said quietly, "Leonie, dear, you must not let yourself be a victim of someone's spite—a man probably hurt by life and hitting back at an innocent stranger. If he approaches you again, then I really shall call the police. In the meantime, I am quite certain you won't leave Rorke. If you did, I could not condone the action. It's old-fashioned to believe in the sanctity of marriage, but then I *am* old-fashioned."

"If I left Rorke, *I* would be the one at fault."

"You are merely splitting hairs. You would both be at fault —Rorke as much as you, for allowing you to go. So, you see, it would be silly and useless martyrdom on your part."

"Oh, I'm no martyr. I'd be leaving Rorke because I'm too proud to live with a man who doesn't want me. Rumors are seldom without foundation." (Once Rorke had said to me, "Whatever happens, she will always be in my blood," and I had never known him to make wild and meaningless statements.)

Berenice was looking at me thoughtfully. "I wonder if you have enough to do here? After all, you worked in London, didn't you, even after your marriage? Here, there is nothing except your painting lessons—and they're only a casual occupation. Perhaps that's the trouble."

"That I'm behaving like a bored wife looking for excitement—however unpleasant? Oh no, I'm not *looking* for it, Berenice, it's there."

But it was like trying to show a blind woman the gathered storm clouds. Berenice would always be deliberately ignorant until the fury was upon her.

I said gently, "I'm sorry, Rorke is more than a nephew to you. I shouldn't have talked like that."

She brightened immediately, throwing off the depression and distaste of the conversation. "No, dear child, you should not. But thank heaven you see for yourself. We all say things on wild, unthinking impulses when we are young. I wish there was more for you to do here; something to occupy you. I wish I knew more young people, but so many of my friends and their families leave Venice for the summer months."

I said with forced lightness, "It's a pity I wasn't born an intellectual; then I could have spent my time here studying Venetian history." I walked out of the room as I spoke, knowing that Berenice would be happy to hear my flippancy as a reappraisal of my dilemma and an acceptance of her faith in Rorke's love for me. I went down the stairs and into the little garden and sat under the awning. The sun was a dazzling fireball just above the myrtle tree, and all was quiet as if everything in the golden surroundings was listening to my thoughts.

When Rorke comes home next weekend, I shall have to know the truth—nothing must be unknown any longer between us.

XIV

There was no moon, and the light over the door was all that illuminated Berenice's garden. It was Friday and I was disturbed and restless. Rorke hadn't come and now, at nearly midnight, I no longer expected him until the morning.

I could see a light in Willy's studio and wondered if he were entertaining friends. I knew that occasionally someone from the old struggling days slipped into the house late at night to have coffee or wine with him. Berenice didn't mind. "Willy is a good man," she would say. "He would never have undesirables in my house."

She had gone to bed some time ago, and as I glanced up, I saw a faint light in her sitting room being flicked off.

People said that given quiet and darkness, one could work

out problems, but neither solved mine as I paced the old stone paths. When I heard a soft rustle behind me, I started round, braced to defend myself. It was Angelo who had followed me out of the house and was brushing the marigold leaves as he ran to join me. I bent and stroked him and heard his gentle, satisfied purr. But my swift reaction to the sound he had made forced me to realize how tense I was and how alert for danger.

I rehearsed what I would say to Rorke when I next saw him, changed the wording, listened to my voice, altered the tone. I was like some inexperienced actress, nervous before an audition. But it was my life and not the public's pleasure that was at stake.

In spite of all my practice I knew that when the time came I would probably be too emotionally involved to remember my lines. I would fluff them, make mistakes, say things I had never dreamed of saying. Defeated, I went back into the house, calling to Angelo, and he came and slunk into a dark corner of the hall where he would happily watch for any venturesome water rat that might wander into the house. "Have fun," I said and left him.

I switched on the staircase light and took the first few steps. Then, looking upward I saw the face of the Floriana portrait staring down at me, not flush with the wall, but at an angle. I checked my steps, reached out and held onto the banister. The edge of a piece of carving dug into my palm as I gripped it, but I was only vaguely aware of it. The portrait, which should be flat against the staircase wall, had swung forward.

I moved cautiously, hand still gripping the banister, toward the painting. I had believed the walls of the staircase to be of stone, instead of which I saw that a panel had been cut out and a wooden door built in. This was covered with some thick substance made to resemble stone. I was looking at a secret door on the staircase that had swung slightly open.

I walked around it and found myself staring into the great

black space on the other side, which was, I realized, the wing over the boathouse. The concealed door could have been made at the time of the Risorgimento when some of the great families had resisted Venice's alliance with Italy as a kingdom. It could have been a hiding place or an escape route.

As I stood there, I was aware of music being played very softly from some room beyond all the darkness. I took a few steps through the opening and could just see the dim outline of some stairs which I supposed led down to Filiberto's rooms. There were also other steps leading up to a room with a partially open door. Here, there was a dim light and piano sounds flowed through the quiet. Someone was playing a Beethoven sonata.

I knew where I was; I had been there before, but I had been taken, then, by the garden entrance.

The steps were of stone and I crept up them making no sound. At the partially open door, I paused. The man at the piano had his back to me. It was Rorke. I should have let him know I was there, walked into the room and sat down in the one armchair and listened. I should have let him play on and then, when he had finished, I should have asked him why he had come secretly to the house. Instead, I stood watching and listening from the door. This was the place he had given me a glimpse of on my first visit—his boyhood room which he had used when he came to stay in Venice for part of his holidays.

I caught sight of a corner of the divan and realized that he could have sometimes arrived, unknown to any of us, on Friday nights, slept in his room and then made a show of having come straight from Milan on Saturday mornings. Memories tore at me: Willy telling me about the light he sometimes saw late at night in the room; Isobel telling me of the time when she had followed her mother as far as the Chiesa San Moisé.

The music stopped. I stayed where I was, scarcely breathing. If Rorke turned, he would see me. Well, why shouldn't

I be seen? I was his wife, and I would stand my ground and wait for an explanation.

But he didn't move from the piano. His fingers ran lightly up and down the scales as if he were loosening the muscles, and then he began to play the Appassionata.

Because of the thickness of the wall, no one in the house would hear his playing and even Filiberto, whose rooms were also over the boathouse, was far away, beyond the flight of steps going in the opposite direction.

Suddenly, Rorke's hands crashed on a chord, his eyes met mine in the mirror on the wall facing him. "Why don't you come in, Leonie?" he said and swung around on the piano stool and faced me.

In the queer semi-darkness of the room, he looked like a stranger, his face in shadow, his hair lit by the lamp glow behind him.

I walked in, saying, "I didn't know there was a door on the stairs. I heard music and I—"

"A door on the stairs?" He shot the question at me. "What do you mean?"

"A door," I repeated. "It's open. It's a panel made to look like stone and the Floriana portrait hangs on it."

He pushed past me and I followed him out of the room and down the short flight of stairs. I watched him at the door, running his hand down the edge. "There's a concealed lock here and it's been recently oiled." He stood for a moment with his back to me, looking into the house beyond, and I watched, hating myself for wondering if he had really known about the door and was only feigning ignorance. I wished I could have seen his face. "Well! Well! These old houses are full of surprises," he said. "We must ask Berenice about it in the morning." He went back up the stairs and into his room.

I followed and asked, "When did you arrive?"

"Some time ago." He spoke calmly, as if my discovery was

unimportant, and went to the piano, fingering the keys.

"Have you had anything to eat?" I sounded incongruously domestic.

"Yes."

I wandered about the room, vaguely noting the dim shapes of the divan, the big chair, the heavy old bookcase. I believed him when he implied that he had not come to his room by the door on the stairs. If he had not wanted to be seen, he would have most certainly used the side entrance from the garden. To enter by the door on which the Floriana hung, he would have to have been already in the house, so what I had discovered on the stairs was suddenly unimportant. It was Rorke's secret presence in the house that was the reason for the outburst of anger which shook me.

"Do you often do this—arrive here and slip up to your old room? Were you going to appear tonight, or were you intending to sleep in this room and pretend to arrive tomorrow morning? If so, for goodness sake, why? Do you think I'd have interfered if you had wanted to play the piano half the night—sleep here, even? Do you think I'd have made some sort of scene and tried to stop you?"

"No."

"Is that all you can say?" I stormed at him.

Rorke reached for the curtains at the window and ripped them apart. He said very quietly, "Stop questioning me, Leonie," and opening the door, stepped out onto the small balcony. With his back to me, he continued, "You know my job, or rather, you know enough about it not to cross-examine me."

"But this has nothing to do with your job, has it?"

He must have heard me, for I had raised my voice, but he didn't answer. A thought ran through my mind, half relief, half pain. At least he wasn't going to lie to me.

"I don't understand. You steal like some trespasser into your own room, play the piano in semi-darkness and were prepared to let us all think you arrived tomorrow morning."

"You exaggerate."

"Then tell me the truth."

"That I wanted to play the piano."

I said, "Why keep it a secret? Why not have dined with us and then said you wanted to come to this room? Why deceive Berenice as well as me?"

He still stood with his back to me, looking out into the darkness. In the distance I could hear the voices of the gondoliers calling to one another. I moved away from the bookcase. My arm jogged a tattered old volume that was jutting out and it fell to the floor. I picked it up, read the title, *The Adventures of Tom Sawyer*, and put it back in its place. The small action gave me time to muster my courage. I walked toward Rorke and felt the soft night air fan my face. I took a deep breath and asked carefully, "Do you want to be free of me? If that's it, then tell me. Rorke, please *tell* me. Let me know the truth. I'm no millstone around anyone's neck."

I was trembling when I had finished. Rorke swung around, his eyes brilliant in the lamplight. "Millstone? Oh, darling, stop asking silly questions."

"There's nothing silly about offering a man his freedom."

He put his hands on my shoulders. "I've not the slightest wish to have you leave me, Leonie. I told you once that I needed you, and that still applies. God knows it applies! And now, shall we drop the subject? It's late."

His words neither comforted nor reassured me. But I knew that he was in no gentle mood, that in his way he was as disturbed as I was in mine—and a name, unspoken between us, could be tormenting him as much as it tormented me.

Was it Catherine who had induced him to play again? And did she sometimes come to him on Friday nights in this room?

Once again, I told myself that it would be too great a risk. But this time I faced the fact that Rorke was used to risks—it was part of his training. Rorke's job was his shield against which no one and nothing had any penetrating power.

I had no idea that I had moved until I found myself at the door. Rorke said my name and came to me, his hands cupping my head, lifting my face to his. "If you break up our marriage, Leonie, you will regret it to the end of your days." His hands drew me roughly closer. "Now are you satisfied?" He didn't wait for an answer but bent and kissed me. I knew he felt my resistance and in a moment he let me go. "I'll be with you shortly," he said. "Go to bed, it's late."

I walked back to the main house leaving the door open, and a terrible thought twisted in my brain: *Of course he can't let me go. He has too much to lose . . .*

And then, ashamed, I fled to the bedroom and flung myself, weeping, onto the bed. It must have been an hour later when Rorke came in. By then I had pulled myself together, undressed and pretended to be asleep.

We lay close and in silence, yet we lay as strangers.

XV

When I finally fell asleep I had a distressing dream about falling, and when I woke, the house was full of morning sounds.

Rorke must have dressed very quietly, for when I stirred and opened my eyes he was already gone. I wondered whether he would tell Berenice over breakfast about my visit to his old room. Perhaps he would make a joke of it.

"Leonie has found out my secret. Did you know that I creep into the house sometimes, unknown to any of you, and play my piano? It's a throwback from boyhood when we often climbed trees and hid for hours from the grownups."

And would Berenice laugh and perhaps be pleased that he was taking an interest in music again? Then, would he make some surprised comment about the door on the landing?

But when I had dressed and entered the dining room, I heard them discussing Eryxa. Rorke was saying: "I'll find out today what Pallamundi plans to do after the drainage of the island has been completed."

Berenice nodded her approval and saw me. "Ah, good morning, Leonie. You slept well?"

I replied that I had with a nod that was, after all, only an implied lie, and reached for a croissant, and answered Willy's question about whether I was going to see the latest exhibition of paintings at the Accademia di Belle Arti. "I may," I said.

"If you can tear yourself away from Adrian's magnificent studio for long enough, you mean?"

"Since I find it interesting to play around with paint, I might easily mean that," I retorted.

He gave a little meaningful smirk which I affected not to see and took my coffee cup from Berenice, whose attention was entirely on Rorke. "You look tired, my dear," she said. "You really should try to get here during the day and not drive through the night in order to arrive for breakfast. I know the Autostrada is a fine road, but you need your sleep."

"I got in unexpectedly last night," Rorke said, "so I went to my old room. It was one of those impulses. And I tried my piano—"

"It must be stiff with misuse, although I have had it tuned regularly just in case you ever wanted to use it."

He said, "It was good to touch the keys again."

"I'm so glad. You were far too fine a musician to give it all up as you did. I've never understood—"

"A combination of impulse, obstinacy and bloody-mindedness," he said quickly.

"None of which," she said with a fond look, "is characteristic of you."

"Oh, I sometimes act out of character."

He didn't once look at me as he spoke, but I had a feeling that telling Berenice about the previous night was for my benefit.

I said, "I heard Rorke playing."

"You heard—through those thick walls?" Berenice exclaimed.

"I found a door on the stairs that I never knew was there."

"A door . . . ?" She blinked at me and was momentarily nonplussed. Then she said, "Oh, you mean the one where the Floriana hangs? But nobody uses it these days, it only leads to Filiberto's apartment and, of course, to Rorke's old room." She flashed a smile at him. "How on earth did you find that, dear?"

Rorke said, "Leonie told me and I went to have a look. The lock has been oiled, so someone uses it."

"I must ask Cèsara and Iolanda about it. Perhaps they use it to come in and out of the house to save going around to the *calle* door. But I don't see how they could know about it unless they accidentally touched the lock when they were cleaning and then went through to see where the staircase on the other side led to." She glanced at Willy. "Did *you* know?"

"About the door? No, but I'm intrigued. I suppose most of the old houses here have secret ways—rather necessary I should think during the dark reign of the Doges." His eyes brightened. "I must go and have a look at it."

"Not now. Not now," Berenice said with rare irritability. "Sit down, Willy, and get on with your breakfast."

He subsided and bent over his plate of bacon; Rorke rustled a newspaper and Berenice slit open a letter. I leaned over and poured out more coffee for myself and felt the unease around me without knowing from whom it came. I couldn't stop the nagging question in my mind. If I hadn't heard Rorke at his piano last night, would he have mentioned it across the breakfast table? Or would he have appeared earlier this morning after a seeming drive through the dawn?

Absorbed in my bewildered questions, I listened only vaguely to Rorke changing the conversation as he laid the newspaper down. "Pallamundi thinks the pier on Eryxa could be shored up and used. It's solid and the foundations are deep."

"I understand, too, that the few buildings there can be restored. That would be a start," Berenice said. "I've already had letters from artists who have heard of the scheme and want to live there. It's so encouraging."

Willy said plaintively, "You won't send me there, will you? I do get terrible rheumatism in winter."

Berenice smiled indulgently at him. "You're part of our life here—my special prodigy. I want to encourage you in your painting, my dear. One day we may be able to have an exhibition of your work."

"You're an *angel* to me," Willy said.

After breakfast, we all separated. I always made our bed and tidied the room, and as I was struggling with the enormous Venetian lace coverlet, Rorke entered.

"Are you going to have a painting lesson this morning?"

"That's right."

He helped me with the bedspread. "Why don't you go to the Lido? It would do you so much more good."

"Painting takes all my attention," I said, smoothing the lace, "and that's what I want at the moment."

He came to me and folded me against him. "I neglect you, don't I?"

"A bit."

"No, not a bit. A very great deal. I'm sorry, sweet."

"My consolation is that it's not forever," I said lightly, and waited desperately anxious for his confirmation.

The little clock chimed and Rorke checked his watch. "I must go. Pallamundi isn't the most patient of people."

The bedroom door was open and Willy was padding by, jerking his head back to look in at us.

Rorke paused in the doorway. "Don't think I've forgotten that it's our wedding anniversary on Wednesday. I can't make any plans at the moment but if I can get away, we'll meet somewhere halfway for dinner. Berenice will lend you the car and I'll call you from Milan."

I said, softly, "There was that place—Riomeyla. You remember, we went there once—"

"I remember," he said, "and if I can get away we'll go and see if it's still there. Would you know the road from here?"

I nodded. "It's straight until you get past Malcontenta. Oh, darling, if you could possibly get away . . ."

"Leave it to me to try."

The door closed and I heard him talking to Willy on the stairs. But Riomeyla came, clear as a perfect photographic print, across my mind: a place so beautiful and so deserted, with asphodels and anemones, ilex and pine—an Arcadia that had seemed to be entirely ours.

*   *   *

Soon after I arrived at the Palazzo Kronos, Adrian said, conversationally, "There was trouble last night. A photographer tried to get a picture of Catherine slipping out of the house about ten o'clock. And she lost her temper with him and tried to wreck his camera."

"Why? She's certainly used to photographers following her."

"My guess is that this was one of the times she didn't want her jaunt to be known."

"On the other hand, she has a right to privacy."

"But why get angry with the photographers? It just calls attention to herself," he said. I must have been looking at him strangely, for he asked sharply: "What's the matter?"

His voice released the mounting tension inside me. I set down my cup and ran to the door. Of course . . . last night . . . Rorke waiting for Catherine. The door on the staircase was unimportant. As Berenice had said, Iolanda, in dusting the Floriana, could have accidentally touched the spring and some night wind could have blown the door open. Catherine had come secretly through the garden to Rorke.

Adrian was calling me. I heard him say: "Have you gone mad?"

I was out of hearing after that. I had a feeling that he followed me into the hall, but I didn't look around to see. I leapt up the stairs, a wild and urgent impulse tearing at me to see Catherine.

My sudden impulse was without plan. I had only a desperate idea that I might find out the truth from her. If she wanted Rorke, she would give herself away far more easily than he, with his iron guard on himself. Catherine would not be able to bewilder and disarm me.

I rang her bell and almost immediately a tall woman with gray hair opened the door.

"Signora Mallory? If she is in, will you ask her, please, to see me?"

My accent gave me away. The woman answered me in English. "Your name?"

I gave it and said, "Please tell her it's very urgent."

I walked, without invitation, into the circular hall and saw that the woman was about to protest. My heart was thudding, more from emotion than my race up the stairs. "Don't worry . . . I'm quite honest and I'm not a reporter. I'm here for a very personal reason."

I sat down on a chair, afraid, now that I'd got so far, that I would be unceremoniously thrown out. The woman looked strong, but she walked quietly away and when she had disappeared, I glanced around the hall. I hadn't been able to see it clearly on the night of the party because of the crowd of people.

Flowers were everywhere: roses in a green bowl, lilies in a bronze urn and, on a carved cassone, a cloud of purple bougainvillaea. Tributes to Catherine Mallory . . .

The curtains at the window were deep blue brocade; the furniture, unlike that in Adrian's part of the *palazzo*, was fragile and gilded; on a portico over the door through which I had entered, golden cherubs entwined each other with vine leaves. To stop my growing alarm, I speculated on the Palazzo Kronos's past and decided that that floor must once have been occupied by the women of the family, in the rich, idle, gossipy seventeenth-century world of Venice. But the past could not hold my attention. I was, now that the impulse had died down, very nervous. If Catherine agreed to see me, what was I going to say to her? A moment's madness had brought me here, but there was still time to escape . . . I rose from the chair.

"The signora will see you now."

I swung round and knew that it was too late. Mutely, I followed the woman down the long passage to the room at the end.

The double doors were open and, where she had sung for us on the night of her party, Catherine waited for me. She wore a green embroidered kaftan and her hair was piled on top of her head like a bronze crown. Whatever she wore, whether it was fashionable at the time or not, Catherine would look right.

"Mrs. Thorburn . . ." She came toward me, hands held out.

The fingers which took mine were cool and dry; the smile, in the dim light, seemed warm. But then, I reminded myself, she was an actress as well as an opera star.

"Please sit down. The chairs here are on the fragile side" —her laugh was low—"and the fat women through the centuries must have been very unhappy in them."

I sat in a straight-backed chair and slid my hands along the arms, which ended in lions' heads. Venice was so full of the lion motif, I thought irrelevantly—fat lions, thin lions, angry lions and benevolent ones. Catherine offered me coffee but I thanked her and refused. To have drunk with her would have been tantamount to the old custom of taking salt at the host's table. Courtesy then would demand courtesy, and I wasn't in the mood for playing polite social games.

I was hot; my dress stuck to me; the palms of my hands clung to the chair arms.

"You must forgive me for this," I began. "I mean I . . . I shouldn't have called without telephoning first, only I was downstairs in Adrian's studio and I suddenly had to see you. I know—" I stopped, not so much to take a breath after my explanatory rush as because I had rehearsed nothing and now that the moment of truth had arrived, I was speechless.

"You had to see me?" she asked quietly. "Why? Mrs. Mackenzie, who let you in, told me that you had something urgent to say to me."

Her voice sounded anxious. I thought: Of course, she knows it concerns Rorke. Perhaps she thinks I've come to tell her he's ill or has had an accident on the Autostrada; but if she had seen him last night, she would know that he had not.

I sat awkwardly in the uncomfortable chair and sought desperately for the right words, the sophisticated subtlety which would enable me to find out what I wanted without being brash about it.

"You know," Catherine said when the silence obviously seemed too long, "I think I'd like some coffee, so you must join me." Without waiting for my acceptance, she rose and went to the door and I heard her speaking to Mrs. Mackenzie.

"Laura Mackenzie makes wonderful coffee," Catherine said, returning to the room. "She travels everywhere with me and I don't know what I would do without her. She's a splendid guardian and she keeps all unwanted callers away."

Catherine was a very unhurried woman. Perhaps so much travel, so much hectic moving from hotel to plane, from car to opera house, had taught her the value and necessity of serenity.

Coffee must have been ready for her, for Mrs. Mackenzie entered with it on a lacquered tray which she set on a low table. Catherine seated herself and as she poured, I saw how beautiful her hands were, smooth and ivory-colored. Rorke would love those hands.

I took my coffee cup and my panic increased. I knew that I must say what I had come for immediately or I would lose the courage to say it at all.

"Mrs. Mallory, I had to see you." My tongue clung to the roof of my mouth as if I had some impediment in my speech. "Rorke," I said indistinctly, "it's about Rorke."

She paused, stirring the cream which I had refused, into her coffee. "Yes, what about him?" She did not look at me.

I put down my cup and gripped the arms of the chair tightly. "You—and Rorke . . ."

"What about us?"

My heart raced and I felt desperately empty inside. I shut my eyes against her level gaze and the words came, like the first deep exhausted breath of a runner who has finished the race. "Do you love Rorke?"

The question was asked and there was silence in the room. I opened my eyes and looked at her. She was resting her coffee cup on her lap, one hand steadying the green and gold saucer. The only sound I could hear was the heavy thudding of my heart and it was like an army pacing the Campo below the windows.

Then Catherine did the last thing I had expected. She laughed. "Oh, how young people these days do fret and probe!"

Her words were like a challenge. I was goaded to defend my youth. "Perhaps we hate secrecy."

"Then speaking personally—and that's what you're here for, isn't it?—you shouldn't have married Rorke, should you? Because that's his job."

"I mean in personal life. I'm not subtle, Mrs. Mallory. I can't live my life pretending that everything is fine when I know it isn't. I'll face facts, even though I know they'll hurt."

She gave me a swift look and then drank some coffee. She seemed adept at knowing just when, and for how long, silences should be held to have the greatest effect. "You're so young," she said. "You ask me: Do I love Rorke? as if it's something that is your concern—or anyone else's for that matter."

"But it *is* my concern."

"Forgive me, but my emotions are my own affair. Now drink up your coffee."

She was so utterly unshaken by my brash question that she floored me, which was obviously what she had intended to do.

I wanted to get up and walk about the room—I could always think more clearly if my body was active. But it was *her* room, *her* floor, and so I sat stiff as a china doll, my mouth dry, my mind empty of any thought except the awful awareness that I should never have come, that I should have stayed in Adrian's studio and checked my insane impulse. I lifted my coffee cup, but my hand shook so much that I had to put it back into the saucer.

I doubted that Catherine noticed, for she had risen and had crossed the room to an ornate table with cabriole legs. There was a low bowl of roses on it. She flicked one gently and petals dropped onto the table top. She scooped them up and held them in the palm of her hand. Every movement was graceful and deliberate, and I had the feeling of being on a stage, part of an act.

"Yes, you really are so young, Leonie." She broke the silence, spreading the dropped crimson petals in her hand as she spoke. "You see love as something you possess completely, absorbing it like the air you breathe, taking it as entirely yours. You see it as something wonderful, like a light inside you. But it's not that, except to sentimentalists. You ask: Do I love Rorke? Why don't you ask yourself that? Do *you* love Rorke? Do you, Leonie?" She lifted her head and looked at me.

Stunned by the switch of the question, I said, blankly, "Of course."

"There's no 'of course' about it."

"If I hadn't loved him, I would not have married him; if I didn't love him now, I would not stay with him."

She smiled and tossed the bruised rose petals into an ashtray. "You make it sound so simple. It isn't. Love is a fierce thing, a battle, if you like. It's a desire which overcomes all preconceived scruples."

"Oh yes." I saw in a flash that she was right. "I understand. That's how it is for me, too. A battle. That's why I shall fight to keep Rorke—that is, until *he* asks me for his freedom." I sat back in the chair and took a deep breath with sheer relief that I could find the courage to speak with such frankness to this intimidating woman.

"You make a brave speech, Leonie. I hope you won't get hurt."

My name, "Leonie," had come so easily to her, as if she had heard Rorke use it many times. I said, "Oh, I expect I shall get hurt. It's part of loving, isn't it?" I saw Catherine's lips twist into a faint smile as if I'd said something corny. It could have sounded that way, but I had been in deadly earnest.

"I'm very much older than you, and I'm more experienced. I knew Rorke long before you did and perhaps I know him better than you."

I said bitterly, "That could be very true!"

"Whether I love him or not doesn't enter into it—"

"Oh, but it does."

Her expression became cold. "If a man wants me, he must be free."

"You have met Rorke recently, haven't you?"

She sat up very straight. "Because you and he are married, does that give you the sole right to his companionship? Or to question his friendships?" There was cool insolence in her words, but before I could think of an answer, she got up and went to the side table on which the roses stood. I thought she just pressed her hands down on it, perhaps wondering how much to tell me, irritated by my brashness.

Then she turned and walked back to her chair. A moment later Mrs. Mackenzie entered.

"Signor Centogufo has called, madam. He says he is a little early—"

"The Maestro?" It was well-simulated surprise. "Thank you. I'll see him now." She turned to me. "You must forgive me for cutting short our meeting. But even on holiday, I have work to do, things to discuss . . ."

I rose. We faced one another and neither of us held out our hands.

"Goodbye," I said.

"Goodbye, Leonie. It's a pity we have no contact. But then, we don't live by the same rules."

I went out of the room and walked down the long passage. I didn't see the Maestro waiting in the hall and I wondered, after Mrs. Mackenzie had closed the doors and I was crossing the Campo in the sunlight, whether there was a bell hidden on the table with the roses by which Catherine summoned Mrs. Mackenzie with a prearranged excuse. The imaginary arrival of the Maestro was the most imposing and imperative reason she could have thought of for getting rid of an unwelcome visitor.

XVI

I went straight to the seat opposite the Palazzo Kronos. The plane tree shaded me, and a woman with a basket of fruit and an old man smoking a cheroot made room for me. I thanked them and sat staring out at the people, at the old wellhead and three children playing some strange game, rather like hopscotch.

My skin burned and my blood felt fiery with anger at my incredible impulsiveness. How deeply was I going to regret what I'd done? Catherine might very possibly tell Rorke. Well, and if she did, why should I mind? Except that in sophisticated society, you didn't go up to someone and demand the truth. You waited and watched and worked out a plan; the process was as subtle as a game of chess. Only I wasn't subtle and so I had lost.

Catherine had told me nothing. Instead, she had generalized about youth and its stupidities. If only she had been angry and lost her temper, the wretched meeting would have been easier. Instead, she had been cool, aloof and patronizing, guarding both herself and Rorke.

"What in the name of goodness are you doing mooning here?"

I looked up and saw Adrian glaring down at me.

"When you come for a lesson, you *have* a lesson. You don't suddenly rush out like someone in a tantrum."

"I didn't mean it to seem like that."

The old woman next to me got up. "Take my seat, signore. I have to get home." She gave us both a smile and I felt that she thought she was witnessing two foreigners in the throes of a lovers' quarrel.

Adrian thanked her and said in excellent Italian, "I'm not staying either, signora. I, too, have work," and then he glared at me again. "What was that wild dash all about?"

"I'm sorry. It was nothing you'd done. I went up to see Catherine Mallory."

"So I observed. But why in the name of goodness did you have to be in such a hurry about it?"

"There was something I had to ask her."

It could have been the gravity of my face that checked his anger. He sat down and touched my hand. "And she snubbed you."

"More or less."

"You're no match for her, my nymph!"

His sudden gentleness was too much. Reaction had set in and I cried, "I know that, now. I've made an absolute fool of myself!"

"Oh, we all do on occasion. What you have to do is learn not to repeat the act." He slid an arm round me. "I suppose I can make a guess what—or whom—you went up to talk about. But I wish you had told me. If you had, I would have held you down forcibly even if I'd been bitten and kicked for my pains. I could have told you Catherine would parry any questions she didn't want to answer. I barely know her, but I can recognize a clever woman. You're a yearling to her."

"Adrian, I'm afraid—"

"You don't have to explain. I know what you mean."

"The gossip—"

"Women in the limelight, like Catherine, are always subjects for gossip, especially in a small city. I don't really listen," he said, "except in this case where you're involved. I know, you see, that there's only one bloody man in the world you'd lose all caution for, and hearing what I have—well, never mind."

"*I* mind. I want the truth," I said. "I tried to get it upstairs just now."

"My sweet, sweet Leonie, you don't get the truth out of reluctant people by demanding it."

In the sunlight of the Campo, with the trees casting dappled shade, the large houses opposite baked in dazzling sunlight, the bright beauty of it all, I felt as if I'd just wakened from a nightmare. Incredible that I should be the victim of someone's hatred. Incredible, too, that I had done what I did that morning.

"How *could* I?" I heard my own involuntary cry. "Oh, how *could* I have been brash enough to blurt out what I did?"

My voice must have risen, for the man smoking the cheroot looked my way and beyond him a woman leaned forward and peered at me. Fortunately, I was speaking in English and I doubted if they understood. What they must have recognized, though, was the agitation in my voice.

Embarrassed, I said quietly, "I can't stay here."

"Come back to the house."

"No." I shuddered. "Not that. I'm sorry. I've spoiled your morning, haven't I?"

"And your own. Well, now you've learned a lesson. Stop and think before you act."

I said soberly, "Catherine told me in an oblique way the very things I went up to her apartment to find out. I think she does love Rorke. But it doesn't suit either of them to tell me." I got up abruptly. "I shouldn't be talking to you like this about my affairs—and Rorke's. *You* shouldn't let me—"

"That's fine, blame me!"

"I'm blaming myself for needing to talk things out. Strong people don't; they cope with their problems themselves."

"Oh, stop wishing you were noble!" he said and took my hand and led me to a café which had a patio screened from the sun by a vine straggling over an open trellis. He chose a corner table. "What you need is a drink."

"A man's panacea for all ills."

"You don't have to get drunk unless you want to. You can have a glass of milk."

"Oh, Adrian, I'm sorry. I shouldn't have dragged you into this."

The drink was brandy and strong, but I was grateful for it. We sat in the shade and talked about people and impulses and I knew that Adrian was trying to help me in his way.

I broke a moment's silence between us and said, "You're so good for me!"

"I know. But I could wish you were good for yourself. As it is, you act on impulse; you regret on impulse . . . Even your marriage," he added, "was probably a wild impulse."

"Oh no. I knew about Catherine before I married Rorke. And I don't regret what I did. I love him."

"Then, from all accounts, God help you!"

"What accounts . . . Whose . . . ?"

"Yours mostly," he said.

A clock struck. Berenice disliked us to be late for lunch and I explained that I had to go. "I'm sorry I wasted the painting lesson today and messed up your morning."

He grinned at me. "You seem to have spent your time this past week or so apologizing to me. Forget it! Come tomorrow —and you'll *paint*, do you hear? Whether you do it well or badly is up to you. The process is as I've already told you, therapeutic, and that's what you need. And don't say 'I can't come to your house any more after what happened today,' because that would be damned silly. I doubt if you'll meet Catherine, and if you happen to see her coming down the stairs, just smile and say 'Good morning,' and walk past."

"All so easy!"

"That's right." He got up, bent and kissed my cheek. "You've finished your drink, so go home. Are you walking back?"

"Yes."

"It's quite a way."

"I want the exercise."

We parted at the box hedge enclosure to the little restaurant. Adrian had taken the bitter edge off my impulsive visit to Catherine. But I knew I would remember all that had been said in that flower-filled room at the top of the Palazzo Kronos and analyze it and find that not one single word would alter my conviction that nothing was changed between Rorke and Catherine, except that she was free.

XVII

When I reached the Ca' di Linas, I let myself in by the garden gate. Willy and Rorke were sitting under the yellow-striped awning. Berenice was wandering down the paths, picking the dead heads off the double marigolds. Angelo lay on his back, paws limp, grinning at the sun.

As I closed the door, I heard Willy's voice talking across to Berenice. "How could a woman like Catherine Mallory have such a daughter? She's discontented and dull."

"Then," came Berenice's faint, patient voice, "why see her, Willy dear?"

"Because I hope she really means that she'll introduce me to her marvelous mother; I'd suffer a lot for that."

"Is Catherine Mallory so marvelous off the opera stage? Or is she just a very fine singer? . . . Ah, there you are, Leonie."

She straightened herself and put the basket of dead flower-heads over her arm.

I waved to her and sat down by Willy's side. He asked me, without any real interest in his voice, how the painting lessons were going.

"I haven't really a gift for draftsmanship; I just love color, and Adrian is very patient. He's too good an artist to be bothered with someone as little gifted as I am."

"He probably wouldn't care if you saw things upside down and suffered from color blindness." He turned to Rorke. "You should be flattered to have a wife other men like."

"Oh, I am," he replied lightly, "so long as 'like' is always the operative word."

I stayed silent, not even trying to find a glib comment to his glib reply.

*   *   *

The siesta hung over the Ca' di Linas like a warm, benevolent cloak.

I undressed and lay on the bed in the darkened room and Rorke came and stretched by my side. I felt a moment's panic. How soon would it be before he learned of my mad visit to Catherine? And when he did, what would happen?

The room was dim, enclosing us in an intimacy which could be beautiful or hateful according to my own choice. Tell Rorke . . . Say: "I went to see Catherine and I asked her if she loved you." What would Rorke do? I had no answer to that. All I knew was that, in strategy, I was no match for them. *If you have no weapons for a battle, then don't start it. Look the other way . . .*

We lay quietly together in the hot afternoon, and at last I fell into a restless sleep. Rorke wakened me with the reminder that he was going to a place on the Zattere where some of the artists who were wanting to stake their claim on studios on Eryxa gathered in the late afternoon. He said, "Do you want to come with me?"

"Yes."

"Then you'd better get off that bed."

The bed was my sanctuary, my hiding place from my fears, my reassurance. I hugged a pillow and asked, "Do you love me?"

"Well, would I be making love to you so constantly if I didn't? Come on"—he gave my thigh a gentle slap—"get yourself up and dressed if you're coming."

I asked, not really caring, but wanting to break my thoughts, "Are we going to have tea first?"

"Yes, if you like. We'll probably be asked to have coffee when we meet up with Paolo and his friends, but we can get out of it quite neatly by admitting, and deprecating politely, our English habit of tea-drinking. Like the grape and the grain, coffee and tea don't mix—not so far as the palate is concerned."

I had a quick shower, slid into a dress and found Berenice and Rorke and Willy in the garden.

Willy was stirring too much sugar into his tea. It startled me to see that he looked ill and a little seedy in spite of the good clothes Berenice bought him. In the house, the dim rooms were kind to lines and shadows, and when Willy was in the garden, he usually sat well back under the awning. But, with his chair pulled out into the sun, I saw in the vivid, revealing light, a new Willy. Hardship had indeed marked his face in ways I had never noticed before.

Rorke and I stayed in the garden long enough to drink small cups of tea and eat macaroons. Then, ten minutes later, we started to walk toward the Zattere. The way zigzagged through the narrow streets, to the Campo Morosihi and then across the Accademia Bridge. The café where the artists awaited us lay beyond the vaporetto stop. A platform had been built over a strip of the Canale della Giudecca and a huge awning was spread over it.

Eight men sat at three tables pushed close together at the far end and when one of them looked up and saw us, he leaned forward and spoke to the others. They all turned and watched us approach.

One of the young men jumped up and brought two chairs from another table and the rest made room for us. The spokesman had dark brown curly hair, a square, ingenuous face and a thin gold chain on his left wrist.

Rorke introduced me to Paolo and he, in turn, introduced the rest. The jumble of names ran into one another. Giacomo . . . Corrado . . . Pietro . . . Giorgio . . .

"Will you have coffee?"

Thanks, but we'd just had tea—our undying English custom! Now, about Eryxa . . .

They leaned forward, hanging on Rorke's words as he explained the plans for the island. There would be studios to rent at a nominal fee and Signora Montegano was certain that, with some publicity in the States and in European countries, she could make Eryxa as much a "must" to tourists as Burano and Murano.

Paolo produced a list of artists from other parts of Italy who, he said, were also interested. And, he hoped, sculptors would be allowed to join the community. There was one—"He is brilliant and very modern in his style, yet not so advanced that nobody can understand his work" . . . *"Magnifico!"* He gave Rorke a wide smile. "He shares my terrible, inadequate studio with me. He is my brother."

Rorke wasn't certain. The Signora had stipulated that the scheme should not become so wide that it embraced other arts. "Painters," she had said.

"I know," Paolo nodded. "She thinks that if we spread too

widely"—his arms shot out to illustrate the width and nearly knocked off the sun-hat of a girl at the table behind him. He apologized charmingly and turned back to us—"if we spread too widely, then there will be people trying to join our Eryxa community who play with—er—er—" His hands made a peculiar movement, twisting round and round and then flopping.

Rorke understood. "Gimmicks," he said. "That's right. The Signora doesn't want people who make pictures out of hairpins or bits of ribbon—"

"But collage?" asked Giacomo hopefully. "I sometimes do such things and people like them. We must not be too narrow in our art on Eryxa."

The conversation continued, animated to the point of being at times utterly unintelligible to me, when they all tried to speak at once, sometimes using the Venetian dialect which I had not yet mastered. This was Rorke as I loved him, taking an interest in these young artists, giving them his complete attention. This was how I wanted it to be: Rorke and I seated together at a café on a Venetian canal, with the sun dipping lower in the sky, burning the rooftops to bronze and copper, the water to gilded aquamarine. This lulled all fears, filled me with a happiness that I refused to see as temporary. I lived for the moment with Rorke's arm touching mine; Rorke picking up the points the young artists made and dealing with them, laughing now and again, turning to me . . .

Suddenly I realized that not only Rorke's eyes, but all the rest, were on me. And I hadn't the least idea why.

"I'm sorry, I didn't hear—"

"The signore says that he will not be able to come to my studio on Wednesday because he will be in Milan," Paolo explained. "But you, signora, perhaps you will come and see my brother's work—he is a fine sculptor. And then you can tell Signora Montegano that my brother, Carlo, also deserves a studio on Eryxa. He would be such an asset . . . he is good . . . You will come?"

I smiled at the anxious face across the table. "Yes, if you will give me the address."

"It isn't far from here—just along a quiet canal behind the church of the Gesuati. And I will show you the Tiepolo ceiling there, if you wish."

"But do not show her the shipyards or she will be disappointed in Venice," Pietro laughed.

"She will never find her way," Giacomo said, "in all that maze behind the Zattere. I will fetch her and bring her."

"No, I have to go to the Merceria in the morning," said Paolo. "I will—"

I sat laughing as they fought over who should bring me to Paolo's studio. And when it was settled that Paolo should meet me in the Piazza outside a shop which sold Venetian glass near the gateway to the Merceria, Rorke packed away a few notes he had made and said that we must go.

As we walked back, through the long shadows, I said, "I would have thought that most artists would prefer to be here among their friends, but they seemed really enthusiastic about going to the island."

"Wait till you see where Paolo and his brother live. I'll bet it's a pretty dismal place. And Eryxa is their summer island in the sun; heaven knows how they will stand the winters there. The more ambitious ones will work, but I can see a great many doing precious little."

I said, disappointedly, "You were so pleasant to them; I thought you were approving. I liked them."

"Oh, I think those we have just met are absolutely sincere. It is the ones we haven't met that I'm doubtful about."

"When I go to the studio, I won't be much of a judge of their work."

"You'd be a better one than I would. Just see that the sculpture isn't a matter of a thousand pins stuck into a piece of wood and given some fancy name."

As I walked with Rorke over the little bridges that curved like stone moons across the narrow waterways and past the Ca' Larga Marzo, I hoped desperately that, in spite of Rorke's caution, the scheme would work—for Berenice's sake.

XVIII

After the shadows of the *calli*, the garden blazed with deep gold as we opened the heavy door. Berenice was crossing the path to the awning under which Willy sat.

"The vine is a little sad this year," she was saying. "I'm afraid it's very old, but I love it and, grapes or not, I'm keeping it."

Willy laughed. "There are so many gorgeous grapes to be bought in Venice, I wouldn't worry about that."

Cèsara shouted from the doorway, "Signore, a call for you," and waved urgently toward Rorke.

Willy said hopefully, as Rorke went into the house, "Eryxa is sinking and so there'll be no artists' colony and all that lovely money will be saved."

Berenice was too far away to hear and I ignored him. The street noises beyond the high wall were the only things that broke the silence. Then Berenice called: "Leonie, dear. Fetch me a nice cool Campari-soda, will you? I can't trust Willy to do it. He makes them too strong for my taste."

I went indoors as Rorke was coming out. He flicked his fingers along my arm as he passed. "You've got a very shiny nose."

"You don't have to look at me until I've done my face. But Berenice wants a drink. I'm getting that first."

"I like looking at you and I don't care if your face shines like a thousand candles."

Not so long ago, the light, charming comment would have made me happy. But that time was past, our life together was now overshadowed by my anxiety over Rorke and Catherine. I simply gave a vague smile and ran up the stairs to the *salone*, opened the drink cupboard, got out bottles and mixed a Campari-soda.

As I passed the alcove on my way down to the garden, Willy startled me.

"Leonie—" He stood in front of the tall, narrow window. "There's something you ought to know."

"I can't stop now. Berenice wants her drink."

"Rorke was talking on the telephone."

"I know." I should have walked quickly past him but, encouraged by my hesitation, he jutted his head toward me like a tortoise coming out of its shell, and whispered, "I heard what he said."

"Do you have to behave like some listening device in this house?" I demanded.

"Please don't be angry with me." His eyes were bulging a little, and pathetic. "It was a woman who called Rorke."

"I'm not interested." I started to move away.

He caught my arm.

"Be careful!" I cried. "The drink—" The golden liquid was swinging from side to side.

"I've got to talk to you, Leonie. I feel you ought to know what I heard Rorke say."

"You needn't feel any such thing and I don't want to listen."

Willy went on, "Rorke said: 'I can't possibly talk to you now . . . You must understand . . .' Then whoever was at the other end must have argued and he said, 'Yes, of course . . . but not here and not at Kronos . . . I'll call you.' He must have heard me outside the door, for he said quickly, 'Just give me *time!*' and put down the receiver."

I lost my temper with him. "If you can't stop snooping behind doors and listening to people's private conversations, then at least keep what you hear to yourself."

"Why turn on me?" he protested. "I'm only trying to help you—" He laid a hand on my arm again and I turned away too quickly. The drink swung high in the glass and spilled over, spurting in a tiny cascade onto the mosaic floor. "There, now look what you've made me do!" I said furiously.

"I'm sorry. All right, I'll get a cloth and mop it up. And give me that glass. It'll be all sticky on the outside." He took it from me, and as I went back to fetch another drink, his voice followed me, pleading, "Leonie, please . . . this affair between Catherine and Rorke—"

"Damn you!" I turned on him. "There is no affair—" I choked over the last word and as Willy shrank away, shoulders hunched, I leaned against the wall just inside the *salone* door until my temper had cooled. The fingers of my right hand were sticky and I needed to wash them. But first, I had to bring Berenice her drink. She had already waited too long.

I tried to keep my hands steady as I mixed another Campari-soda. Then I took it downstairs to the garden, passing Willy, who was on his knees in the alcove, rubbing the floor with a damp cloth. He looked up at me, but against some inner urge that made me sorry for him and his tactless concern for me, I ignored him.

Down in the garden there was laughter. I gave Berenice her drink. "I'm sorry. I spilled the first one. Willy's mopping it up for me. I must go and rinse my fingers; I hope I haven't made the glass sticky."

She felt around the edge and smiled. "Not in the least."

I escaped into the cloakroom off the cool hall and dabbed my face as well as my hands with cold water. Over the washbasin was a mirror. I looked at myself and in the poor light there was something about my face that reminded me of my mother. She had had wild impulses, too.

I gave a swift thought to the man who came after my father, Elliot Jerome, Berenice's brother. How strange that, had Mother married him, Rorke and I might have been distantly related by that marriage!

I flung down the towel, let it lie untidily across the rail and went quickly through the vast dark hall, my loose sandals clattering on the stone floor, out into the sunshine to Berenice and Willy. Rorke was on the other side of the garden and he called to me. When I joined him, I saw a butterfly with iridescent violet wings and splashes of royal blue resting on a flower.

Rorke said, "It's a purple emperor. I didn't know it was ever found in Italy."

I said, laughing, "Perhaps it's on an exploration to find new places."

Above me, he said quietly, "Did you introduce Isobel to Willy?"

The question was so unexpected that I jerked upright and startled the purple emperor. "Yes, yes I did. Why?"

"I don't know that it was particularly wise."

"Why not?"

"Isobel is difficult and rebellious, and we know very little about Willy's life."

"He lives here—"

"And spends most of his day with his art pals at the Zattere. And now he has some crazy dream that Isobel could be his entrée into another kind of world."

"It wasn't an 'arranged' meeting," I said, "and anyway, why are you so angry about it?"

"I'm not angry," he said quietly. "Isobel is nothing to me. But I think it was an unwise act."

"For whom? Willy? Isobel? Why don't you want them to know each other?"

He looked away over my head, suddenly withdrawn, impatient. "I don't think we'll have an argument about it. It's not *that* important—only Willy happened to mention the meeting just now while you were fetching Berenice's drink."

I hated Willy for having told me what he had; I longed for the serenity that ignorance brings.

XIX

Walking with Paolo, from the Piazza where I met him to his studio in the Zattere district, was like running a race which I was obviously losing from the start. He didn't have very long legs, but he seemed to leap ahead like a gazelle. And I, small and never a fast walker, arrived breathless at the house in the *salizzada*, the paved alley where he lived and worked.

The buildings stood like seedy drunks near a beautiful little stepped bridge where gondolas, piled with unsold fruit and vegetables, lay still on the water.

"You must be careful, signora," said Paolo. "The steps are a little—" He waved his expressive hands.

"Rickety," I said in English.

He grinned, not understanding, and I climbed the twenty

or so stairs to the studio which jutted out, precariously, like something a child had built, over the narrow street. I thought as I reached the top, thankfully, that the light must be pretty poor for painting since the houses on the opposite side over-shadowed the grubby studio windows and the patched roof.

The door was open and then I saw that the studio had a cool north light that filtered through from a gap in the house-tops round the bend of the alley. There was a smell of turpentine and dust in the great untidy room. Paolo's sculptor brother was, I thought paradoxically, a miniature giant—short but immensely broad-shouldered and thick-hipped, with a head that was made larger by the wild hair that stuck out from the skullcap which I guessed he wore to protect his scalp from the stone dust of his art. Wiping a hand on the back of his trousers, he extended it to me in a warm greeting; the fingers were rough-skinned, yet gentle. I was offered coffee and drank it wandering around the studio, with both men talking to me at once so that I began to feel like some mechanical doll, my head twisting this way and that, looking first at brilliant abstract paintings, then at beautiful little stone figures. Some benefac-tor had made Carlo a gift of a huge chunk of stone and he was busy carving figures in bas-relief which, he told me, repre-sented the elements. I, who had only a few weeks of Adrian's artistic training, thought it a powerful piece of work, but could not assess its real merit. The stone, Carlo explained, was so old that it had matured and that was why there was a patina over it that gave a glow to the figures and the unfinished block. Did I notice it? I did.

He said, longingly, "If I could have a studio on Eryxa, a *real* place where I could expand—"

"I'll tell the Signora that if I were rich, I'd buy that carving from you."

He had an almost childlike artlessness and his eyes lit up. "You really like my work?"

"I think it's beautiful," I said. "But you must realize that it's not for me to promise you a studio on the island. The Signora has said 'Painters,' although I'll do all I can to persuade her to take sculptors as well."

Carlo was as happy as if he had already been promised his studio on Eryxa. He and Paolo didn't want me to go, and touched by their genuine charm, I looked at everything in their studio. There were two paintings facing the wall. I turned them around.

Paolo said, "Oh, they're sold. I have a private buyer who is convinced that I'll be famous one of these days and he has bought a few of my works. He doesn't pay much for them. Somehow, I don't think he's got a lot of money to spare for long-term investments—and it may take years before I am recognized. But any money is good money—it buys me bread and wine."

I said, "Perhaps he shows them in a shop in the Piazza."

"Oh no, I'm certain he doesn't. He's just a private collector and he comes occasionally, selects anything he takes a fancy to, and pays cash." He stood back and added gloomily, "*I* don't think much of my work . . . not yet. But I shall improve—I shall be good one day."

To me the wild colors of the two paintings that were sold could be of volcanic eruptions or streets in hell. The paint was laid on thickly, the colors obtruded almost offensively. I moved away, glanced at my watch and said that I must be going.

Paolo saw me to the end of the *salizzada* and I told him that I knew my way from there. I had no difficulty until I reached a meeting of two *calli* and a narrow *riva*. I recognized none of them, and I stopped a woman holding the hand of an immaculately dressed little girl and asked her the way to the Piazza San Marco.

She turned and pointed. *"Giù il ponte."*

Down the bridge with the many worn steps. The expression was so typical of the Venetians: you never went across a bridge—the steps gave a kind of other direction; you went up, over and down. I thanked her and she smiled.

"*Inglese?*"

"*Inglese,*" I admitted, acknowledging what was probably my awful accent.

It was then that I saw the man I called Charon. I forgot the bridge and began to run after him along one of the narrow *calli.* He was walking fairly quickly away and I had no idea whether he had seen me or not. But I had to catch up with him, and find out who he was and what he knew.

"Signore . . . Signore . . ."

People turned and looked at me, as I sped through the crowds. But the man was even further ahead of me, as if he were floating out of my reach.

"Signore . . ."

He turned a corner and although I reached it only seconds later, he was not in sight.

It was a winding street lined with shops, and he could have gone into any one of them. I slowed down, breathless after my chase, and peered through doors—the wine shop, the shop that sold pasta. I even looked into one that had nothing but women's blouses in the window. The man was nowhere to be seen and when I reached the end of the *calle*, I gave up. He must have gone into one of the houses or down a side alley. Wherever he was, I had lost him.

I wondered, as I turned back, if he had deliberately outdistanced me because he didn't want us to come face to face again. From that came another thought. *Because I was in no danger on this journey, he had no intention of shadowing me.* As if he knew from day to day, hour to hour, what was in store for me: a strange, bright-eyed, rather shabby man in touch with some unknown manipulation of my life.

I returned to the bridge, crossed it and when I was on the other side, I recognized the street that led to the Merceria. After that, I would be almost home.

*   *   *   *

The house seemed very quiet and empty as I let myself in, but Cèsara heard me and called out: "Oh, signora, I have a message for you."

I paused on the stairs.

"The signore, your husband, telephoned you twice. He asked for you, but I said that you were out. The second time, he asked me to give you a message. Would you meet him at Riomeyla this evening? He has to go to Padua and it would be quite easy for him to drive from there. He said that he knew the Signora would not mind you taking her car from the Piazzale."

"That's wonderful," I cried. "You see, it is our wedding anniversary. Did he say a special time?"

"Eight o'clock. But it is a long way, signora."

"I don't care."

She asked eagerly, "There is something I can do for you for this very special occasion? Your dress to be pressed? Your shoes cleaned?"

I said gratefully, knowing her rich, sentimental streak, "You're so much better than I am at doing up parcels. Would you make up a very special one for me, please? It's my anniversary present for my husband."

"You give it to me." Her black eyes danced. "I will make you a beautiful parcel. And the signore said, 'Tell her to meet me at the entrance to the glade. She will know the place.'"

"Oh, I know!" I said in a voice that rang across the huge, dark hall.

I was quite certain that Berenice would let me use her car.

It was kept in a garage at the Piazzale Roma, just beyond the causeway that led to Venice. Berenice herself seldom used the Ferrari although Filiberto went regularly to give the car a run.

I took the stairs two at a time and nearly collided with Willy, who was arranging lilies and delphiniums in the stone urn on the half-landing. It was a job he loved doing and Berenice indulged him.

Berenice was sitting at her desk writing checks and when I rushed my request out, she said, "Of course you can use the car. You have your driving license?"

"Yes."

"It will do the Ferrari good to be driven. I'll give you a letter to Vascalli and draw a plan to show you where the garage is."

"Oh, I remember. We used the car when I was here before. Rorke took me to Vicenza."

She nodded. "I remember. All the same, I'll give you directions." She took a piece of embossed notepaper and drew a rather wild little map on it.

*   *   *

It was half past six when I left for the mainland. I was far too early, but I decided that I would rather be on my way than wandering about the house, fretting for the time to pass.

I wore Rorke's favorite color, green, and an old Victorian brooch that had belonged to my great-grandmother. I also carried a long silk scarf in case the temperature should drop when darkness fell.

At the boat station, I waited with the crowd as the ferry edged its way to the landing stage. A bell rang out an order and a guard then opened a section of the rail. We moved forward in a mass onto the deck, and I made my way toward the front of the boat and waited with impatience for the latecomers to run along the landing pier, collect their tickets and board the ferry.

At last, with a churning of light-suffused water, we were away into the Rio Nuova Lagoon, which had an uncluttered run, free of gondolas and small boats.

I looked westward, the way we were going, into the glitter of the evening. I had a lightness of heart that erased all the negative devils of fear and doubt and suspicion. Curious how the name of a place could hold such magic, how a remembered scent could bewitch. Riomeyla and rosemary and wild thyme . . .

XX

I found the garage without much difficulty, and the proprietor brought the Ferrari into the street for me.

For the first few miles I drove along the banks of the Brenta, following the road sign to Stra and treating the beautiful giant of a car with respect until I became used to its power. Once past Stra, I turned inland, past white Palladian villas and stretches of slender birch trees standing very still in the evening air.

I began to look for landmarks which I remembered from the times Rorke had driven me to Riomeyla: the stretch of marshland, above which birds I could not name wheeled and circled in the burning light of the sinking sun; the old stone well set in the middle of the road; the white villa with gables and the rose trees that might have been lifted straight out of England.

Everything I passed became vaguely familiar: the twisted olive trees, the shuttered windows of the houses, the goats and geese and dogs going home. And all the time the sun sank lower and the sky was stained flame and purple above the distant hills. Darkness was creeping swiftly from the east and when I rounded a bend in the road and saw the sickle moon, I wished it had been full—the small, Arcadian grove of Riomeyla with its tumbled mass of stones, its broken statuary and the thyme-scented earth needed moonlight to reveal its magic. The moon: the astronauts' dead place, the sentimentalist's silver witch-ball . . . I began to sing as I drove toward Rorke.

It took me longer than I had expected, because the shadows lengthened so much in the places between long stretches of trees and I lost my way, and twice I had to stop, ask at a cottage and drive back to the turning I had missed.

Then, quite suddenly, I came upon the acacia wood on my left and knew that I had arrived. There was a path that ran through it to the glade. I turned the Ferrari with difficulty into the narrow lane, only a moment or two before the brief Venetian twilight was blacked out by night; I saw below me the glow of old stones picked out by the car's lights and the scattered flowering bushes bleached white by the gathered darkness.

I got out of the car and, before starting my walk down to the glade, felt on the passenger seat for the flashlight I had brought with me. Then, turning it on, I looked around for Rorke's car but couldn't see it. Of course, he had had a much longer drive than I and I'd have to wait with some sort of patience for him.

The evening was warm and there was no wind. I was wrapped around with the scent of thyme and pines. The last few feet of the way were so steep that I clutched at bushes to keep myself from falling. I reached the glade and walked a little way across the serene, scented grassland. I thought what I heard was only the rustle made by my own footsteps, but when I stopped to look about me, the sound continued—the soft persistent hissing of disturbed grasses. Someone walked behind me . . .

I swung around, but I was too late even to cry out. A hand clamped over my mouth, dug into my skin. As I tried to wrench myself free, the flashlight dropped from my fingers and the switch must have been jolted at the fall, for the light went out.

I tried to scream, but an arm was pressed sickeningly against my throat and I breathed the horrible smell of what I thought was ether.

I gave a last desperate struggle. My eyes opened in terror and saw something leap out at me. Panic and rapidly losing consciousness had unhinged me. My last wild thought before I blacked out was that it was a white wolf or a ghost, or a werewolf with red eyes—but it didn't have red eyes . . . I knew no more.

꙰

I recovered consciousness in a small, stuffy room. There was a smell of cooking and a woman dressed all in black was standing by the hard couch I lay on, looking down at me. My mind was boiling with jumbled fears, like the bubbles in a witch's cauldron, but one thought leapt clear of all the rest.

Now I'll know who wants me dead . . .

I stirred, put my hand over my eyes and asked where I was. I must have spoken in English, for the woman said in Italian, "I do not understand, signora."

I struggled to a sitting position and felt terrible. My throat hurt and I felt sick. I said in a slurred voice in Italian, "Where am I?"

"You are at our cottage."

"Whose?"

"I am Lucia Tortelli. My husband works for a farmer over the hill. Do not look so afraid. You are safe with us."

I said faintly, "May . . . I . . . wash? I need cold water . . ."

The woman bent and helped me to my feet. The room spun around. I swallowed three times and then said faintly, "I'm . . . sorry. I . . . I can't walk . . . on my . . . own."

She led me into the garden. There was a pump there and she filled a bucket. Reeling, I dashed ice-cold water over my face and the shock took the feeling of sickness away. I reached thankfully for the coarse linen towel she held, and wiped my face. I stood leaning against the pump and, eyes closed, took in deep gulps of air. The woman stood by, watching me anxiously as I collected my wits and fought off the nausea that had swept over me.

After a few minutes, I opened my eyes and said, "I feel much better now. But who attacked me?"

Without answering, she took my arm and led me carefully back into the house. I sat on the hard couch again and put my hands to my throat.

I asked again, "Who attacked me?"

"We do not know. My husband was out walking and he saw someone come behind you and saw you struggle. He called his dog but the dog is a fool. He sprang at you to welcome you. The man who attacked you, though, became frightened and ran off."

I gathered that her husband had given chase but had lost the man in the darkness of the woods, and that the dog was no use at trailing a scent. "*Stupido*," she said with impatience and affection.

"You came in a car, signora, and it is quite safe. If the man who attacked you is waiting to steal it, he cannot, for my husband has driven it into our yard at the back. He is waiting for you to be well enough to tell him to call the police."

"Oh no," I said. "Not the police . . . But I must telephone someone."

"There is no telephone nearer than a kilometer from here," she said. "My husband would take you but he has no license to drive and you are not well enough, and you surely cannot walk all that way."

"I'll be fine if I can just rest a little."

"Coffee," she said. "Strong coffee. That will help you. But, signora, you must have someone to take you to your home."

"I wasn't affected too badly by the ether," I assured her. "It *was* ether . . . he . . . used? Your dog, jumping out like that, saved me from the full dose." I could even manage a small laugh because of the relief of my momentary safety in this tiny cottage.

"But I think Mario should go for the police. Someone attacked you—"

"And will be miles away by now," I said, "and there will be no fingerprints since your husband was there and whoever it was, ran away before he could take the car."

As if the car had been the objective! I lay back, resting my head against the thin cushion on the couch.

"Coffee," said the woman. "You will excuse me while I get it for you?"

I thanked her, but the smile I gave was a tremendous effort, for I knew that what I had been saved from here would only be a postponement. If Mario Tortelli and his dog hadn't arrived at that moment, what would have happened to me? I didn't know the terrain of the place. Perhaps there were deep chasms between the hills and I would have been flung into one; or perhaps I would have been taken, unconscious, and dumped in the Brento to be found lying face downward somewhere where it flowed into the sea near Chioggia.

Who had made those two telephone calls that had brought me to Riomeyla? It couldn't—it mustn't—have been Rorke.

Someone else knew of the proposed meeting, knew the time, the circumstances, and had got there first. So far as I was aware, only three people knew of my journey. Rorke, Berenice and Cèsara.

I sat on the settee, my hands gripped together, my flesh clammy and crawling with fear.

"The coffee is hot and strong." The woman came back into the room carrying a little tray. "And perhaps you could eat some bread and cheese?"

I shook my head but I took the coffee gratefully. When Mario came in with his dog after searching the area, I tried to make him understand that I didn't want the police, and that, given a little more time, I would be perfectly fit to drive home. "Home," I repeated, keeping from them the fact that my home was more than an hour's journey away.

I knew I couldn't remain too long at the cottage because I had no idea what time the last ferry left the Piazzale Roma. I knew, also, that I wanted to make the journey as soon as possible, while there were other cars on the road. Whoever had attacked me knew he had not succeeded and might be waiting for me on the lonely track back to the main road and Stra.

When I felt strong enough, I thanked the couple for all they had done. I also took a note of their address and decided to send them a gift—I noticed the thinness of the matting on their stone floor and knew that the winters in the Venetian estuary were cold. I would find a warm rug for them.

Neither of them was happy about my leaving, and I made a tremendous effort to seem bright and unafraid. They came out with me and waved as I drove off into the dark, and the dog stood by them, tail circling.

I drove slowly, headlights full on, forcing my wits to stay alert. If anyone stood in the road and tried to stop me, my foot would press down on the accelerator and they would have to leap for their lives. I was in no mood to help any stranded traveler, however harmless, along the road back to Venice. At the same time, although I felt reasonably clear-headed now, I hoped the aftereffects of the shock I'd had wouldn't slow my reflexes if a crisis arose.

I had locked the car doors so that I was garrisoned, and I kept looking in the rear-view mirror to see if I was being followed. But the road seemed fairly deserted and I reached Stra, passed through the town and drove toward Venice without incident. Whoever had tried to drug me and then dispose, God knew how, of my unconscious body, had failed this time and had gone into hiding.

Over and over again, with a kind of wild monotony, I kept asking myself why someone hated me. Only one person could hate me for something—*someone*—who was mine. Catherine Mallory. But the very idea was ludicrous. Catherine did not belong to the world of the maniac or the psychopath.

If only the moon had been fuller, the cottager might have seen the face of the man who had attacked me; if only the dog had been trained to hunt . . . If only I, and not Cèsara, had answered the telephone that morning I'd have known if it had been Rorke's voice.

And then another thought struck me. Perhaps it had been Rorke who had telephoned; perhaps he had come to Riomeyla but had been delayed and had arrived late, after I had been taken to the cottage and the car driven into the yard. He could be still there, waiting for me. But I felt certain that he would have looked around, found the cottage and inquired if they had seen me pass by.

Whatever the possibility, I lacked the idiot courage to turn the car around and return to Riomeyla. Instead I kept on and saw a restaurant where lights shone brightly. No harm could come to me so long as I parked the car right in front of the entrance, and I knew that I must find out if Rorke was in Milan.

I pulled in as close as I could to the open doorway, entered the half-empty restaurant and asked if I might use the telephone for a long-distance call. I explained that it was urgent. The thin red-haired woman behind the desk looked me up and down, and I was aware that my dress was crumpled, that I hadn't bothered to do anything to my face after dousing it in cold water and that my hair probably looked as if I'd rough-dried it after a dip in the sea.

I said, as she hesitated, "My car is outside."

She looked through the window and saw the long, splendid lines of the Ferrari and looked at me again. For a moment I was afraid she would think I had stolen it. "I've had an accident and I want to telephone my husband in Milan. I'm English," I added, "but I'm staying with my husband's aunt at the Ca' di Linas on the Grand Canal."

Something in all my rapid but ungrammatical explanation must have convinced her that I was no criminal escaping justice in a stolen car, for she relented, jerked a finger toward the telephone and said, "Long distance? You will not use it for many minutes, signora?"

"Only to try and contact my husband."

While I waited for the connection with Rorke's hotel, my heart was beating so loudly that it was like some interference on the line. Then, once connected, I could hear rapid conversation, someone calling to someone, and I guessed that Rorke was not in his room and was being paged.

I looked at my watch. It was only nine o'clock. He liked dining late; he could be in the restaurant. I clung to the receiver, standing first on one leg and then the other. At last a voice said, "I'm sorry, but Signor Thorburn is not in the hotel."

"Have you seen him recently? I mean, did he come in and then, perhaps, has gone out to dinner?"

"I saw him at lunchtime, signora, but not since."

I thanked the desk clerk, replaced the receiver and returned to the red-haired proprietress, opening my purse. "If you would please give me some small change, I'll call the operator and find out how much I owe you."

"There is no need. I know what it costs to telephone Milan; I do it often for business." She named a figure which I thought very fair and I thanked her, paid and left. I saw her peering at me through the window as I steered the Ferrari away from her front steps.

Of course, Rorke had gone out to dinner. Why should I expect him to dine in solitude at his hotel? He knew a lot of people in Milan and he had either forgotten our wedding anniversary in the rush of some important assignment, or he could not make Riomeyla and took it for granted that if he didn't ring me to arrange the meeting, I would understand. The car purred on at a minor speed I knew it hated, its powerful engine fretting to be let loose. And all the way back to Venice, I kept asking myself who it was who could have called while I was out that morning, acting the part of Rorke and convincing Cèsara that he was my husband. Someone who knew everything about me, everything about both of us.

XXI

I reached the Piazzale Roma and put the car away. Then I crossed to the ferry station and waited. The boat was a long time coming, and I kept looking over my shoulder. My attacker could have fled from Riomeyla and driven here while I was lying in the cottage. He could be anyone among the crowd of strangers. I deliberately wedged myself between four women also waiting for the ferry and felt grateful for their unconscious guardianship as they surrounded me. At the back of my mind was a determination, if I saw a *carabiniere*, to go to him and tell him my story.

But when the ferry arrived, I turned and saw one, carbine over his shoulder, watching us idly, his thin, dark face disinterested. Without knowing why, I didn't fight my way through the people back to him; I let myself be carried forward onto the boat. After all, what could I give as evidence of my danger? Nothing but what could seem a couple of near-accidents and what would be considered an attempt to steal a car by someone utterly unidentifiable who had been thwarted by a man and a dog.

I was careful not to stand at the rail on the ferry, but chose the covered saloon. Now that I was released from the need to concentrate on driving, I found that shock was gathering momentum inside me so that I felt weak with it, sick and terrified and wanting only the safety of Berenice's house. I sat watching the reflected lights of other craft, like golden lizards darting through the water.

The sense of peril was still with me as I got off the ferry. Each time I turned a corner, I looked behind me. There were plenty of people about: tourists glancing in at the brilliantly lit windows of jewelers and shoe shops; Venetians pausing to gossip with friends. A light rain had begun to fall as I turned the final corner and saw the side door of the Ca' di Linas ahead of me. I took the last lap of my return at a run, feeling for my key as I went. I plunged it into the door, turned it and walked into the dim, dank-smelling hall. The door, slamming behind me, echoed like thunder in a cave.

I was safe.

I fled up the stairs into the *salone*, where Berenice was alone watching television.

"You're back very early, my dear!"

I sank down on the settee opposite her and told her what had happened. She listened to me first with incredulousness and then, when I mentioned the name of the man who had seen the attack, she was convinced.

"What can I say? Oh, this is terrible—terrible! It was the car, of course. You were a girl alone in a very isolated place—"

"I don't think it was that."

"But there is no other explanation."

"Perhaps it wasn't Rorke who called me on the telephone, but someone pretending to be him."

"Why?" She didn't wait for me to answer but got up and pulled an old-fashioned bell-rope by the fireside. "We must ask Cèsara if she's quite certain that the voice was Rorke's."

Cèsara entered and her bright smile faded at seeing me—I probably looked more ill than I felt, or perhaps half-witted with latent shock.

"When you took the message for Signora Leonie this morning," Berenice said, "were you sure that it was the signore's voice?"

She nodded vigorously. "Oh yes, he spoke so nicely to me as he always does and was sad that the signora wasn't home. He speaks very good Italian, but then he was here so much as a little boy. Of course, he has an accent, but"—she shrugged—"it is not easy to speak another's tongue like a native. And the—"

Berenice cut her short. "Many people speak with an accent. You are quite certain that it was the signore?"

Her bright black eyes shot from one to the other of us inquiringly. "Of course. But it is strange that she is back so soon. I thought—"

"She is back early because she did what your message told her to do. She went to Riomeyla. But my nephew wasn't there—"

Cèsara's hand went to her mouth. "Oh, but I know the message was correct. I do not make mistakes."

Berenice nodded. "The fact remains, the signore wasn't there. Instead, she was attacked—"

"*Dio mio!*"

"She is not harmed, fortunately, because someone came along and the attacker fled. But we must report this to the police."

I said quietly, "And what help will that be after all this time?

Whoever attacked me will be safely away by now."

"Nevertheless, it must be reported."

"No," I said. "Please, not until . . ."

"Until what?"

"Until I've spoken to Rorke. I tried to ring him on my way back to Venice, but he wasn't at the hotel. Let me call him again. Let me see—"

"But what good can that do? We're only wasting time," Berenice said with a touch of unusual impatience. "No, I shall phone Basilio Nebiole myself. He is one of the chiefs of the Venice police force and a friend of mine."

As she rose to go to the telephone, I reached the door first. I stood there, rather as if I were guarding something or someone—in my heart, I was terrified that I was. "Please," I pleaded, "let me speak to Rorke first." I saw with dread the obstinate set of her usually kindly face. "Berenice, this concerns me." I persisted. "Please understand. It's no use reporting this until I know whether Rorke telephoned me or not."

"But a car thief attacked you. That's all Basilio needs to know."

"I must speak to Rorke first."

She gave way merely because I was fleeter of foot than she and reached the telephone before her. I knew, as I asked for the number, that both Berenice and Cèsara were standing motionless in the next room listening.

I waited, aware of the silence at the other end while the operator tried to connect me. Then, with a tremendous feeling of relief, I heard Rorke's voice.

"Leonie. I suppose you're wondering why I didn't call you."

"You didn't?" My voice was a croak.

"I couldn't get away. Something important cropped up. I hadn't forgotten the date, darling, but I thought you would understand if we celebrated at the weekend. I'm sorry, but that's the devil of my sort of job."

"You rang this morning while I was out. Cèsara answered and took the message that I was to meet you at Riomeyla at eight o'clock. I went."

"I don't know who's playing games, but I most certainly didn't ring you up. I've just told you, I couldn't make it. What *is* this, some fool joke? If so—"

I interrupted him. "No one's joking. I went to Riomeyla and I was attacked. Someone stuffed a handkerchief soaked with ether over my face."

"Good God! Leonie—where are you?"

"Home. I got back somehow. Rorke, I'm scared."

"Hold on, will you? I'm using the phone in the lobby; I'll go up to my room and then we can talk in more privacy. Stay by the telephone—"

I sat waiting and in no time at all I heard him. I gave a brief thought to the fact that I did not know if the elevator was taking him to the first or the top floor. I had never been to his hotel; I had no idea how it was furnished, what it looked out onto, or how large it was. In Milan, Rorke was a man living a life about which I knew scarcely anything.

"Leonie?"

I realized from the sharp impatience in his voice that he had spoken before.

"I'm still here."

"What exactly happened? Are you hurt?"

"No, just shaken. A man with a dog came along and the attacker was scared away. Then I was taken to a cottage and a couple were very kind to me. When I felt better, I just drove back to Venice."

"After being attacked with ether? What the hell were the people at the cottage thinking of?"

"They couldn't stop me. I wasn't badly affected—the man came along in time."

"Why didn't you call me from Riomeyla?"

"There wasn't a telephone."

"There was at that restaurant we went to before and where I would have taken you to dinner if I could have managed to get away."

Of course, less than a kilometer the other way, past Riomeyla. I cried, "Oh, Rorke, I'd forgotten! It went right out of my mind; I was so badly frightened. The couple at the cottage wanted to call the police, but it would have been ages before they arrived and I was quite certain the man, whoever he was, was already a long way off. I did find a place from which to call, somewhere along the road to Stra, but you were out."

"I had gone out to dinner; dining in the hotel bores me. But to come back to Riomeyla. You must have had a flashlight with you—did you manage to see the man's face?"

"It all happened so quickly."

"And the car? Did he touch it?"

"Not that I know of. He shot off as soon as the man and the dog appeared."

"So there'll be no fingerprints."

"Why should you take it for granted that it was the car he wanted?"

"Then what, in heaven's name?"

"To harm me, just as someone wanted to harm me at the Accademia. I *know* it's true. I know—"

He interrupted the high note of fear in my voice with gentleness. "Calm down. Let's take it logically. But first, you're sure there was nothing that could give a hint as to the man's identity?"

"No." I waited and then added, "Berenice is sending for some police officer who is a friend of hers."

"Basilio Nebiole? And what good does she think that will do now?"

"Perhaps someone living near the glade saw a man prowling around and saw his car."

"Why should he have one?"

"Because I can't think it was anyone local. Someone from Venice followed me there."

"Not necessarily. It's far more likely it was a man living in the neighborhood who knew where he could sell a valuable Ferrari."

I was tired and frightened and angry and I stormed at him. "Didn't you hear what I told you? *I was made unconscious.* Car thieves don't wander around isolated places with bottles of ether in their pockets."

"I'm sorry, darling," he said. "You are right, I'm not making sense. But neither does your theory: somebody knew we were talking of meeting at Riomeyla and deliberately went there to attack you. For God's sake—" He paused and then asked less explosively, "Who knew you were going?"

"Berenice. And Cèsara spoke to the man on the telephone who used your name."

"Also, anyone in the house who lifted the receiver on an extension and listened in."

"Cèsara, Filiberto, Iolanda and Willy," I said. It was horrible that I was in a state where I could suspect people of trust. After the pause in which I faced the wretchedness of suspecting anyone, I added, "But none of them have cars."

"Then we return to my theory that it was someone prowling around that place, intent on stealing a car, perhaps from someone who had gone to the restaurant for dinner."

"I don't believe—"

He cut in sharply. "What else, then? Who would follow you to Riomeyla to harm you?"

"I don't know."

"Darling, nor do I. But when Basilio arrives, tell him everything—try to remember the smallest detail. If I can, I will get home tomorrow and we'll talk more about it then." I thought he said "My love . . ." before he rang off.

It's all too late. I sat with the receiver still in my hand and heard the summer rain beat against the windowpane. It would probably be raining at Riomeyla too, and any trace of a man's footprints in the glade would now be eliminated. My only hope was that the police would perhaps be able to trace the two telephone calls; but I doubted even that.

"What did Rorke say?" Berenice's voice startled me. She was standing behind me, her pretty square forehead puckered.

"That it must have been a car thief and that the important thing is to find out who telephoned this morning."

"You must tell Basilio everything."

A small panic rose inside me. "At the *questura*?"

"No. Basilio is a friend; he will come here if I ask him, and he won't talk to you like a policeman. He is a kind man, though strict with criminals. I'll telephone him now and ask him to come immediately, but not to make it one of those formal occasions when he brings his two state policemen with him."

I was grateful to her. I had a feeling that if I went to the *questura*, I would be in greater danger, for whoever watched me would make certain that I was silenced before I could turn the tables and be a danger to my attacker.

❦

Basilio Nebiole was a huge man. His mustache was black and beautifully trimmed; his hair was tinged with gray and his nose was like some proud and powerful weapon. As I was being introduced to him, I gave an irrelevant thought to his wife. I hoped she wasn't a small woman—in one great hug, he would crush her delicate bones. But when he sat down, accepted a brandy and began talking to me, I knew what

Berenice meant. He was gentle, although I was certain that this disarmed many amateur criminals.

He sat, overspreading one of the not very comfortable chairs, and fixed his black eyes on me as I told my story. His attention was complete. When someone slammed a door below us, he didn't even flick an eyelid.

I was in the middle of my story when Willy entered. He looked surprised, turned his head from one to the other of us, saw our grave faces and said, in bewildered surprise, "Oh . . . oh, I'm sorry," and disappeared. If Basilio heard Willy, he gave no sign.

I left nothing out and when I had finished, he sat back, drained his brandy glass, smacked his lips appreciatively and said, "Your servant, Cèsara. Signora, may I please speak to her?"

When she appeared, he was as kindly and relaxed with her as he had been with me, but she finally burst into tears. The man had spoken fluently, but with an accent, just as the signore did. The man had seemed to know Signora Leonie's movements and had asked if she was back from her visit to some artist's studio. "Then, when he rang a second time, he said he had to go out on business and couldn't wait in to speak to her, so would I give her a message? Did I do wrong?"

"You did what you were directed to do," said Basilio. "You could do no more and no less. What we have to discover is who telephoned, and from where."

Berenice, who was sitting a little way from us, leaned forward. "Leonie can't possibly have enemies here in Venice."

"There are people who foster imaginary wrongs. Can you think of anyone?"

Before I could answer, Berenice said urgently, "But the car, Basilio. It's worth a lot of money. It *must* have been the car."

A thought flashed through my mind. Why were we all assuming the attacker was a man? A woman's hand could be just as deadly with an ether-soaked handkerchief . . .

Berenice was leaning forward, her voice almost pleading, her face anxious. "Perhaps he didn't mean to harm Leonie, just to put her out long enough to make off with the Ferrari."

Basilio Nebiole gave her a reproving glance. "Carrying around a bottle of ether when a blow would have been sufficient?" He turned to me. "On the face of it, signora, what I am about to ask you may seem absurd in someone so young and charming, but can you think of anyone who may, perhaps, dislike you intensely? Hate you, even?"

I shook my head. My fingers were tearing at the clasp of my purse, which I had picked up for no other reason than that, like the Chinese with their fidget beads, I had to do something with my hands.

I was wondering whether to tell him about the attack near the Accademia and in the church near the Zattere. But I decided that he might well see them as Berenice and Rorke had done, as near-accidents which my imagination had built up into sinister drama. I had no proof of the deliberate malevolence of anything that had happened to me, except the attack at Riomeyla—and that only because of a man and his dog.

Basilio Nebiole made notes in a little book, and all the time I was saying to myself, "It's too late—it's too late . . ."

I felt that if I had to get up, my knees wouldn't bear me. I had reported the incident at Riomeyla to the police because I was afraid for my life, and now I was even more frightened, enveloped in a kind of miasma of horror. Perhaps it was exhaustion, or perhaps the aftereffects of shock, that made the people in the room seem to advance and recede, made Basilio's black mustache stand out like something stuck on a paper man and Berenice look like a little fat doll in a blue dress. The figures moved, grew larger, blocked my view. I felt myself swaying; lights danced before my eyes and I felt as if I were dissolving.

"Are you all right, Leonie?" Berenice had risen and had put an arm around me. "Tuck your head down, dear . . . right down . . . yes, like that. You should never have attempted the drive back to Venice after what happened. They shouldn't have let you."

"They couldn't stop me, and anyway I had to get back." My words were slurred together like someone drunk. I heard Basilio ask the name of the couple in the cottage at Riomeyla.

"Tortelli," I told him with my head on my knees.

He closed his notebook. "I will have inquiries made immediately. And you, signora, you must get some rest."

Berenice, who still had her arm about me, asked, "What do you think, Basilio?"

"Conjecture is dangerous, signora. Only facts matter. I will be in touch."

"You see," Berenice said when he had gone and I stood at the door to the terrace taking deep breaths of warm night air, "It was so easy, wasn't it, my dear? He is a good man, and clever. He will have questions asked everywhere and eventually he'll find who did this dreadful thing to you. And now, Leonie, you must go and sleep."

I had slept the sleep of the ether-drunk in the Tortellis' cottage. I wanted to lie down and find some release from the exhaustion and queasiness I felt, but I was quite certain that I wouldn't sleep.

I kissed Berenice and went to the bedroom, switched on the light and wondered whether to have a bath. But I was too afraid of fainting and sliding unconscious under the warm water. I thought grimly, "And if I *did*, what a way out for whoever hates me! Death by my own stupidity!"

I cleaned my teeth, undressed and then stood before the long mirror of the dressing table staring at my own reflection. My robe was dark blue with wide sleeves and elaborate braid; the lamplight gave my tired eyes a sharp brilliance and exaggerated the mauve shadows. My hair fell heavily about my shoulders. Given a crown to raise above my head, I could have been Lady Macbeth, fierce and haunted.

Haunted, I certainly was. But fierce, no. Only frightened.

Rorke had been at his hotel when I had telephoned the second time; but two hours or more had elapsed since the attack on me—just long enough for a journey from Riomeyla to Milan.

I sank down on the carved stool in front of the dressing table and dropped my arms onto the cool surface. Rorke was not involved. The thought was both a statement of fact and a prayer—a confusion that shook me so that I lost all sense of time until I heard a knocking on my door.

Willy called softly, "Leonie?"

I got up and went to the door. "What do you want?"

"Just to know that you're all right. Berenice told me what happened and I'm so worried. I can't bear to think of any harm coming to you."

"Nor can I." A quiver of wry amusement lifted me out of my depression. "I'm no martyr."

"Are you *sure* you're all right?"

"Thank you, yes." One had to be very patient with Willy. He could drive a subject to exhaustion. "And I'm going to try and sleep now."

"Is there anything I can bring you? Some hot milk, a cool drink . . . ?"

Funny, anxious Willy. I said, "I've had a drink and I really am going to try and sleep."

"Then, goodnight."

"Goodnight." I turned from the door. The shaft of light from the uncovered top of the lamp near the bed shone upward, onto the part of the fresco where the girl with streaming hair rode the white dolphin. It was odd, the affinity I felt for her. But then she didn't belong in that painting of Olympians any more than I belonged in Rorke's world, beyond the closeness of our physical love.

I paced the room as if I were caged in its huge space. I turned to the childish habit and began biting my thumbnail. A despair had taken hold of me so that I kept thinking: *I wish Rorke would leave me, then I'd be free at least from this terrible bondage of doubt and suspicion.* If he rejected me, I would suffer the hurt of it for the rest of my life because of the depth of my own love for him. But at least the break would be clean. At the same time, I knew I couldn't send him away. He must leave me.

But he has too much to lose . . . The thought rocketed round the room as if I had spoken aloud and found echoes, wild and bitter and despairing . . . There must be no divorce . . .

So, it seemed, only my death could free him.

I flung off my robe and climbed into the wide bed. The sheets were cool, the pillows soft; but I lay tossing and making myself hot and uncomfortable, listening to the hours chiming away until, just before dawn, I fell into a restless sleep.

XXII

I overslept next morning. By the time I was up and dressed there was a very faint mist, like spun pearl, on the distant houses across the Giudecca. Berenice met me by the landing alcove where she was putting fresh flowers into an antique bronze urn. "I've told Cèsara that you will breakfast in the garden this morning, Leonie. I think it would do you good."

I was grateful and told her so. I had a stifled feeling, as if I had spent the night sleeping with my head under the blanket and my lungs were starved of fresh air.

Cèsara must have heard me come down the stairs, for she appeared out of the dining room with china and cutlery and gave me a small, anxious half-smile. She obviously hadn't recovered from the shock of being interrogated by one of the hierachy of the Venetian police the night before.

I went out into the soft morning light; because of the opalescent haze which dimmed the sun, the awning hadn't been drawn over the part of the garden near the house. I sat in one of the rattan chairs, leaned my head back and waited idly, with a curious sense of being in a dream state, for my breakfast.

Cèsara brought it out: hot coffee, croissants, apricot jam. She set the tray on the small round table, pushed the butter dish into the shade made by the myrtle tree, took the lid off the jar of jam and then put it firmly back again. "The wasps, they love it too much!" she said. "And I think it is not too early in the day for them. You be careful, signora, that you are not stung."

I thought with a spurt of bitter amusement that a wasp sting would be an anticlimax after having been nearly asphyxiated on the previous night.

"You feel better this morning?"

I looked up at the broad, kind face. "Yes, thank you," I lied politely.

Her swift, sun-dappled smile broke out. "I am so glad. I was thinking so much about that terrible thing last night. I believe someone knew of the Signora's beautiful expensive car and followed you to Riomeyla intending to steal it and planned, if you did not leave it somewhere where they could drive it off, to attack you and steal it that way."

"It could be, Cèsara," I said. "Thank you for thinking of it."

When she had gone, pleased with herself that she had hit on a solution, I poured out strong black coffee, the way I never really liked it.

I was due to go to Adrian's that morning for a lesson but as I sat in the garden, I began to think up some excuses I might make on the telephone: I wasn't feeling well; I had something important to do; Berenice wanted me to go shopping with her that morning . . .

But I knew that I would go to the Palazzo Kronos and that

I would tell Adrian of the horror of the night before. He was my good listener, my uninvolved friend. Uninvolved? True enough from my angle, but I wondered how deep his affection for me went and as I sat drinking black coffee, I visualized him against the brilliant background of marigolds.

Adrian and Rorke . . . If there had been some stern judge by my side explaining them to me—"This one will give you gaiety and a happy life; that one will give you flashes of joy, but you will have doubts, too, for you will never really know him"—then I would choose "that one." Rorke.

I sat in the garden until a distant clock chimed ten. The strokes seemed to beat out Adrian's name like a summons. Suddenly restless, I rose from the chair and stepped over Angelo. The telephone rang.

Berenice called from the house, "It's Rorke, for you."

I sped to the telephone, picked up the receiver and said his name.

"How are you, Leonie? Did you sleep well?"

"I'm all right and I slept."

"So Berenice called Basilio."

"How did you know?"

"She has just told me and I've had a visit here from a policeman who likes garlic. He was very polite but we got exactly nowhere. He left, telling me that they would continue their inquiries. Stay in Venice, do you hear? And you are not to use the Ferrari again. I can't have you taking the risk."

I said mechanically, "Lightning never strikes the same place twice."

"But thugs who like expensive cars can strike a dozen times. And if you get another telephone call asking you to meet me somewhere, don't go, because it won't be from me. We'll make our arrangements privately in the future."

"I'll contact the police, instead."

"Do that." His voice was suddenly far away as if he had turned his face from the telephone.

I clung to the receiver. "Rorke—"

His voice came back strongly. "I must go, but we'll talk about it when I get to Venice. I'm afraid I can't get away today as I had hoped, but tomorrow—tomorrow, Leonie . . . Good-bye—and take care of yourself." I thought he said "darling" before the line went dead.

*   *   *

I went to Adrian's studio with a knowledge that only hard, concentrated work could exorcise fear. But trying to paint the light that shone onto my reflected hair in the mirror made me remember how, at Riomeyla, a strand of it had been caught up with the soaked handkerchief. I turned away from my own indifferent painting and watched Adrian putting the touches to the rich blue silk background for Isobel Mallory's portrait.

He said, without looking up, "Get back to work."

"I can't concentrate."

"You're not trying hard enough." He slashed sapphire shadow at the bottom left corner of the canvas.

"Someone attacked me last night."

For a moment I thought he was too absorbed to have heard me. Then, my words seemed to penetrate, and he turned his head in slow motion and said, "Oh, not another near-accident! What's the matter with you, girl? Are you a subconscious suicide? Which is, I suppose, a contradiction in terms."

"This time there's no question of accident. I lost consciousness."

I had his complete attention. "Start at the beginning."

I put down my brush and went to the low window seat and curled up there and told him.

He listened with growing fury. "You came here prepared to try and settle down to painting without telling me a word about it for"—he looked at the clock—"a whole half hour? What in the name of hell cats are you thinking about?"

"You don't have to be angry with me," I retorted, angry myself. "I told you about those other times and you had a ready answer. I was accident prone."

"This is different; it was an actual attack. What have you done about it? What has Rorke's aunt done—or come to that, Rorke himself?"

"Berenice called a friend of hers who is a high-up policeman."

"And what's *he* doing?" Adrian demanded.

"Everything he can. But he hasn't got much to go on. Someone attacked me and escaped before anyone could see his face. It's rather clueless, isn't it?"

"With Cèsara, and not you, taking the message, I'll say it's clueless! Except that Rorke—" He stopped abruptly.

The sound of my heart hammered in the moment's shocked silence. Then I cried loudly, "No, Adrian. *No!*"

"What are you being violent about?"

"The way you're looking, as if—" I couldn't say it.

He said, "All right, we'll keep to facts. And one is that car thieves walk around with skeleton keys, sweetie, not bottles of ether."

"Nor do I believe it was the car."

"So, if it wasn't a chance encounter with a thief, someone went to that place with a prearranged plan."

"You're implying that it must be Rorke." I had said it at last, fiercely, my voice filling the studio with violence. "You're trying to tell me in that damned calm way of yours that my husband went to that place to kill me. It's monstrous!" I caught my breath and gasped. "And don't stand there looking at me in that pitying way as if I were a child you'd like to knock some sense into. You didn't really mean, did you, to imply . . . to imply . . ." I stumbled over the words and quite suddenly I became engulfed in a flood of tears.

Weeping was not my way and I turned my back on Adrian, fighting for some sort of control. I found a handkerchief and clutched it to my face to stifle the awful hiccuping sounds I was making. Then, despairing and embarrassed, I rushed into the hall.

There was a big bathroom at the end of the passage. I made for it, closed the door and in secrecy gave myself up to tears. When the flood was over, I bathed my eyes and then sat on the edge of the bath, waiting until I was sure I was completely calm before returning to the studio.

The window was open onto a well between the Palazzo and the next house. Two women were having a heated argument, their voices beating against the wall opposite and bouncing back to me, the words clear and easily understood, for they were quarreling in English.

I got up and moved to the window. The voices were coming from somewhere above. Catherine and her daughter were having no cozy chat.

"A girl of your age talking of boredom! I shudder to think what life will be like for you when you are middle-aged." Catherine's voice came, richly and clearly.

"It's all very well for you; you have your—amusements."

"I have my work, my singing."

"And more," Isobel shouted.

"What do you mean?"

"You know, and *I* know. Oh, Mother, don't pretend to be so innocent! There's someone here, someone you are having an affair with. You may think you are being so discreet, but all Venice knows—except the one person who *should* know, the man's wife. Do you want me to tell you his name? *Oh . . . Oh, don't! . . .*"

What Catherine had done to Isobel for her to break off and give that sharp, wounded cry, I had no idea. Perhaps she had slapped her face. All I knew was that there was a sudden, quick weeping and then the slam of a door. I thought: *Above and below, women sobbing their hearts out . . .*

I put back the towel, did my face and then returned to the studio.

Adrian was standing in front of a painting he had propped on a chair.

"I'm sorry," I said. "I shouldn't have flown at you. Only when you realize that you're going in fear of your life, something happens to self-control."

"It snaps," he said briefly. Then, more gently, "The trouble with me is that I like you too much. Or no, damn it, it isn't! Anyone with a spark of humanity would be anxious when a girl is set upon."

I went to the easel, cleaned my brushes very carefully and dumped them in the turpentine jar. Then I looked at the portrait of myself. "It's bad, isn't it? Perhaps I should be painting flowers and bowls of fruit instead of myself seen in a glass—darkly." I stared at it. "I *have* made it too dark, haven't I? As if I'm trying to paint the shadows that are around me. Oh, heavens, stop me from being morbid!" I walked away from the portrait and straight into Adrian's arms.

"You're not morbid," he said. "Just naturally frightened. And I'm scared for you—and bloody angry, too—" He broke off and listened. Someone was clattering noisily and with wild haste down the stairs.

"Oh, hell!" Adrian muttered and sprang to the studio door, hand ready to close it. But he was too late. Isobel, her face contorted with misery and anger, pushed past him into the room.

"I can't stand her any longer. Adrian, may I stay down here? *Please?* You've got loads of room and I wouldn't be any trouble—" She had seen me in the far corner of the room and she let out a wail, "Oh no, not you again!"

"I'm sorry you're upset"—Adrian seized her arm—"but if you're going to be rude to my very welcome guest you can take yourself off. Go on, o-f-f . . . *Off* . . ."

"But I can't." She was openly weeping. "I haven't anywhere to go."

"Back to London."

"Mother has my passport. She'd never let me have it." She looked at me and something of her mother's imperiousness crept into her voice. "I'm sorry to have to oust you, Leonie, but I want to talk privately to Adrian. Do you mind?" She indicated the door.

Adrian, more irritated than sympathetic, slapped her hand back to her side. "You don't order people out of my house, my dear Isobel. So just relax. And for the love of all the saints, don't start crying again. There's enough water in Venice as it is."

She turned her back on me with a slow, deliberate movement, pretending that I wasn't there. "I've just had an awful row with my mother. Why did I have to be born to such a horrible parent?"

"Oh lord, not that again!"

"It's all very well for you to be impatient, but what would you do if you were my age and had a mother who was having a marvelous time herself and didn't care how bored you were?"

"I'd be glad she's having a good time."

"With someone's husband—" She didn't look my way.

"If it's true," Adrian said, "then that's her business."

"Oh, it's true, all right." She faced him like an antagonist. "I told her I knew who the man was—"

Adrian said, with undisguised distaste, "You're really enjoying your own imaginings, aren't you?"

"I'm imagining nothing. I know. Adrian, I *do* know. . . . And so do you."

"What I know"—he gripped her so hard that she winced—"is that if ever you come in here again uninvited, I'll have the law on you. Do you hear? This is *my* house, *my* studio and your outburst is just damned nonsense. Now, stay away from me."

"But my portrait . . ."

"Damn the protrait."

"You're going to finish it?"

"It'll find a home in the Canal, my child, unless you do what you're told. You'll continue your sittings for it when *I* tell you, and it won't be yet." He began to push her roughly to the door, and she fought him every yard of the way, wailing his name, sobbing in anger and frustration.

With one final thrust she was outside and Adrian locked the door. Then he turned to me, but before he could speak Isobel shouted through the white panel, "Leonie, do you know that my mother has just made a date with Rorke on the telephone?"

A long silence filled the room, and I knew that Isobel was listening tensely for me to speak

I leaned my head back against the wall and closed my eyes and said slowly and loudly, "She must be lying, Adrian, because Rorke rang me not so long ago."

"From Milan?"

"Yes," I said and realized that I didn't know. He could have called me just as easily from some place not too far from Venice and, after our conversation, he could have got into his car and gone to join Catherine. Where? Not at Kronos and not at Berenice's house in broad daylight. In some secret place.

I put my hands to my face. "The awful thing is, I can't think straight. It's like seeing a mass of paths and not knowing which one to take and where to go for the truth." I took care to speak quietly so that no one outside the door could hear and was relieved when angry heel-taps receded down the hall.

210

"You *could* decide that Isobel was lying," Adrian said.

"Out of jealousy, because she's in love with you?" I spoke before I thought.

He shouted at me, "That's damned ridiculous. She's lonely and is hanging her emotions onto the first male dummy that comes along."

I astonished myself by bursting into laughter at Adrian's description of himself.

"That's better," he said.

But when the laughter was over, I felt worse than ever.

"You've got a problem, darling girl," Adrian said. "If you were in England you'd have close friends to talk it over with. Here, you've only got me—and I'm prejudiced, anyway. There's Inez, of course, but she's a charming gossip. Berenice Montegano is your 'family' out here, so you could talk to her."

As Adrian had said, he could not help me . . . and who could? Only Rorke himself by telling me the truth.

XXIII

Berenice was becoming vague about time. The following morning I went to tell her that lunch was nearly ready and found her at her desk. She turned and saw me at the same moment her hand dug into the inner drawer of the Sheraton desk. She withdrew her fingers quickly as though they had been burned.

"Again," she cried, "again everything here has been touched . . . disarranged!" She looked up at me, expecting me to speak. I stayed silent, but the memory flashed through my mind of the night when I had walked in the garden and had seen the light go out in Berenice's sitting room long after she had gone to bed.

"I had to look through a list of my shares the other day," she said, "and I know I put them back under here—" She tapped the square of parchment tied with red tape. "There's also—this—" She picked up the thick gold ring. "I remember putting it right at the back of the drawer." She lifted her head and I saw that her face had a bruised, frightened look.

I said faintly, "Who?"

"Certainly not the servants, nor Willy. They wouldn't know how the drawer is worked anyway. But someone—" A look of incredulity crossed her face. "It couldn't—it couldn't possibly be Rorke!"

"Why . . . would he want to . . . search your desk?" A question so often avoided a lie, played for time. I guessed that the drawer contained her will as well as a list of her shares in various companies.

"Yes, Leonie, why would he? Except . . ." She rolled the ring over and over in her palm, looking down at it. Suddenly she lifted her head and her expression hardened. She rose, went to the window and pushed open the shutters. Her arm came up in a great wide sweep and I saw the ring's golden glint catch the sunlight for a fraction of a second before it hurtled out of the window and down into the Canal.

"*What have you done?*"

She stood with her back to me. The quiet was intense; the sun dazzled. I saw Berenice set her shoulders as if throwing off a burden. "Did you know that in medieval days there used to be a ceremony of marrying Venice to the sea, and the Doge threw a ring into the water?"

It was not the time to be interested in an ancient ceremony. I was concerned only with Berenice's incredible action. "Why did you do that?"

She turned away from the window. "Leonie, my dear, please don't ask me to explain. Just put it down as an impulse."

I had no intention of being put off. "You think it was Rorke who searched your desk!"

"Oh, Leonie, no! Of course not. I spoke thoughtlessly, stupidly. Just forget—" She broke off.

213

"But that ring must have been valuable—"

"Leonie, would you mind?" She made a small gesture with her hand. "I'd like to be alone just for a while." The vitality had gone out of her, and she sank heavily into a chair and stared at the far wall.

I left her and went to the garden door. Something about the small, desperate scene nagged at the back of my mind, but as I walked the garden paths, it remained as unformed, as vague as a dream I tried to seize on waking, and failed. Perhaps there was nothing to remember, after all. Perhaps it was only my own imagination, intrigued and stimulated by the strange incident. And Berenice could have acted in a panic that was quite unconnected with the ring. But what panic? And why?

There was movement at the far end of the garden, and my heart leaped with relief as I saw Rorke sitting on the seat under the vine. Then my eagerness to rush to him was stifled by the thought that Isobel had said she had heard her mother making a date with him. For yesterday? For that morning? Had he just driven from Milan, or had he spent part of the previous day with Catherine? How could I ask him without sounding what I was, a suspicious wife?

I joined him slowly, speaking as casually as I could. "You're very early. Have you just arrived in Venice?"

"No, I've been sitting here worrying about you." Then he said sharply, "I thought you were at the studio."

"I was there yesterday."

"I thought you went to the studio most days."

"Oh no, usually three times a week." *He should be asking me about the attack at Riomeyla instead of making light conversation.* I said, "Isobel came into Adrian's studio while I was there yesterday, and she was very upset because she had had a quarrel with her mother."

"Had she?" He sounded disinterested.

"Rorke, I've got to ask you," I burst out, knowing that I

could only find the courage if I spoke on impulse. "I don't want to sound like a wife who wants to keep tabs on her husband, but"—I laid a hand on his arm and felt it like granite beneath my fingers—"have you seen Catherine today?"

"As a matter of fact, I have."

"Why?"

He released his arm gently but firmly from my hold and got up and walked the length of the garden. So he had no intention of telling me and resented my asking.

After his quiet rebuff, the next step was going to be difficult —either I became angry and demanded the truth or I capitulated. The one needed courage; the other was so temptingly easy. I watched him and felt that he was withdrawn as if he were enclosed in thoughts a long way from our brief, unhappy questioning.

The vines made a partial curtain softening the sunlight, dappling my dress with shadow as I sat hunched in a corner of the seat. A wasp explored me and flew off; a tiny ant crawled up my arm. I flicked it onto a vine leaf and watched Rorke light a cigarette. I gave no thought to subtlety. I went to him and put my hands on his arms, pinning him with a rather puny effort to the place where he stood.

"Rorke, why aren't you honest with me?"

"About—?"

"Catherine."

His blue eyes looked down at me, and I felt the muscles of his arms tighten as if he resented my grip. "I've known Catherine for a long time. Do you resent my seeing her occasionally?"

Question for question, making me seem like a narrow, suspicious wife . . . then I would behave like one. "I hate secrecy."

"I'm making no secret of it. You asked me if I had seen her and I told you I had."

"But if I hadn't asked?"

He moved away from me without answering.

"What do you want, then, a life with me and another in which I can take no part?" I demanded. "A kind of mystique in our relationship so that I'm never allowed to know, completely, the man I married?"

"Catherine asked me to see her about something on which she needed advice. Does that satisfy you?" I remained silent and he smiled suddenly at me. "How do you manage to make your eyes flash like that when you speak so quietly? It's a complete contradiction."

"Rorke, *please* . . . I thought sharing and understanding were the basic things about marriage. But if I'm wrong, then let's break it up, cleanly and finally. I must be at ease with someone I'm living with. If you don't want that, then you know I would never come begging you not to leave me if you wanted to go—"

There was plenty of time for him to give me his answer before a voice said, "Forgive me if I'm interrupting."

I swung around. Willy was smiling at us from the doorway. "It's after one o'clock, and you know how Cèsara hates us to keep lunch waiting. It means that cleaning up makes her late for her siesta."

"We're coming now," Rorke said, and walked ahead of me toward the door.

So the answer I demanded was to be postponed unless I wanted to make a scene with Willy as onlooker.

The two men waited for me to enter the house. Cool, polite, restrained, we walked into the dining room.

Berenice turned to Rorke. "I'm so glad you managed to get here. Will you go and see Basilio about this horrible attack on Leonie?"

"I went to the *questura* this morning," he said, "and I've told the police that I didn't call her. It is now up to them to find out who did. In the meantime, if anyone telephones her and

uses my name, she is to ring off and then call me, just to make
certain that it was I who rang her."

"But she knows your voice," Berenice said.

"Cèsara thought she did, too. And the line isn't always that
clear."

Willy gave a huge sigh. "It's all so terrible!"

Berenice turned to him. "None of us can bear the thought
that Leonie was in danger. But she'll be safe from now on
because I won't let her risk driving the Ferrari again."

꽃

After lunch Rorke disappeared and I wondered if he
had gone into the garden or to his old room in the wing. I
knew that from now on, whenever he was missing, I would
imagine him there. It was ridiculous to feel that the room was
out of bounds to me, but that was exactly how I did feel.

I went into the bedroom, took off my dress, kicked off my
shoes and lay on the bed. I must have slept, for I opened my
eyes with a start as if something that had scared me in a dream
had been carried on in my mind into wakefulness.

Rorke was standing by my bed. Without a word he lay down
by my side and took me in his arms. Usually, I needed nothing
more than his touch to respond. But now there was no answering passion in me. I let him kiss me; I felt his hands at first
gentle and then urgent over my body. But the barrier of suspicion and despair made it impossible for me to feel anything,
though there seemed to me to be a deepened intensity about
his need for me that afternoon. In a limbo of despair I thought:
*He dare not let me go . . . he has too much to lose . . . So he plays
a loving game with my body . . . Oh no!*

Rorke had always been sensitive to my slightest movement.
Sometimes in the past, a little tired, I had half turned away
and immediately he had let me go. But every time that had

happened it had been I who had eventually drawn him back, wanting him in spite of tiredness, hating that small act of rejection that I hadn't really meant. This time, he ignored my rejection, and there was no gentleness—only a need which seemed to set him on fire. Need for my absolute trust? To dissolve my suspicions? I wanted to push him violently away, to shout at him across a distance, "And an hour or two hours ago, were you making love to Catherine Mallory?"

"Leonie . . ." His hands were asking me for the response I could not give.

I turned my head away but he gripped my chin and forced my face around so that he could look at me. His eyes burned; his fingers hurt my flesh.

"I love you . . ." he said.

I wondered if I had dreamed the words. I lay quite still in his arms and listened to the echo inside me. Words could lie, words *did* lie . . . I knew it, but I was helpless against their magic. I heard my own wild involuntary cry. For one terrible and wonderful moment I forgot everything else. I knew *only* the moment; Rorke's need, *my* need. He was hurting me and I didn't care. I wept as he made love to me.

I pushed open the shutters and looked out at the late afternoon. We were dressed and I had smoothed the bed-clothes. Rorke came behind me and drew me against him, took my hand and laid a parcel in it.

"The wedding anniversary present you should have had at Riomeyla," he said.

I turned back into the room and found my gift for him. "I took it to Riomeyla."

I watched him unwrap it, then exclaim, "It's beautiful, Leonie." He held the small carved jade figurine in his palm.

"You've always said you would like to collect jade," I said, "so I thought you had better begin."

"Thank you." He kissed me. "Aren't you going to open your parcel?"

A large delicate pink stone gleamed in its setting of small diamonds—and the jewel could be worn either as a pendant or a brooch.

"It's a pink topaz," Rorke said, "and Victorian. I wonder whose great-grandmother wore it?"

I took it out onto the balcony and let the sunlight play on the rich peony-pink. "It's so lovely . . . Oh, Rorke, thank you." I stroked the stone and glanced down at the end of the *calle* where it met the waterside. Someone was watching the house, leaning against a stone bollard as if he had been there a long time. At that distance I couldn't see his features clearly, but I knew him too well by sight. It was the man I called Charon.

I called to Rorke. "That man—the one who spoke to me the other week at the newspaper kiosk. He's down there looking up at the house."

"Perhaps the stone animals interest him." Rorke stepped forward and peered down. "No one is there now."

He was right. The place where Charon had stood was empty. "But I *saw* him!"

"Are you sure he's not a fantasy?" Rorke spoke lightly, but his eyes narrowed as people's did when they didn't quite believe what was said.

"My fantasy! My imagination!" I cried. "Do you think I made him up? If so, I created a kind of guardian angel, didn't I? Because it was he who saved my life at the Accademia."

Rorke flicked my hair and laughed. "I don't doubt it. But what he saved you from was the pressure of people and someone so tipsy that he fell against you."

219

"And the attack at Riomeyla? Did two of us—a rather simple country man and myself—imagine it? Did I make myself unconscious through sheer hysteria?"

The laughter went out of Rorke's face. "No, darling. That's different. But let's leave it to the police, shall we?"

I laid the jewel on its velvet bed. Like black dreams, all my dangers were without trails or traces. They came, and left nothing behind but fear.

"By the way," Rorke said. "I may have to go to Eryxa during the week. There are some builders in Milan who are excellent and very reasonable. I want to get an estimate from them for restoring those two houses on the island and if I make some preliminary sketches to show them, it will save time."

"Then you'll be here that night?"

He shook his head. "I'll probably get a water-taxi from the Piazzale Roma to Eryxa and return to Milan the same night. Anyway, if I can get over to the island, I'll ring you. Perhaps you'd like to meet me there. But I'll understand perfectly if you would rather go to the Lido."

I laughed. "As if there's any question!"

"And by the way, just for safety's sake, we'll have a code word. What shall it be? I know. The name of our street in London. I'll just say 'Sorrel.' Will that do?"

"Sorrel Street . . . Sorrel!" I nodded. I was suddenly very happy.

XXIV

The voice called my name clearly and melodically: "Leonie?"

I was walking across the Piazza, dodging the photographers, weaving between groups of tourists who stood in wonder before the confused architecture that made up the glory of San Marco. A small boy tossed a red balloon my way; I tossed it back, laughing. The sun was sharp on the golden domes of the Basilica.

"Leonie—"

The second time I was too near to ignore the clear, carrying voice. I turned and saw Catherine sitting alone at a table outside Florian's.

My first instinct was to walk on; I couldn't understand why, after my impulsive onslaught on her privacy at the Palazzo

Kronos, she would want to see me. But I guessed it was a pretty strong motive and I couldn't resist knowing what it was.

She patted the seat beside her. "If you are not going anywhere special, sit down and have a coffee with me. I escaped this morning from the telephone and from possible visitors. The worst of being international is that wherever you go, you know people and they want to get in touch with you."

I watched her hand, with a single emerald on her marriage finger, curl around the coffee cup. I sat with my purse on my lap, feeling awkward and angry with myself for not walking past her, pretending I hadn't heard her call me. I was intensely aware of the two of us—one perhaps Rorke's mistress, the other his wife—sitting together like casual friends in a Venetian square. It was possible that Catherine saw nothing strange about it; it would be merely sophisticated behavior.

"Venice is a wonderful city, isn't it?"

The banal opening surprised me, but before I could agree, she continued. "I envy you. You have so much time to see everything here. Although this is supposed to be a holiday for me, I'm hemmed in by people and plans, future engagements, celebrity-seekers."

So, we were to start by being social. I decided to play her game. "But to have something that you love doing must give you tremendous happiness."

"Yes. Music for me isn't just a need for artistic self-expression. It is an obsession. Rorke had it once, too. He had so much talent."

So here it was!

"If music had been an obsession with Rorke, he wouldn't have sold his piano in London. He would still be playing—or composing, or both."

"There has to be stimulus, too, to nourish the need."

And I'm no stimulus. And you are?

I peeled the paper off two lumps of sugar, then realized that I didn't take it in coffee and set the pieces in my saucer. "If Rorke wants music, then *I* want him to have it, too." My voice sounded belligerent. I said more carefully, "He's perfectly free to give up his job and try to make a living composing, or accompanying, or anything that will give him happiness."

Catherine watched two women pose in front of the colonnade for a photograph. "Why don't you try to understand him?"

"For heaven's sake!" The deplorable impertinence of her question after what I had just said roused me to sudden helpless fury. "Understand him? What do you think I've been trying to do all this past year? I don't want to change him any more than I believe he wants to change me. We have to accept each other."

Her hands lay calmly in her lap. "I wonder if you know what 'acceptance,' as you call it, really is?"

"It is knowing that you can't expect people to think and act exactly as you would yourself."

"How very simple you make it! But, then, there is a fundamental simplicity about most people. They like, they dislike, they laugh, they cry and everything reflects their inner mood. But there *are* people who are not like that at all. They guard themselves; they're devious. And they have to be handled carefully or they are dangerous when something—or someone—denies them what they want."

"Beware of the hidden tiger!" I murmured flippantly after her voice had trailed into a significant silence.

"You see it as a joke, my dear, but it isn't."

"Are you trying to give me a lesson in understanding?" I asked. "If so, I'd better tell you, I've got beyond the beginner's stage. And anyway, all that you've been saying is really to tell me that Rorke won't be happy without music. Well, I'm not stopping him."

She was silent, and I knew she hadn't been thinking of music at all. There was no need to make such hard work of trying to convince me that music was an obsession with him. For "music," I thought, substitute "Catherine."

I moved suddenly, jerking round in my chair, and faced her. "What you really called me over for was to find out how successful my marriage is. That's it, isn't it?"

"Rorke and I have known each other for a long time. Naturally, I want to know if he's happy."

"Why don't you ask him?"

She gave me her calm, slow smile. "Oh, Leonie, how young people these days do pride themselves on their directness!"

"Yes, we do. And I'll tell you quite frankly that if Rorke is unhappy with me, then he knows he can get free any time."

I had angered her. Her eyes went cold; her mouth settled in a tight line. "What do you think I'm trying to say to you. 'Give up your husband because *I* want him'?"

"Aren't you?"

"You more or less accused me of that when you came bursting into my apartment the other day. I told you then, however much I may love a man, I'm only interested in him if he is free. I'm too busy to have my life complicated by other women's husbands." She paused and we both looked out at the crowds thronging the Piazza, and I guessed that she was as little aware of them as I. She said after the long silence, "On the other hand, no one—no man or woman, however determined—can stop the inevitable."

"What is—the inevitable?" I hadn't wanted to ask, but the words came.

"I don't know. I just . . . don't . . . know. But whatever it is, you have to accept it."

"I'm accepting that I love Rorke." I reached over and grabbed my purse and got up, scraping back my chair. "This conversation is horrible." Shaking, I walked away from the table.

She called me back and said gently, "*I* didn't bring the subject up, Leonie. You did. I was talking generally; you made it a personal thing. You really shouldn't, you know. It only ends in misunderstanding."

"Oh, there's no misunderstanding." My legs were suddenly steady, my whole body controlled. "The first time we met, I deserved any anger you felt. I apologize for my incredible brashness. This time, I have no need to apologize." I took two steps backwards and said very clearly, "You are outrageous, Catherine," and then I turned and left her.

I had gone some way before reaction set in, and I found that my knees shook and pigeons scattered as I went blindly across the Piazza and blundered, without really seeing them, into a party of tourists. I gave one irrelevant thought to the fact that I hadn't left money for my coffee. But that was a small price for Catherine to pay for warning me that Rorke would move heaven and earth to get her because she, and not music, was the obsession.

I walked as if I were late for an appointment, through the Merceria, down the *ruga* toward the Rialto, turned and wandered through streets I'd never seen before, feeling as if I were on the edge of living—like a sleepwalker whose nightmare refuses to end.

A woman was scolding a young boy, giving him a small, sharp slap. *"Stupido!"*

He turned on her and shouted and wept with rage and humiliation. I translated his words as I passed. "Are you not sometimes stupid too, Mamma?"

For all her sophistication, Catherine had been that, I

thought, calling me over to discuss Rorke. Why? Was it that even clever people did foolish things when they were desperate?

.ʃ.

I seemed to have been walking for hours, and at last I could bear the confusion of the narrow, busy streets no longer. Even two caged canaries, out-singing each other in a window over a *trattoria*, became arrows of pain stabbing through my tension. I turned around and made my way back to the Ca' di Linas.

I was too early for lunch and went into the garden and sat on the far seat shaded by the vines. A tendril brushed against my arm, cool to my hot flesh, and I leaned my cheek against the leaves.

I had no idea how long I sat there, but Cèsara came to the door and looked in my direction. I glanced at my watch and saw that it was lunchtime. She waited for me at the door.

"Signor Willy is late and the scaloppine will spoil."

"I'll find him," I said. "He won't be far away; he loves his food."

He was in his studio at the top of the house.

"Willy?"

He looked over his shoulder at me. He had two brushes held between his teeth so that his mouth was set in a comical grin.

"Stop working and come down to lunch."

On the canvas were vivid splashes of purple and crimson with blobs of deep gold. One thing I knew as I stared at the painting. Willy hadn't done it. I had seen it, with another, face to the wall in Paolo Vagnuzzi's studio, waiting for the mysterious buyer to collect it.

I put out a finger and touched the canvas. One small corner had a smear of wet paint. "So this is Willy, the artist!"

"I was just putting in a few finishing touches—"

"To someone else's painting?"

He blinked at me. "To mine, of course."

I shook my head slowly. "Someone goes to the studio of an artist called Paolo near the Zattere and buys an occasional painting cheaply. Paolo believes that this man is a collector and that one day the paintings will be worth a lot of money. But he's not that sort of collector, is he, Willy? He collects in order to pretend he's an artist, to put his name, and a few strokes of paint, to another man's work."

"Leonie, how *could* you think—"

"It's too obvious."

He went very red and said with an angry stammer, "You c-can't know anything of—of the k-kind. I've always b-been an artist. I—"

"Oh, stop lying to me." My temper, already roused by my meeting with Catherine, made me snap at him. "I saw this very canvas at Paolo's. If you like, I'll tell you what I thought when I saw it. 'Is it a volcanic eruption or the artist's interpretation of hell?' *You* don't know either, do you, because you didn't paint it. But you took a risk and you've been found out."

"It was such a small risk," he said, beaten. "Paolo Vagnuzzi is so prolific. His paintings are everywhere and there's nothing very original about them, so he was an obvious source. I thought I'd be safe; I never realized that he'd contact Berenice as soon as he heard of the plans for Eryxa."

I said, "He's charming, but ambitious; he's exactly the kind who'd want to know all about the scheme from the beginning. You should have studied his character before you chose him for your deception."

"I'm not very good on character. And Paolo is cheap because he paints so fast, and he's very unoriginal."

"So you said. But he was original enough for me to remember that particular painting."

His mouth was down-drawn in an adolescent pout. "You're

trying to make out that I'm a cheat, that I—"

"You are," I said softly. "Why did you do it, Willy?"

I watched his face. The startled indignation with which he had first listened to me gave way to pathos. His mouth quivered like a hurt child's; his eyes watered. "If I told you, you wouldn't believe me."

"Try me and see."

"It was Berenice," he said. "She has such admiration for artists and she's so kind to the ones who are unsuccessful. I'd heard about her interest in modern art before I was brought here and so when she asked what I did, I said I was an artist. I thought she'd be good to me if she knew that. And she has been. And I love it here, Leonie. I'm so happy. I can't bear to be sent away."

"Where do you get the money to buy these paintings? Oh," I added before he could answer, "of course, Berenice gives you an allowance."

He nodded, ran the back of his hand across his sweating forehead and looked like a mournful boxer dog.

"But suppose Paolo strikes lucky and finds someone who will pay him more than you do for his paintings?"

"I shall find another artist."

"So the deception will go on."

"What else can I do?"

"You aren't old or decrepit. Find a job." I walked away from him as I spoke. At the door, I paused. "I shan't tell Berenice. Oh, not for your sake, but for hers. It would hurt her to know that she had been made a fool of. Now, let's go down to lunch and hope that there'll always be some artist willing to sell you his abstracts. By the way, how do you manage to get through so much paint if you never use any? Berenice says you lap it up like a hungry mongrel—*her* expression, not mine, and spoken with sympathy."

"Oh, I . . . I just . . . throw some away."

I didn't believe him. Perhaps he sold it or spent what she gave him for it at the cafés. He walked behind me down the stairs to the dining room.

Cèsara came out and beckoned me aside, waiting until Willy passed us into the darkened dining room.

"The Signora has one of her bad headaches and will not come in to lunch."

"I'll go to her."

"No. I asked if she would like me to call you but she wants to be alone." Cèsara hesitated and then said, "Signor Rorke telephoned her this morning. I took the call and put it through. Before I could replace the receiver—you know how quick the signore is—I thought I heard him say that he is going to Eryxa this afternoon."

I nodded. "He told me he might. I wonder if he gave the Signora a message for me?"

Cèsara shook her head. "I think she would have told me so that I could tell you."

Or had she forgotten because the pain of her headache tore out remembering?

In spite of Berenice's instructions that she was not to be disturbed, I would have to try to see her for a moment after lunch to find out if Rorke had left a message for me to meet him at Eryxa . . . A message with some reference to the code we'd agreed upon—to "Sorrel Street." I was certain that he had.

A thin shaft of sunlight caught my face as I entered the dining room, and I saw that Willy had opened the shutters a little.

He touched my arm. "You aren't still angry with me, are you, Leonie?"

His pathetic deception had gone out of my mind. "Oh, forget it," I said crossly.

Over lunch we made sporadic efforts at conversation, but

I knew that Willy was as relieved as I when the meal was over. I left him pocketing two peaches and went to find Berenice.

I paused at the double doors leading to her bedroom, knocked softly and waited. Then I knocked again. Nothing disturbed the stillness of the house; the great walls were like monstrous ears listening, as I was, for a sound. None came. I tried the handles of the doors, turning them, pushing on them. They didn't yield an inch. Berenice had locked herself in.

I knew that her rare headaches were violent. She had probably heard me knock but couldn't bear to talk. I left her in peace, knowing perfectly well that I was going to Eryxa.

Berenice always telephoned her orders to Filiberto, but she was mistress of the house and I felt that I should not be so peremptory. The door on the staircase was firmly closed, so I went out into the garden, through the door that led to the wing over the boathouse, and tapped on Filiberto's door.

"*Avanti . . . Avanti . . .*"

A newspaper was spread over the table and there was a glass of wine in his hands.

He got up quickly when he saw me. "Signora?"

I said, "Would you mind very much taking me over to Eryxa this afternoon? I haven't asked the Signora's permission to use the boat because she has a headache and doesn't want to be disturbed—"

"Of course I will take you, if you wish to go, but"—he looked doubtful—"it is a long way and the lagoon tide will begin to go out in another hour and a half."

"I promise I won't be long," I said, "but I think that perhaps my husband is going there."

He looked surprised. "He is?" Then he gave me an indulgent smile and I read his thoughts. I was lonely and very much in love and for that he would happily forego his siesta.

XXV

Scaramouche sped past the lagoon traffic and into the calm beyond. I sat with my back to the sun, watching the distance, already feeling as we left the life of Venice behind that I was in a world that was entirely mine except for the silent man at the wheel. It seemed almost profane for our speed to churn up the gentle, milky waters and startle the silence—like shouting in church. At last Filiberto cut the engine and we drifted toward the broken-down landing place. There was no water-taxi to be seen.

Filiberto said, "The signore has not arrived and if he does not come soon, his boat will be out there"—he jabbed a finger into the lagoon—"on the mud."

"Perhaps there is another landing place on the island," I said.

"Perhaps. I do not know. The Signora has never asked to be taken by boat round Eryxa."

As I stepped onto the reedy bank, the light, accentuated by space and the surrounding glitter that the sea so abundantly gave back, dazzled me.

From the boat, Filiberto called, "Remember, signora, the sun is high. Take care."

My skin pricked with the sudden motionless heat after the slight breeze with which the little boat's speed had kept me cool. I slid my scarf over my head to protect my neck, and put on my sunglasses.

Filiberto said, "You understand that you must not stay long or we shall be aground on the shallows and we will not be able to move for many hours. So, please do not stay more than half an hour."

If there was a danger of being marooned for hours, then Rorke must have already arrived or would do so very soon.

It was quite possible that there was another landing stage on the far side of the island. Rorke could have found it and the water-taxi from the Piazzale Roma could be tied up there.

First, I went to the ruined farmhouse and found it empty; then I followed the overgrown path through the dry, prickly grass to the villa at the far side of the island. I went through the arched entrance and into the first stone room. The place was not only deserted, but the food we had seen on our first visit was gone. No bread moldered on the improvised table; no cheese had been nibbled at by water rats; no empty wine bottle; no newspaper. Of course, Rorke had been over since then with the surveyor and must have tipped the whole lot into the lagoon.

"Rorke . . . ?" My voice hit the stone walls emptily. Nothing moved; no one answered me.

I went out into the sunlight and walked across the island to the north side. The reeds growing all along the bank were too tall and too thick for me to see if there was an old landing place there.

The sun beat pitilessly down and I walked back to a group of stunted pines, sat under one and, leaning my head back, closed my eyes.

So Rorke had either not arrived yet or had been dissuaded when he reached the Piazzale Roma because the time was wrong and the tide ebbing. If the latter were the case, how mad he would be at himself for not thinking of it before he made the long journey from Milan. He had probably telephoned the Ca' di Linas again, this time from the Piazzale Roma, and finding Filiberto and me gone, would guess either that I had heard that he was going to the island and so had already left in *Scaramouche*, or that I had decided against going and that Filiberto had taken me to the Lido.

I glanced at my watch. Filiberto had said "Not more than half an hour." I was well within that time, and I would rest for five minutes and then go back.

A small sound, no greater than the snap of a twig, startled me. There was a crunch as if someone had stepped on gravel, and I scrambled to my feet.

"Rorke?"

Ahead of me, right at the edge of the island, stood a man. He was hatless and he wore a blue shirt. I had never seen him like that before, but I knew him. My private name for him leapt to my lips and I cried it out into the blazing sunlit silence.

"Charon!"

I scrambled to my feet. "Wait. Please, I must talk to you. I must—" My voice carried over the empty island and startled a sea bird, which rose, screaming, into the still air. *"Wait!"*

For a moment Charon stood poised against the sky. Then he leapt into movement and was running down toward the water. There was a grass rise, so that I had no idea how near the water was. But I saw him disappear.

I raced over the rough grass, tripped, nearly fell and righted myself. The man was already in a small boat. I saw a rope hurtle through the air from the rough mooring-post hammered into the foreshore; an engine started up. I put my hands to my mouth and shouted, "Wait . . ."

The man had heard me. He turned, one hand on the wheel, and looked at me. Then he swung the launch around and made for Venice.

I watched until the boat was a speck between Eryxa and the distant horizon. I had a curious sensation that was part fear and part reassurance. Surely he could not have followed me here; I would be in no danger on a lonely island where there was nothing but sea and sky, lizards and crickets, dry grass and a few ruins. It could, of course, be just a coincidence that Charon, too, on a hot day, needed the quiet of an island and had resented the sight of another human face. But although coincidences happened in life, I mistrusted them—this one, in particular.

I got up and walked across to the actual spot where I had seen him disappear and noticed, between the tall reeds, the broken spars and rotting wood planks of another landing place. The boat was now so far away that it was like a dot on a piece of blue rippled paper. As I watched it, I thought of the unfinished meal at the ruined villa. Was the man Charon camping out on Eryxa? But if he was too poor to pay for lodgings, how was it he could afford a motorboat? Then was he hiding out here? But, again, if that were the case, he would surely not walk the Venetian streets.

The sense that he could have been watching me for some time before I saw him was unnerving. The man seemed benign, but his presence threatened danger even on this hot island with few shadows.

Suddenly Eryxa became unbearable. I began to run back along the ragged track to the boat, but the heat defeated me and I had to slow down. When I reached *Scaramouche* I felt as if I had just come from a dip in a hot bath.

Filiberto was standing in the bow of the boat watching for me. He held out his hand as I scrambled along the wooden landing pier.

"The signore was not on the island?"

"No." The boat rocked gently under me and I felt safe. I pushed my damp hair back from my face. "I was sure he was coming here this afternoon, but I must have been mistaken. I'm sorry I dragged you from your siesta."

"It is nothing. And now, we must hurry or we cannot leave for many hours." He started the engine.

"Someone was on the island," I said. "He left when he saw me, from a landing place on the north side."

"There are always a few boats around," Filiberto said without interest. "Perhaps it was a visitor stopping to look at the place."

I left it at that and went and sat on the shady side of the cabin. There was every possibility that if Rorke had not found a water-taxi to take him to Eryxa, he would be at the Ca' di Linas. Or, perhaps, I should have waited to talk to Berenice, to hear exactly what message Rorke had left. I peered out of the cabin windows onto the white glare of the lagoon, impatient for my first glimpse of Venice.

*   *   *

Rorke was not at the Ca' di Linas, but Berenice was up and sitting in the *salone*. I asked her if her headache was better, and she said that she had slept for two hours and the pain had almost gone. "But you, Leonie, have you been to the Lido?"

"To Eryxa. I thought Rorke would be there. He said last weekend that he might be going to the island and that if he did, I might like to join him there. He rang you this morning, didn't he? I thought perhaps he told you that he was going and—"

She said in surprise, "Rorke didn't ring me this morning."

"But . . . but Cèsara said that he did, that she put through a call; she recognized his voice."

Berenice looked down, playing with her rings. "Oh, that! Yes, I did have a call this morning from a man who always speaks to me in English. A . . . a kind of courtesy to me, I suppose—or more likely his own little vanity in showing off his mastery of my language. Anyway, it was just a small business matter concerning this house."

"Cèsara thought—"

"Cèsara was wrong," she said briskly. "Rorke did tell me last weekend that he would telephone if he could get away from Milan today. And obviously he couldn't because he has not called—" She broke off. "Oh, Willy! How you do startle people!" She frowned at him. "I do wish you'd wear proper shoes in the house instead of those awful slippers."

"I'm sorry." He sank into a chair, his eyes resting mournfully and a little reproachfully on Berenice. "I wear slippers because I respect your floors."

"The mosaic has been laid down for hundreds of years. Shoes aren't going to damage it now." Berenice passed a hand across her forehead. "Take no notice of me, Willy. You know I am always short-tempered when I have a headache." She looked up as Cèsara entered. "Ah!" she exclaimed with exaggerated brightness. "There's something so *civilized* about tea, isn't there?"

No one answered her.

She drank three cups and ate nothing; Willy sulked and ate enough for all of us; I sat, half facing the Chinese screen, counting its golden dragons and feeling the tensions in the room, some of which I knew emanated from me.

I fretted for tea to be over, and then, when it was, Berenice announced that she was going to church. Willy said he was meeting some friends at a café in the Zattere district. "I want to tell them about Eryxa," he said.

When the door had closed behind them, the house was empty except for Cèsara singing in the kitchen. The great stone walls, the high painted ceilings, the very age of the place, all of which I normally loved, became suddenly oppressive. I had to escape and the best escape of all was in painting. I would never be good at it, but it absorbed me and that was all I wanted at the moment.

Adrian had told me that I could work in the studio any time I liked, whether he was there or not. I found a clean linen smock, slung it over my arm and caught a water-bus to the Accademia. Adrian was out when I reached the Palazzo Kronos, but Nicolo welcomed me.

"I thought I'd work a little on my portrait," I said.

He smiled, showing his beautiful teeth. "Of course, signora."

In the studio, I crossed to my easel and pulled the sheet off my half-finished painting. As I turned to get my brushes, I heard a sound in the hall.

"Why, hullo!" said Isobel.

I had left the door open and she walked in. "I've just been shopping," she said, "and I've bought something lovely. It's some jewelry I'm going to wear tonight."

"You're going to a party?"

Her eyes shone. "It's one of those very exclusive ones—and I'm being taken to it"—her manner indicated her small triumph—"*by a man.*"

"I hope you have a lovely time."

"Oh, I will." She gave a sharp, unlovely laugh. "*I* will, but Mother won't."

"Your mother . . . ?"

"The party is at the Villa Vastomoli and everyone who is anyone will be there. Mother doesn't know I've got an invitation; she'll be furious when I turn up. You see, I'm her 'little daughter'; I mustn't be sophisticated or it'll make *her* seem old. I'll enjoy watching my elegant mother's face." She came close to me and said, "Would you like to see what I've bought?" She didn't wait for me to reply but unwrapped the parcel she was holding.

The earrings lying in their green velvet bed were far too elaborate for a young girl. They glittered in the light. "Aren't they beautiful?"

"Yes."

She seemed too delighted with them to notice my half-hearted admiration. She closed the little leather box and said, "The man who is taking me is marvelously good-looking and exciting to be with. He tells me he's a bad character, and laughs about it. He said I'd find out tonight what he meant by describing himself that way, but I like him and I don't care what his badness is."

"Perhaps he's not bad at all, but thinks telling you that will intrigue you."

That didn't please her; she wanted to think there was a touch of danger in what she was doing. "It's time something exciting happened to me, so let's see what tonight has in store." She tossed me a smile. "Goodbye, Leonie. Maybe you'll see me in the newspapers tomorrow."

I picked up a tube of bright blue paint, unscrewed the cap and squeezed some onto the palette. But as I worked on the background of the portrait, Isobel came between the canvas and myself.

Had this man who was taking her to the party at the Villa Vastomoli really admitted to being a bad character, or was it her own piece of make-believe in order to dramatize herself?

I couldn't be certain. Although I didn't really like her, I felt a strong sense of compassion for Catherine's daughter, with her uneasy adolescence and her isolation from a mother who was so absorbed in her own fame that she had no time to notice her daughter's loneliness.

XXVI

That evening Berenice and I watched television. She went to her room very early and I remained in the *salone*. If Willy had been home I would have suggested that we go out for coffee and cognac in the Piazza, but I was nervous walking through Venice on my own after dark. The shadowy colonnades, the twisting streets, the little side canals, safe as they were for everyone else, were places I wanted to avoid.

"If this man annoys you again," Berenice had said, "we must go to the police."

But Rorke hadn't said that. Did he really know me so little that he believed I was exaggerating, turning near-accidents into imagined attacks? Or? . . . Or what? I didn't dare answer my own question.

When Willy returned I greeted him, for the first time since I had known him, with relief. But he was restless and quite unable to settle to talk, wandering around the room, continually glancing at the clock until at last I asked impatiently, "What *is* the matter with you?"

He stopped pacing, and ran his fingers through his hair. "I'm worried about Isobel Mallory."

"Why? You scarcely know her."

"I've met her a few times in the Piazza and she always drags me off to have coffee with her. Not that she interests me," he added quickly, "but her mother—"

"And you're worried about Isobel." I brought him back to the starting point.

He gave me his narrow, sideways look. "I . . . I think I've done something awful."

"What have you done?"

"Well—" He went to the mantelshelf and leaned against it. "Isobel was depressed and lonely and so I . . . I . . . introduced her to a man I know only slightly. He—er—he hasn't got a very good reputation."

"Are you talking about the man who is taking Isobel to the party tonight?"

"You *know* about it?"

"I met her late this afternoon at Adrian's. She told me about the party. She even knows the man's reputation. What is he, Willy, a young delinquent?"

Willy's face was very red. "He has had two jail sentences for robbery—in Rome and Florence—but he says he's going straight now and—"

" 'He'. . . 'He'. . ." I said sharply. "What's his name?"

"Pietro. That's all I know him by. Just 'Pietro.' And when he heard that I knew Isobel he—er—wanted an introduction."

"And so, knowing that she was a young girl and he a proven criminal, you brought them together!"

He winced at my tone. "I like to do people a good turn—"

"You mean he saw to it that you did. I wonder why?" I considered him. A mild blackmail? Or just Willy's inability to stand up to someone with a stronger will than his own? "Go on."

"Pietro is very amusing and good-looking—and those are the things that would attract a girl like Isobel. He had an invitation for himself and a guest for this party tonight—it's a rather exclusive affair, and so I thought it must be all right; but I did warn Isobel that he was a bit wild."

"You utter, unmitigated ass!"

"I suppose I was. But I thought I was doing her a kindness."

"If Pietro whatever-his-name-is is going to the Villa Vastomoli, what for? Theft?"

"I told you, he has an invitation," Willy said indignantly.

"Probably stolen."

"Oh, I don't think . . ."

"Oh, you *do*!" I snapped. "And he's taking a sixteen-year-old girl to this elegant party where there'll be plenty to pocket if he's light-fingered enough." I moved across the room. "We'd better call the police."

"For God's sake, don't do that! You can't have a man arrested without cause. If the police search him and find nothing, you could be prosecuted and I would be involved and it would upset Berenice—"

"Then what do you propose we do? Take a chance on Pietro going innocently to a party in a great house?"

"No. I thought . . . I mean since I've realized what . . . er . . . might happen I thought we—you and I—could call at the Palazzo Kronos and stop Isobel from going."

I glanced at the clock. "At this time?"

"The party doesn't start until half past nine."

"It's a quarter past nine now."

242

And she would probably be at the Palazzo waiting for her mother to leave, her dress on a hanger, the too-sophisticated earrings in their elegant box.

"It might work, Leonie." Willie was watching me, his eyes gleaming as if trying to hypnotize me into agreeing. "If we hurry—"

"You're really scared that this man, Pietro, isn't going to the Villa Vastomoli tonight just to be social, aren't you?" I didn't wait for an answer. "Heaven knows what we can do about it, but come on."

I raced up the stairs to fetch my purse because I was fairly sure that Willy wouldn't have money for water-taxis if we needed them. I gave only a vague thought to the fact that Pietro might possibly be a harmless guest at the party, his criminal rocord behind him, so that all our effort would not only be unnecessary but deeply embarrassing. It was better to be suspicious with no cause, than to find a young ingenuous girl involved, through her own loneliness and boredom, with a possible criminal. I had a vague feeling also that I was glad to be able to be active, to forget my own alarms in the consideration of someone else's danger.

We ran all the way to the boat station and caught one for the Accademia with half a minute to spare.

Willy said, "We may be too late. Or Isobel could tell us that what she does is none of our business."

"Of course! But we'll take a chance. I'm not giving up now."

The vaporetto was crowded and I sat wedged between two people while Willy wriggled into a place opposite me. Once or twice his eyes slid along the line of people, caught me watching him and slid away, as if ashamed. That was typically Willy—you mistrusted him and yet felt compassion for him.

When the boat pulled up at the Accademia stop and the guard rails were opened, we were carried forward with the crowd. We rushed across the Campo to the Palazzo Kronos and I pulled the great bell and heard it jangle through the house.

Nicolo opened the door, flicked a look at Willy, then smiled at me.

"Signorina Isobel Mallory?" I asked.

She had gone out only a few minutes earlier, Nicolo said, and Signora Mallory had left some time ago to attend a party at the Villa Vastomoli. He did not know where the signorina had gone. A young gentleman had come for her.

"A gentleman!" I commented as we thanked Nicolo and walked away. "*Now* what do we do?"

"If Isobel has only just left, we might be able to catch up with her."

"And drag her forcibly away with us? Don't be silly!"

"Then perhaps Mrs. Mallory will be at the Villa. We could ask to speak to her and tell her."

I had no wish to have any more contact with Catherine, and I said so. "I'm going home. Isobel must learn her lesson the hard way. I have no intention of interfering when the whole thing may be nothing more than an embarrassment to Catherine Mallory. She must cope with her daughter herself."

"Oh God." Willy brushed his hand over his face. "*Oh God*, Leonie . . . I—I've got to tell you—"

"Go on."

"I think there really is a plan to—to—er—'lift' a few things at that party."

" 'Lift'. . . steal . . ."

"And Isobel is so young, there'll be a hell of a lot of trouble over it. If you'd just come with me to the Villa, I'll find her mother and explain."

"Fine! You started this; you go and do the talking."

He stopped quite still. "Look at me, Leonie. Just *look* at me!" He glanced down at himself and the street lamp overhead shone onto his expression of abject distaste. "The men at the door—butlers, footmen or whatever the rich call them—would just throw me out. But if *you* were there, you're known as Berenice's niece from the Ca' di Linas, you'd be listened to."

He had a point. "Oh, come on then," I said wearily. "But you do the talking. Where is this Villa Vastomoli?"

"Over the bridge and past the Chiesa San Vitale."

As we crossed the bridge, I glanced at Willy. Sweat was pouring from his face and I suspected that he desperately regretted, for his own sake, the impulse that had led him to introduce Isobel to a convicted criminal. Why had he done it? Not, I was certain, out of any kindly feeling for Isobel. Knowing his character, I suspected that the whole thing had been some malicious impulse on his part—the rich girl and the crook. Put them together and see what happens. Have fun watching the result . . . and now he was frightened.

When we were past the church, I paused. "Now which way?"

He looked to the right and the left and chose the left *calle*. The tall houses hid the moon so that the darkness was thick. Twice, as we were about to turn a corner, I thought I saw a shadow move as if someone unseen waited for us. But each time, Willy reassured me. "It's all right, Leonie. Don't be scared. If you could see these buildings in daytime you'd realize they were very respectable." His laughter was on a high note and he kept running his hand over his face.

We came at last to a corner of a street that had no lights. All I could see was a high wall directly in front of us that obviously enclosed a large house. It barred our way and I said, "We're up a blind alley. Let's go back."

"It's all right. I know exactly where I am." He walked ahead of me, brave now that I had made a decision for him. He stretched out a hand, feeling along the blank stone wall.

"What are you doing?"

"It's so dark, but there's a gate somewhere here."

"You seem to know the place well."

He said bitterly, "Along that *rio* and around the corner is where I once had a room, a broken-down, rat-ridden—oh, never mind, I want to forget it. Actually, the main entrance to the Villa is on the other side, but you can only get there by water-taxi. Behind this wall there is a courtyard; I've seen it sometimes when the side gate is open."

We crept like conspirators, rounding a bend and finally finding a heavy, wrought-iron gateway backed by dark wood. A lamp shone over it.

I leaned against the wall. "Now what do we do?"

"Get inside," he said and pulled something that looked like a file out of his pocket.

"Willy! For heaven's sake! If you use that thing and someone sees us, we could be arrested for breaking in."

He said softly, "Everyone will be arriving by the front entrance; you can see by the glow over the wall that it's all lit up. So, there'll be no one at this door. It's the tradesmen's entrance, anyway."

"Willy, this is silly. Don't you dare break in!"

"It's our only way." He turned a desperate, sweating face. "Leonie, please understand. I've made a terrible mistake; this is the only way I can try to put things right—and *you* can help Isobel."

His pleading caught the right note. I would have been less than human if I didn't try to help, even if it meant facing Catherine. "And, heaven forbid me that!" I thought.

Willy fumbled around with the file. At last I heard a click and as he put his shoulder to the door, it opened.

We were in a large courtyard with trees in tubs and flowers cascading from stone urns. From a fountain, the water danced like jewels in the brilliant lights from the house. The wall of the Villa that faced us was entirely of glass, folded back so that house and courtyard were one. We stood in the shadow of the outer wall looking at the elegant, animated scene: the rise and fall of voices, the laughter, the uniformed servants moving among the guests with trays of drinks.

"Let's get closer," Willy said. "Then when we see Isobel—or Mrs. Mallory . . ."

We crept toward the house, and I felt utterly embarrassed at playing Willy's furtive game.

"Careful! Don't go too near," Willy hissed at me. "If we stand here, the bushes will hide us and we can see right into the room."

I was pressed uncomfortably against a bank of camellia shrubs facing the vast interior of the house where carved doors had been flung open to make the three splendid rooms into one. Crystal chandeliers gleamed; gilded mirrors reflected the kaleidoscope of movement and color. Leaning forward, I searched the rooms and at last saw Catherine, glorious in sapphire-blue. It was obvious from her relaxed and laughing manner that either Isobel had not yet arrived, or that she was, for the time being, hidden from her mother by the crowds.

A servant carrying a tray of champagne glasses moved toward some people near the flung-back windows.

"Now is my chance," I whispered. "I'll give him a message for Catherine. I'll say it's urgent, and then when we see her, *you* warn her to find out if those invitations Pietro has are genuine or stolen."

"Wait!"

I shook off Willy's hand. "I'm here and I'm going to carry this through however much I detest doing it. Isobel is a minor and—"

Afterwards it seemed that time had telescoped a dozen subsequent things into one appalling moment of action.

A hand shot out from the left of the bushes where I stood, and, conditioned to be alert to danger, I ducked as a liquid spilled in front of me. There was a sickening smell and then the scratching of a match. A small light flew through the air, went out and another followed quickly.

Willy cried, *"In God's name. . . No!"* He seized me and flung me away from the bushes with such force that I slithered onto the courtyard stones behind him. At the same moment, the small light burst into a huge flame.

Someone screamed; Willy leapt at me and without giving me time to get to my feet, dragged me like a sack further from the blaze.

"Get up. Get up and run . . ."

The stones scraped my arms and legs, my eyes were dazzled as I scrambled to my feet. Smoke choked us, I flew to the fountain, dipped my skirt in the water and held it over my mouth and nose and looked back. There was nothing in the courtyard for the flames to attack, but tongues of fire had reached out and caught the curtains inside the room, curling and leaping up them to the ceiling. Inside the great rooms was a wild, tangled surge of color as the women, pushed forward by their men, rushed for the doors. I heard shouting and one or two isolated screams; I heard a thud as if something heavy had overturned. If the great wall of glass had not been pushed back, the fire could not have reached inside the Villa; it would have blazed outside near the camellia tree, *on the spot where I had stood . . .*

Willy clutched at me. "Run, Leonie. You aren't hurt, are you? Even if you are, *run . . ."*

As we made for the gate, I said, "They'll all escape. . . They will . . . won't they?"

Willy answered, gasping and choking between the words, "There's the water-door and another on the far side. The p-place . . ." he was stammering, "is stone. The walls . . . w-will . . . stand."

"Damn the walls. The people . . ."

"What the hell do you think you can do, anyway? Move!" He opened the gate and gave me a violent push through it. The small side canal was stained with the reflected crimson of the fire. I leaned, fighting for breath, against the wall and wondered how the blaze could have spread so quickly. But of course, fire created its own wind, urging the flames before it.

"Surely someone must have seen and sent for the fireboats?"

"Yes . . . Yes . . ." His nails dug into my wrist.

I dragged my arm away. "I can't leave. There might be people who have been hurt. We might be able to help."

"You can't stay, God in heaven, you mustn't!" His voice rose, screaming at me, "Don't you know? That fire wasn't meant for the house, *it was meant for you.*"

I must have gone limp with shock, for I came to, after what seemed an age, to find myself being pulled along like something only half alive, stumbling, my lungs gasping for clean air after the killing stench of the smoke.

As Willy dragged me away, I lived again the moment before the flame burst in front of me. I saw the swift movement of the arm shooting out, probably to stun me before the petrol was tossed onto the spot where I stood, close to the bushes. And in the split second before the hand could strike me, Willy had seen, and flung me to safety.

Crowds were pushing past us, drawn to the blaze. I heard the wailing notes of the fireboats, the scream of police sirens as their launches edged up the Canal behind the Villa.

"So now you know."

I stopped and turned slowly, looking at him.

"I meant what I said!" His whole body was shaking. "That fire wasn't meant for the people at the party. And we've got to get away; every corner here is dangerous—for you—*and* for me. We'll get a water-taxi or a gondola—anything we can find to climb into. Only hurry . . ."

I dragged my feet in a nightmare of unreality, so that when

Willy's grasp on me relaxed, I almost fell. I put my hand to a wall to steady myself and turned to look at him. He was shaking even more violently, his body twisting right and left in a queer, crab-like contortion of a walk.

Suddenly I was the strong one. "Willy, it's all right! We're safe. Sit down. Look, on this step . . ."

"No. No. We've got to find a boat . . ." He swayed. "You didn't see, did you?"

"What I saw I'll never forget."

"You didn't see—*him*?"

"Who?"

"Rorke."

The Canal was just ahead of us. A woman scrambled awkwardly into a gondola drawn up by some steps; a man steadied her and I heard her high-pitched laugh. Or was it mine? Had I laughed at Willy?

I wove my way toward the water's edge, clutching Willy. "Double!" I said. "Rorke has a double . . . You see him here; you see him there . . . Rorke's double!" I heard my mockery, loud and cruel since Willy had saved my life. "How ridiculous you are, Willy!"

"Leonie, I *saw* . . . You must believe . . ." The sentence was cut off. His fingers dropped from my arm and the sound he made was a man's scream: throaty, wild, horrible to hear.

I turned swiftly, fear turning my heart over, and saw the man I called Charon stand with his arm raised. Then he struck. It was a lightning movement, a strange slanting chop.

Willy fell like a stone.

We were like people petrified in a moment of time. The man and I standing on each side of Willy, who was sprawled on the dark stone. I moved first, dropping to my knees, feeling for Willy's pulse. "You've killed him—"

"I hope I have." He began to walk away.

"*Wait.*" I got to my feet and ran after him. But the dark

alleys of Venice defeated me and, once again, I lost him at the corner of a *calle*.

I raced back to Willy. A small group of people had gathered around him, and a man had opened his shirt and was feeling his heart. Someone had put a folded coat under his head.

"Don't just stand around; get help," I shouted in Italian, and a man raced toward the *rio* where the water ambulances stood.

I gave a shocked thought to the fact that if Willy's neck had been broken, they had done the worst thing they could by lifting his head onto the cushioned coat.

Willy was not dead. I remained, kneeling by his side watching for a flicker in his eyes, impatient for the ambulance men.

Why had he been attacked? He had done precisely what the man, Charon, himself had done at the Regatta; he had saved my life.

A policeman arrived, asking for witnesses, and took a statement from me. He wrote down Willy's name and address and I realized that when Basilio Nebiole heard about this, he would be thinking that the English girl really did attract trouble.

"You were at the Villa when the fire occurred, signora?"

"Yes, the signore and I came together to . . . to look for someone we thought might be there."

He did not question my statement although I noticed that he gave a faintly surprised look at our day clothes.

"And the man who attacked the signore?"

I said I did not know who he was. He had very bright gray-green eyes, a beard and, on other occasions when I had noticed him in Venice, he had worn one of those·broad-brimmed hats artists wear. "But he had no hat tonight," I added. "And his hair is very dark and thick."

The policeman scribbled in his notebook. I inquired if I should go with Willy to the hospital but was told that it would be necessary to get in touch with Signora Montegano. I protested that if he should regain consciousness, Willy would need to see a familiar face near him.

"I do not think the signore will be in a state to worry very much about that," the policeman said gently. "All we want to know is who his relatives are. Signora Montegano will tell us."

I was certain that she could not, but I made no comment. The ambulance men had arrived and carried Willy to the launch. I had a swift idea of asking for police protection back to the Ca' di Linas, but the policeman gave me no opportunity. He was striding after the stretcher men, and I saw him in the distance get into a police boat, which followed the ambulance, sirens at full blast as they wound out of the narrow waterway and into the Grand Canal.

The crowd began to disperse, and I knew I must keep with them and not walk alone down the dark streets. I began to run and caught up with a group of people at the water's edge. A tall, fair couple next to me asked in tentative Italian if I were alone and when I said I was, asked where I was going.

"To San Marco."

"So are we. Perhaps we could give you a lift."

The colloquial expression translated into Italian would have amused me in less tragic circumstances. As it was I said, "You are English?"

The man relaxed. "Yes. And you? Oh, that's fine. Now I don't have to stumble through my doubtful Italian."

The grapevine that served the water-men of Venice must have been busy that night, for gondolas and water-taxis queued along the side of the Canal.

When we finally managed to get a boat, I felt safe at last. The woman drew her lovely, inadequate chiffon wrap around her. I saw her eyes flick over my short day dress. "You were at the party?"

"Oh no. I—I just happened to call there with a message for a friend."

My answer satisfied her. "It was horrible," she said. "The flames spread so quickly. But I think everyone escaped. The doors in these great houses are so wide and there are so many of them. It is such a lovely house. I do hope some of it has been saved. I wonder how it could have started? It seemed to have come from outside, but I can't think how. It couldn't have been an electrical fault, could it? It *smelled* like burning oil—or petrol—"

The man with her said, "We'll know in the morning. But let's stop talking about it or we'll all have nightmares."

When we landed, I thanked them and the man suggested that they walk home with me. I said it was such a short way and I'd be quite all right. But when we parted I sped across the *fondamenta* and down the *calle*, arriving breathless at the door of the house. I didn't even look for my key but rang the bell. I wanted to be reassured by Cèsara's kindly, familiar face before I entered that huge hall.

The door opened and she was there, wearing the shawl she always put around her shoulders when she went out.

"*Perdio*! What has happened to you?"

"There's been a fire at a house near the Zattere. Where is the Signora?"

"In the *salone*. She was awakened by the sirens."

"Has Signor Rorke arrived?"

"Tonight? Oh no, you were not expecting him, were you?"

"No." I sped up the stairs, aware that Cèsara was watching me.

XXVII

Berenice was standing on the balcony. She turned as she heard me, saying, "There's been a big fire somewhere. It looks to be somewhere beyond the Accademia."

"The Villa Vastomoli. We were there—"

"*We?*"

"Willy and I." I had felt calm as I sat with the fair couple in the water-taxi. Now I realized that I could no longer contain the effort I had been making in front of strangers. Shock broke out again and my limbs trembled. I slumped down on the settee and gripped my hands together.

"You and Willy saw the fire? Why—" She crossed the room and peered at me. "You're ill. My dear, what is it?"

I closed my eyes. "As we came away from the fire Willy . . . was attacked."

"Where is he?"

"In the hospital. He was knocked unconscious. They . . . they wouldn't let me go with him, but the police said they would get in touch with you. I gave them your name."

"I must go to Willy at once. He is quite alone and so I must take responsibility."

"Could I go, perhaps, for you? It's late and—"

"I must go," she said very firmly.

From below came a loud knocking.

"That's probably the police," I said. "I'd better warn Cèsara—"

Berenice put out her hand to stop me. "I'll answer the door. Cèsara was going out to get a little air before going to bed, and I think I heard the door close soon after you came in."

I was past arguing and sat staring at nothing. Berenice could have been gone five seconds or five hours—time, for me, was dissolved in the shock of the remembered holocaust.

She came back, bustling into the room. "I'm going to the hospital. Filiberto is bringing the boat around. You won't mind being alone for a while, will you, Leonie? I'm sure Cèsara won't be out long."

"Of course I don't mind."

"There will be things Willy will need in the hospital. I'll find out what they are and then get Filiberto to take them to him. He must have the very best attention. Poor boy; he is so alone."

I went downstairs with her and stood at the door to the water-steps watching her climb into *Scaramouche*. She went straight into the cabin and sat there and didn't look back at me. I watched the launch until it was just a black shadow between the dancing, glittering patterns of light on the lagoon.

Then, closing the heavy double doors, I crossed the hall and made certain that the door to the *calle* was firmly shut. On my way up to the *salone*, I paused on the staircase by the Floriana portrait and felt for the spring that must open the door. It was a small knob partially hidden by the carved frame. I pressed it, and nothing happened. I tried to twist it, first to the right and then to the left. It held firm. Then, impatiently, I pulled it and the knob came slowly out of its well-oiled socket so that I could grip it like a handle. It turned and the door opened and I stood at the entrance to the wing.

The light switch was difficult to find, but my hand, snaking along the wall, found it at last and turned it on. The forlorn, naked glare lit up the two staircases, one going down to Filiberto's rooms and the garden door, the other up to Rorke's old room.

I went down the stairs to the door that led into the garden and locked it. As soon as I heard the steady beat of *Scaramouche*'s engines, I would unlock the doors, but until then I intended to barricade myself in the house. At least I would see to it that I was safe for the rest of the night.

When the police came—and I was certain that they would want to ask me more questions about the attack—I would tell them what Willy had said. *"This is for you."* When he regained consciousness, he would confirm it and would be forced to tell all he knew.

Back in that splendid house where an elegant party had been in progress, had all the guests escaped? The fair Englishman in the water-taxi, and Willy himself, had reassured me by telling me that the house had many doors. As for me, a camellia bush could have been my place of cremation. Only Willy had saved me. *But how did he know the fire had been meant for me?*

I closed the door on the staircase and leaned my weight against it until I heard the click of the lock.

More than anything else, I wanted human contact without having to go outside my stronghold to get it. A voice on the telephone would help. I ran into the small room behind the *salone*, sat down in the yellow brocade chair and called the Carters' apartment.

Rosetta answered and told me that the family was out. I thanked her and called Adrian. He answered immediately.

"It's Leonie. I know it's late, but—" I said.

There was a pause and then he exclaimed, "Well, Leonie! Don't tell me you have a sudden urge for a painting lesson—not at the moment."

I heard a soft rustling sound like material stirring and settling as someone sat near him—or lay near him on his bed, listening in.

"You aren't alone?"

"As a matter of fact, I'm not. But what is it? Did you want to talk to me?"

"It doesn't matter. I was just a bit bored."

"Darling Leonie, come tomorrow and I'll 'un-bore' you."

I thought I heard another sound, a tiny sibilant hiss.

"I can't come tomorrow. But it's all right, boredom won't kill me. Goodbye." I put the receiver down slowly.

Adrian loved us all and was kind to us all. When we were with him, we were the one and only in his life, the last, the loveliest . . . But we said "Goodbye" and the next one came and the pattern was repeated.

I sat and felt loneliness creep deeper inside me.

Restless as a cat at nightfall, I wandered from room to room. I had made certain that every door was locked, yet, beleagured as I was, I listened, nerves taut, for the slightest sound, as if my unknown enemy had a ghost's ability to walk through walls. I kept looking at the clock, wanting Berenice, Cèsara, Filiberto. And most of all wanting Rorke—and afraid of my need for him.

I could still feel the smoke curled in my lungs, and I thought coffee might at least take the taste of it away.

The sound of my own footsteps on the stone stairs comforted me. But for someone wearing sandals, I seemed to be making a great deal of noise. I stopped still. The footsteps continued.

Someone was coming up, or going down, the stairs on the other side of the wall.

Ice-cold needles pricked the back of my neck, my heart leapt and lurched as if I had just completed a too-long marathon. Filiberto could only just have reached the hospital with Berenice, and I would have heard Cèsara had she returned. I had locked all the doors, so that no one could have turned a handle and walked in.

But someone had.

The footsteps stopped. I stood where I was. When people had talked about being frozen to immobility by fear I had thought how stupid they were; they should have taken to their heels and run. But suddenly I understood. I remained rooted with the Floriana's catlike gaze on me.

There was a small scraping sound; the door opened and I stared like a hypnotized rabbit at the eyes of the woman in the protrait coming slowly toward me as the gap widened. If an ax had shot out from behind the door, I could not have avoided it. I watched and waited for God knew what.

"I thought I would find you here," said Rorke.

I made a swift, involuntary movement, crouching against the carved banister.

"Come here, Leonie." He spoke gently, but I was suspicious of gentleness.

I clung to the banister.

He said, "Don't be silly," and reached out and plucked me from my desperate anchor.

"How did you get in?" I barely managed a whisper.

"You ask that as if I had no right." His voice had an odd withdrawn note as he were only half aware of me. "The door to the garden was locked, so I climbed up and got through the window."

His fingers still gripped my wrist, and I walked by his side up the bare stone steps to his room, a curious sense of fatalism quieting me. Whatever was to happen must happen sooner or later. In a limbo of despair that was even beyond fear, I pulled danger nearer to me, saying: "Willy saw you . . . at the Villa Vastomoli."

"Did he?"

"Why were you there?"

Instead of answering me, he said slowly, like a man going to meet a shocking fate, "God forgive me for what I have to do!" He moved like lightning, pushing me into his room and slamming the door. I heard the key turn rustily in the lock, and hurled myself at the door, hammering with my fists and shouting, but there was no response from the other side. The noise I made must have drowned Rorke's footsteps going away from me. *To where? To what?* I leaned against the wall, listening. The silence around me was so heavy that all I could hear were my own heartbeats like drum rolls.

When I could think clearly I knew I had one chance of escape. I ran to the tall windows, dragged them open and went out onto the balcony, measuring the distance to the ground. It would be a soft landing on the marigold beds, but the height was too great. The garden was in darkness and beyond it I could hear voices and footsteps along the *calle*. If I could only project my voice so that someone would hear. *And rescue me from whom? Rorke?* I drew back, leaning against the cool stone wall and wondering how long it would be before Berenice and Filiberto returned. One thing I knew: I would not go back into the room. If Rorke came to me I would stay where I was on the balcony. The fact that there were people in the distance gave me a greater sense of safety than the interior of the vast, lonely house.

Venice, shadowy and beautiful, lay around me under the dark sky. My ears were tense with listening, with willing Berenice to come back. Every time I heard the throb of an engine I darted forward trying to see the lagoon from the balcony, but only a small wedge of it was visible from this side of the house.

At last I heard a boat draw up to the water-gate. Berenice had returned. My heart raced and I gripped the iron balcony rail, waiting. I felt sure that I had more chance to call Filiberto from where I was than to summon anyone at the locked door. I heard *Scaramouche* being eased into the boathouse below and waited until the sound stopped. Then I shouted.

"Filiberto! Filiberto!"

I listened. There was no answering call, nor did he come out into the garden to see who wanted him. There was silence for a few more endless minutes, and then I heard the clump of heavy-shod feet coming up the first part of the stone steps that led to Filiberto's rooms. I flew to the door and banged on it, shouting his name.

"Filiberto! Filiberto! Let me out . . ."

The footsteps paused. I called again, and to my wild relief I heard them coming up the flight of steps to Rorke's room. A key turned in the lock; the door opened.

"*Dio mio!*" Filiberto cried, staring at me.

I pushed past him, crying, "Thank you. Oh, thank you."

"But signora—"

"No . . . time . . . now . . . to explain." I was at the staircase door. Rorke must have closed it, but, fumbling around the edge, I found the hidden lock.

Filiberto was behind me. "What are you doing? What is happening? I do not understand—"

"I'm terrified that *I* do!" I said and pressed the tiny spring. The door swung heavily open.

I left Filiberto confused, muttering to the empty air, as I raced to find Berenice. A murmur of voices in the *salone* led me up the staircase. Whatever danger there might be for me, I would stand a better chance of not being attacked if there were more than one person in the room.

I reached the curve of the staircase from where I could look up to the next floor. The door of the *salone* was partially open, and I was near enough to hear Berenice's high-pitched agitation and a man's quick interruptions. I leaned over the banister, glancing upward. Even then, I could not see into the room, but someone was standing just outside, in a patch of deep shadow.

"Rorke!"

He swung around as I called his name, and the chandelier high above us shone onto the top part of his face, highlighting his eyes, which were full of brilliant, angry fire. Although he watched me as I climbed the remaining stairs, I knew that he was still listening to the conversation, and as I reached his side, he gripped my wrist.

"Don't . . . you're hurting me."

He reached out with his other hand and pushed the door wide and walked with me into the *salone*.

The effect was electric. Berenice cried out and put her hands up with a queer, instinctive gesture as if to ward us off. The man who had his back to us, wheeled around. I knew him. It was Charon.

Rorke let me go and in one leap was on the man. There was a jumble of movement; a hand came up with the swift, chopping karate movement. I screamed; Rorke's reflexes had the speed of lightning. He ducked, dived for the man's legs and threw him to the floor.

They struggled together with Berenice's moaning protests like some eerie background music. Then Rorke pulled the man to his feet and pinned him against the wall. He had his knee in the man's stomach and for the second or two that he was pressed there, the man Charon looked like something painted on the wall.

Berenice found her full voice and cried out, "No, no, Rorke! . . . This is my house . . . whatever quarrel you have . . ." She flung herself at him and, in brushing her aside, Rorke must have relaxed his hold on the man momentarily, for he broke free, leapt across the room and was away with the grace and speed of a panther.

I heard his feet pounding the stairs that led down to the hall. There was a shout and a woman's sharp cry. Cèsara must have just come home, and the man had probably cannoned into her.

Berenice was clinging to Rorke's arm. He pushed her aside and raced from the room as she fell against a chair.

"Oh, Mother of God, help me!" She sank down on her knees, her skirt billowing round her, her face buried in the seat cushion of the chair.

Everything swam round me. I wished I could conveniently faint or will myself into stupidity so that I could come to when everything—whatever that ghastly "everything" was—had been resolved. When I had described the man Charon to Rorke, he had dismissed him as a crazy stranger, yet all the time he had known him.

XXVIII

I could not have followed Charon and Rorke even if I had wanted to, for I was drained by the accumulated shocks of the night. Berenice had deceived me, too. I looked across at her. She had lifted her head, and I saw that she looked suddenly old, her cheeks gray-tinged, her hair untidy, her eyes dulled.

I went over to her and bent to help her to her feet. She yielded without protest and I led her to the settee and put cushions behind her head. "Now tell me, who is that man?"

Her lips moved but the words would not come. She shook her head.

I said harshly to break the shock that was numbing her, "I have a right to know. I'm involved."

She burst into sudden heavy sobs which shook her and her voice came, thick and cracked. "Leonie, save him from Rorke. He'll kill—"

I bent down and seized her shoulders. "What are they to one another? Tell me. *Tell me.*" Without really realizing what I was doing, I began to shake her.

"Signora!" Cèsara swept up behind me and tore my hands from Berenice's shoulders, her face contorted with anger. "How can you behave like that? You are young; she is old—yet you—"

Berenice gripped her hand. "You don't understand, Cèsara. Leave me."

"I shall not leave you," Cèsara said firmly, "and certainly not to be tortured like that."

"Tortured?" I cried. "I'm only trying to get her to tell me—"

"She is too upset to tell you anything. Can you not see?" Cèsara put her hands under Berenice's shoulders and urged her gently. "Come, *povera signora*, come with Cèsara. She will take care of you." Her great arms enclosed the small woman; her eyes glared at me. Berenice resisted her from some desperate, dredged-up strength, and all Cèsara could do was to enfold her and croon as to a child. "You must not cry so! No one is going to hurt you while I am here. And you have Filiberto, too; he is strong. We will look after you. Come to bed now and I will tuck you in and bring you what you would like. A little brandy, perhaps?"

Berenice broke away from her. "No. I don't want to go to bed. I can't—not yet. I must wait—for them."

"For who, signora?"

"Never mind."

"Who was that man who ran past me?" Cèsara demanded. "He almost knocked me over when he tore at the door and vanished. Is he a thief? Has he broken in and frightened you? I call the police, yes?"

"No!" Berenice sat down on the settee, hands tearing at her damp handkerchief. "It's all right, Cèsara. Leonie was not ill-treating me, if that's what you think. She is as upset as I. As I say, leave us, please."

Cèsara looked at me as if she thought she were abandoning her beloved mistress to a viper. "Very well, I will go and make coffee for you and I will bring brandy. I will not be long."

"I don't want anything."

"You do not think you do, but *I* know." She bent and smoothed Berenice's hair back gently, looked at me again and said with reluctance, "I will bring coffee for both of you."

Our voices clashed, Berenice repeating, "No . . . I want nothing," and I saying gratefully, "Thank you."

Cèsara left us, muttering that she didn't know what it was all about and it was terrible that the Signora should be so unhappy, but the dear Saint Anthony would protect the house. She crossed herself and plodded down the stairs to the kitchen.

I felt that Berenice had really only been half aware of what had been said. She lay back on the settee and shaded her eyes. "I'm not afraid," she said softly and slowly, as though forgetting me and thinking her thoughts aloud, "not for myself . . . only for him."

"Who is he?"

She dropped her hand from her eyes and looked away over my shoulder, still seeming to be talking to herself. "Rorke has this streak in him . . . this violence . . ."

"*Who—is—that—man?*"

Her eyes focused on me at last. For a moment I thought I had her confidence, then she turned her head away and struggled to her feet, hanging onto the side of the settee with a shaking hand. I went to help her, but she brushed me away. "I'm all right," she said and wove past me to the window.

I followed her, distressingly aware that I was behaving like a bee buzzing round something that was rejecting it. But I had to wear her down; I had to know.

"When I told you about the man at the newsstand who had given me that odd warning, you said you didn't know him. But you do. Berenice, *you do*."

I was talking to an empty room. She was standing on the balcony, looking up at the stars.

I said loudly, "I gave that man a fancy name because I had to identify him to myself somehow, because he was important. He had saved my life. He . . ." I waited. There was no sound from the little figure outside, hands on the stone balustrade, head lifted to the sky.

I tried again, my voice even louder, firmer, demanding an answer. "You know him and you like him—"

"I love him."

I caught my breath, and my words came as a whisper. "You love him—and he saved my life. Who was that man?"

She turned and glanced beyond me and I looked, too, and saw Cèsara enter the room carrying a tray with coffee pot, cups and a little plate of macaroons. "Now sit down, signora, and drink and eat a little, then you will feel better."

Berenice went obediently back to the settee, which was so huge that it made her look small and vulnerable as she sat there clutching the handkerchief, her toes turned slightly inward, her eyes dry now but blank as if she had reached the end of feeling.

The question "Who is the man?" had to be asked again and again, until she explained him. But I gave her a few minutes' grace after Cèsara had left us. I poured out coffee for her and for myself and drank mine bitingly hot. The minutes ticked by and the house was full of a ghastly silence.

I broke it, asking, "How is Willy?"

"He had not recovered consciousness. The police were there, and I told them I would be responsible for him."

"He knew this man, too."

She gave me a startled look. "Willy? Oh no, he—" And then she stopped.

"Please go on," I said gently.

She looked about her in a distraught way, ignoring what I had asked her. "Where have they gone? Where are they?"

" 'They'? One of them being Rorke, and the other—?"

"Sometimes men hate so much that they take the law into their own hands." Suddenly she seemed to pull herself together; her shoulders straightened, the numb fear left her eyes. "All right, Leonie, you will have to know. The man who saved your life at the Regatta—your mother loved him."

"Mother knew him?" I said bewilderedly. "But how could she? If she knew him, I would have and I had never seen him before I came to Venice."

"It was through you that they first met. Elliot," she said. "Elliot Jerome—my brother."

Shock must have deranged her. I said gently, "Elliot is dead. He died in that car crash in the Pyrenees."

She shook her head slowly. "It was someone else. Elliot escaped."

"And let everyone believe it was he who died? Why?"

"He *had* to escape."

"From whom?"

She swallowed before she said his name, as if her throat hurt. "Elliot was terrified of Rorke."

"Why, in heaven's name?"

She shook her head. "He only said that Rorke was planning to get him in some trouble at Melarper's, but that he was innocent. He said 'The guilty are so very clever. They can lay the blame on others and often get away with it.' "

"What blame?"

"I don't know. . . . I don't know! Elliot wouldn't tell me."

"You mean you didn't try to find out?" I asked incredulously.

Her small plump hands were twisting and turning in her lap. "Elliot said it was best for me not to know. I remember him saying, 'You are fond of Rorke and so I would rather not tell you everything. One day you will find out for yourself. That's the way it has to be because I can't hurt you with the truth. Only, take care!' I thought: 'It must be just a terrible misunderstanding.' I knew, though, that whenever Rorke came here—and I couldn't bear to stop him from coming—I had to be careful that he never knew that Elliot was in Venice."

"Even while we've been here, you met Elliot."

"Before you came to stay we used to meet in Rorke's old room—nobody knew because I used the door on the staircase where the Floriana hangs to go to see him. Elliot had a key to the garden door and he would come late, after Filiberto was in bed and asleep. The walls and floors of the wing are as solid as in the house itself, so we would never disturb him. Elliot was afraid that the servants might talk if they ever saw him; and Rorke would get to hear about it."

"But he sometimes came when we were in the house," I insisted. "You know I found the door on the staircase open one night."

She shook her head. "At some time or other, I must not have fastened it properly and perhaps, in cleaning, Iolanda unconsciously opened it a little and a draught swung it right open that night when you saw it. But Elliot never dared come here while Rorke and you were staying with me." She put out her hand. "Leonie, I don't understand Rorke's hate; I've tried to make him tell me, but it's no use. I'm in the dark. I don't understand their mutual hatred. Yet I love them both so much."

"When I described the man at the newsstand, you pretended you didn't know him."

"How could I from your description? Elliot does not have gray-green eyes and you were very sure of that; you stressed the point. They were very bright, you said."

"The man who gave me a lift at Melarper's was fair, like you."

"Elliot bought a wig and grew a beard. That was all I knew. But there are so many dark men with beards in the world. Besides, how could I possibly imagine he would contact you when he was so afraid of Rorke and of you coming here?"

"Of course, I see it now!" I said. At some time or other Elliot must have bought contact lenses to change the color of his eyes. And in that disguise, how could Rorke ever find him in this city of a thousand little alleys? "How did Elliot live?"

"I gave him money."

"With which he bought a boat."

"A—a boat? What would he want one for? He has a room near the Rialto—it's small but comfortable, and he always uses the water-busses whenever he comes to see me."

But he had a boat—or had hired one. To follow me to Eryxa? Because he was afraid, not only for himself, but for me, too? He had loved my mother and whatever he had done to make Rorke hate him, whatever wild despair had sent him into hiding, he had watched over me.

Berenice was holding her hands tightly against her and the old-fashioned claw setting of one of her emeralds caught in her dress. She extricated it roughly, pulling at the threads of the silk. "I threw Elliot's ring away. . . . You remember? You saw me."

"Because someone had been at your desk drawer twice."

"Rorke," she said. "I'm sure of that now!"

"Because at some time or other, he had seen Elliot's ring there. Why did you have it?"

"Elliot couldn't wear it—it was too distinctive—but it was his small vanity and he loved it. It was the only thing he possessed from the past."

A deep purple amethyst buried in the mud of the lagoon. Elliot Jerome's jewel.

Suddenly I knew what had puzzled me for so long. It had started in Berenice's private sitting room at the open desk. The link went back more than a year. In fact, to that foggy morning when Elliot Jerome had given me a lift home from Melarper's. The headlights from an oncoming car had glimmered for a moment on the vivid purple stone of his ring. I had glanced at it, interested that a man of Elliot's conventional type should wear anything so curiously ornate. But it had been a passing thought and, as I had never seen Elliot again, it had gone out of my mind. But at some time in that year, between then and now, either my mother or Rorke must have mentioned that nothing had been found on the man burned to death in the car . . . on Elliot. Nothing.

"It *must* have been Rorke who searched my desk." Berenice's voice broke the silence, startling me.

Yes, it was Rorke . . .

The room was stifling.

"Leonie, is Rorke *really* in Italy because Ferris Caretta sent for him?"

"That's what he told me."

I got up from my chair and Berenice cried, "Don't leave me."

"I'll be back."

"Do you think you can go and look for them? You can't. You'd never find them."

"I'm not going to try." I went to her and put an arm around

her. "There is nothing we can do but wait. I'm only going to the garden for a little while."

I heard her murmur as I left her, "They will both come back. . . . Please God, let Elliot be safe!"

I had to escape the house, but I was afraid to go beyond the garden. In the beautiful city where, but for someone's private hatred of me, I would have walked without fear, the streets were malevolent, the shadows full of threats.

The night was clear and the flowers were blanched by the brilliant three-quarter moon. But being alone gave me no peace, either. I could not sort and clarify the jumble of fear and shock that tore at me. Elliot was afraid of Rorke: Elliot, who had perhaps saved my life at the Accademia . . . and yet had struck Willy down . . .

In the end, defeated, I went back to the house and found Cèsara hovering over Berenice, avid to know what it was all about, trying to drag the truth of the night's strange happenings out of her without direct and impertinent questions. But Berenice just lay back on her cushions, saying, "Yes, Cèsara" . . . "No, Cèsara."

"Go to bed," I said to her. "I'll stay with the Signora."

"But she must rest, too. She cannot sit up all night."

The argument was broken by the great bell at the door of the Ca' di Linas which crashed through the house. I had my hand on Berenice's arm and I felt her go suddenly rigid.

"I'll go." I said and flew past Cèsara, taking the curving staircase with suicidal speed. Rorke . . . Rorke, in his mysterious fury, forgetting his key.

The man who stood at the open door owned the shoe shop at the top of the *calle*. He smiled.

"Good evening, signora." He always spoke to me in English. "Your husband stopped me a while ago and asked me to deliver this note to you."

"Thank you, thank you . . . Where did you meet him?"

"He was coming up from the Palazzo Bernado near the Campo San Polo and we just went—so!" He banged his hands together. "He recognized me and said, 'Wait, please,' and then wrote something on a page torn from a little notebook he carried, and asked me to bring it to you."

"And—and then—?"

"He thanked me and walked away toward the *rio*." The man was looking puzzled and I realized why. I was trembling violently.

"It's very kind of you." The piece of paper seemed alive, burning and fretting to be opened. *Go. Go. Go*, I urged the man in silent despair and said aloud, quietly, politely, "Thank you very much for your kindness."

He gave me a friendly smile and walked away. I closed the door and sat down on the stairs and unfolded the paper.

It was a scrawled note: "I shall not be home tonight. Just keep quiet and send no one looking for me." No signature. Nothing. But I knew Rorke's rushed, impatient handwriting.

Keep quiet and send no one looking for me. No police interference. I'm on my own in this. And so are you, my darling . . .

Oh no! I was putting thoughts into his mind that couldn't be there. Rorke wouldn't mock me. My imagination was becoming a second enemy. This violent hatred that was between Rorke and Elliot had nothing to do with the things that had happened to me.

I sat where I was with the piece of paper gripped in my fingers. The hall, as always, smelled of damp stone and as I crouched on the stairs, a dreadful thought struck me, hitting me in the stomach with a pain like a sledge hammer. *Will Rorke ever come back?* Was this some terrible crisis that had thrust itself, not only between him and myself, but also between Rorke and Catherine? In the end, would some irony make us mutual losers?

*　　*　　*

I sat hugging my arms round my body, not so much because of the chilly air of the hall as because I felt that if I relaxed, I would disintegrate physically. Another thought hung at the back of my mind, beyond all the pain. *No one should be permitted to love so completely. Love should have a few reservations, an armor to protect it.* I had none.

"Leonie. Leonie. Who was it?"

Berenice was calling me. I came to partial life, screwed the note into a ball and, holding it tightly in my hand, went into the *salone.* Although it was a beautiful warm night and the shutters were closed, Berenice was lying on the settee shivering. I went to fetch a blanket from the gilded cassone down in the alcove and covered her with it.

"Oh, nothing . . . nothing. Won't you let me help you to bed?"

She moved her head from side to side. "I couldn't sleep. I've got to stay awake, to wait—"

"Then try to sleep here. I'll stay with you. Don't worry, I'll call you if they come back."

She clung to my hand. "Where are they, Leonie?"

"I don't know any more than you. Now try to rest."

She closed her eyes obediently and I heard her sigh. While I was in the garden she must have got up from the settee to turn out the lamps because the lights hurt her eyes. Now, the glow from the chandelier in the gallery outside was all that lit the room.

I pushed the shutters open just a fraction and then crept to my room, took my coat from its hanger and returned with it to the *salone.* Pulling a footstool up to the largest armchair, I settled myself as best I could with my coat over me.

Someone, somewhere, was playing one of those light,

charming instruments I could never distinguish—a guitar, a banjo, a mandolin? What did it matter? I hid my face in the cushioned side of the wing chair, and the only sound in the room were the tiny cries, like an animal dreaming, that came from Berenice. She was always so animated that one forgot how old she was, and the old cannot always receive shocks without physical damage. Could the young?

XXIX

For the rest of the night we turned and twisted and fretted. I fell into short, exhausted sleeps, waking with a jerk, opening my eyes to look around me, startled and alert. The silence was like a threat and I longed for something to break it—the doorbell ringing; a footstep; Cèsara creeping in to see if the Signora needed her.

I knew that Berenice, too, merely dozed like a cat, an ear listening all the time for one of her men to return, yet terrified of the news either would bring of the other. I had deliberately not told her of the note I had received from Rorke in case his message might alarm her still further. It was better that she should spend the night expecting his return.

Cèsara woke me from my last short sleep, hustling past me

to the windows. I heard her, through the last moments before complete waking, saying *"Bah!* It is bad—this air coming onto the Signora, bringing in the fog!"

I opened my eyes and stretched my stiff limbs and started up.

Cèsara turned on me. *"Zitti! Zitti!"* She glanced at Berenice.

But there was no need to be quiet; I saw by the flicker of her eyelids that she was awake.

Cèsara fastened the shutters and then looked over her shoulder at me reprovingly. "The Signora should have gone to bed properly and rested."

"I know, but I had to let her stay. She wanted to."

"And you left the shutters open." She came up to me and, taking up my coat, shook it and replaced it carefully round me.

"Only just a very little," I said.

"But there is a fog this morning. The Signora"—she glanced across at her—"should not have been breathing the damp air that comes from the sea."

"I don't think it will hurt her."

Cèsara gave up. The ways of the English often made little sense to her and I couldn't explain that I had left that chink in the shutters to ease the claustrophobic feeling in the room, the sense of being shut away from the people we were waiting and listening for.

"You think I should bring in tea now?"

"Yes, please. And make it fairly strong, will you?"

"If you wish, if you wish." She padded out of the room and I got up and went over to Berenice.

She lay very still, but her eyes were open. "They didn't come home?"

"No."

"What is happening—what *did* happen last night when they left us?" She ran her fingers distractedly through her hair. "There's a fog this morning, isn't there?"

"Yes."

Cèsara entered carrying a tray of the early morning tea Berenice had insisted upon from the day she had set foot, as a bride, in Venice.

"You will ache so badly after sleeping uncomfortably, signora. Here, let me help you sit up."

Berenice waved aside her attempts to help. "I'm all right. Open the shutters wide, please."

Cèsara stared at her as if she were out of her mind. "But the fog—"

"Do as I ask you."

Cèsara stalked across the floor and pushed them another inch apart.

"No, *more.*"

"You will catch cold."

"Nonsense. I must have the shutters open." Berenice struggled to her feet. "If you won't do what I ask, then I must do it myself."

"Oh, very well then, I will open them. Wide? Like that?" She flung them defiantly backwards so that they clanged against the wall.

Berenice said, "Yes, like that."

Cèsara gave me a long, meaningful look, and I knew she was wondering if Berenice had taken leave of her senses. I drank my tea standing up.

"It's so solid," Berenice cried, staring at the thick white morning. "Like a wall. And they are out there, Rorke and Elliot. But where? *Where?*"

I could give her no answer.

"It was good of you to stay, Leonie dear," she said. "And even when I slept, I felt you were there. Thank you. Now go and freshen up and get some breakfast. I'm all right—" she urged, as I hesitated. "It's morning—and that is never so dreadful, when you're afraid, as night. Go, dear."

I bathed, dressed and went down to the empty dining room and stood for a while at the window. All I could see were the dim outlines of the adjoining buildings like the spires of a floating city. I heard the melancholy sound of a foghorn, but the gondolas and the motor launches would be lying at their moorings in the opaque light.

"Signora—" Cèsara entered, looking across at me. "It is Filiberto. He wants to speak to you. I said he must wait, but he says it is urgent."

He hovered behind Cèsara and I called, "Come in, Filiberto," and sent Cèsara unnecessarily for more hot milk. "What is it that's urgent?"

"The signore gave me a message and told me to deliver it to you this morning."

I swallowed the rest of my coffee in a gulp. "When did you see him?"

"He woke me in the early hours of this morning to take him to Eryxa. It was mad, signora, and I told him so. It is not always correct to follow the *bricoli* at nighttime. It is the fishermen's fault; they put extra lights on their poles to mark the fish traps and even I, who know the channels so well—"

"Filiberto, *please*—"

He said, reprovingly, "I am coming to the point, signora. I took Signor Rorke to Eryxa and he asked me to leave him there. I called, 'But not for the rest of the night!' He did not answer me. I thought—forgive me, signora—'There has been a little love trouble between them and he wants to be alone.' So I leave him. But it is a long way back, so I rest a little and smoke a cigarette. Then, as I am casting off, I hear the signore say 'Bring Signora Leonie over in the morning, early. I will wait for her at the villa—she knows where it is.' He was somewhere quite near me, but I could not see him. I thought: 'It is not good for him to frighten the little signora like this by staying out all night, but angry men do foolish things.' Forgive me."

I didn't care how Filiberto interpreted Rorke's night vigil on Eryxa. "We must go," I said and pushed back my chair.

"The fog!" he cried. "Even the vaporetti have cut their services and the gondoliers hang around the steps, not even bothering to polish their boats."

"I must get to the island."

"I am a good navigator. I have always said that if you cover my eyes *so*"—his huge brown hand covered the top half of his face—"I will find the channels of the lagoon." He spoke as if his protest a moment earlier had been merely a gesture to authority; no one must ever think Filiberto servile. But his eyes were bright with the idea of a challenge. He had so few in his quiet life with Berenice. "If you wish to go now, signora, then of course, we go."

"Thank you."

Whatever happened to Elliot Jerome was no longer of importance. Rorke could have lost him in the search last night and given up the hunt. Or perhaps his hate had cooled; or perhaps they had met and argued it out, or fought it out, and the antagonism was over. But why did Rorke want to see me on Eryxa? He could have spent the night there because, with a decision to be made, on that isolated island he felt free from us and our influence over him. I faced up to what the decision might be: Catherine . . .

"You must wear a coat, signora. The fog makes everything damp. Later, when the sun comes out, it will be hot."

I flew up the stairs and seized the white coat that lay on a chair.

Filiberto was waiting for me as I dragged open the double doors to the water-steps. I tried to close them quietly behind me but the hall was like a hollow shell so that the sound ran echoing far into the raw, damp corners. Filiberto had eased *Scaramouche* up to the lower step.

He helped me into the boat, saying, "It will be a very slow journey. I will have to crawl."

"I don't mind." I sat in the cabin as he stood at the wheel, sounding his horn continuously, so that it was as if I had an invisible toad in the boat, croaking its lungs out.

XXX

As Filiberto had said, we crawled, and how we kept within the poles that marked the water lanes between the mud flats I would never know. Minutes in that milky whiteness stretched to half an hour, an hour; then at last the little island loomed up before us and Filiberto cut the engine and edged into the muddy channel. He got out first and stood for a moment, looking about him, calling. It sounded to me like: "Oi-lè! Oi-lè!" He waited a moment and then repeated the call. Another silence met us.

I said, "I'll go to the villa. That's where my husband told you he would wait for me."

Filiberto shook his head. "I should not leave you here like this, signora. I should wait." He lapsed into Italian. "The fog will clear very soon and the day will be beautiful. I think I will wait. It will be easier for me, too, or I must crawl back and some idiot will run into us and damage her."

"Her," his beloved *Scaramouche*.

I hesitated for a moment or two, half hoping that Rorke would materialize out of the opaque light. But there was no movement.

I walked slowly, dreading my arrival, my mind revolving around one thought: *This is just the kind of morning for bad news—a ghost morning as blank and dead as if the world had melted away.* As my world could melt away when I finally faced Rorke and in all probability read in his proud, withdrawn face the fact that he had chosen this place in which to tell me our marriage was over. I could only think that he must have spent the long, lonely hours on Eryxa facing his problem and realizing that his obsession for Catherine was too great to overcome.

*　　*　　*

I walked along the path, the damp grass whipping my ankles, facing the finale—the emotional ruin from which, at God knew what distant date, I would have to pick myself up and start to live again.

One thing brought a modicum of comfort, like an anesthetic. I was accepting the shock of truth now, so that when I joined Rorke the worst of the experience would be over. I would be able to seem brave. But only seem . . .

The white mist curled round me gently. Nothing else stirred. Near the villa, I called his name.

"Rorke?"

There was no answer. He must have gone inside to wait for me. I walked on toward the broken building, feeling nothing, as empty inside myself as the soft Venetian morning. I called again and stood, listening.

This time I heard his answer, faint and very far away. "Leonie . . ."

I could tell nothing from the disembodied voice and as I reached the ruined building, I had an odd feeling that I was encased in armor that made my limbs feel leaden. I ran my hands down my dress to dry my wet palms; I tried to shake my hair back from my shoulders, but it clung, pasted to my neck. If there had been anyone there, I would seem, in the translucent mist, like some curious wraith risen from the sea, an Undine without a heart, possessing immortality . . . But I had a heart and I was mortal. I was also very exhausted, frightened and urged on, illogically, by despair.

"Rorke?"

"Over here."

I went through the gap where the door had once been. The place struck cold and no one came out of the shadows toward me. I turned, and immediately a hand covered my mouth so that my scream was stillborn. "I've got to talk to you," said a voice.

But it wasn't Rorke's.

I managed with frantic effort to open my mouth against the rough hand and bite the fleshy edge. The man's free arm swept round me and crushed my ribs.

"It is a long time since our first meeting on the steps of Melarper's, isn't it, Leonie?" said Elliot Jerome.

I did what I had done at the Accademia on the night of the Regatta and kicked back, feeling the heel of my shoe catch Elliot's shin. He flinched, but he held onto me.

"That's vicious, and it won't help you. You can scream if you like, but no one will hear you." The hand moved, splaying out to cover my nose as well as my mouth. "You came here expecting to see Rorke, didn't you? Well, you shall. I'll take you to him. But there is plenty of time. The tide won't move him for a long while, so he'll still be there after we have had a talk. You see, he is dead."

My head was reeling; my hands were dragging at the palm clamped over my face. I kicked out again, even more wildly. Rorke was dead . . . A wild tornado of fury swept over me, outstripping shock. So there had been a fight and Elliot had killed Rorke. I would make him pay; I would kill, too. Grief and rage turned me into a virago. Some conjured-up power gave me a swift burst of abnormal strength and I flung myself free and faced Elliot.

The man Charon, gray-green eyes, beard, dark hair, utterly unlike the man who had driven me home through another fog, watched me.

"I don't believe that Rorke is dead."

"Eyes don't deceive and I'll show you—later. I killed him. He is lying face down in the lagoon. Only the dead, the drowned, do that."

"You're lying. Rorke is stronger than you . . . you couldn't—" I broke off and sprang, trying to pass him. But he just reached out and flung me back as if I had no more weight than a puppy.

He didn't take his eyes off me, but his face crumpled and his voice became a whine. "If things could only have been different; if your mother had married me—"

"What has my mother to do with this?"

"A great deal."

There were fallen stones everywhere. I wondered if I could distract his attention while I picked one up and aimed.

"Your mother," he was saying. "I loved her; I would have married her. Instead, she kept telling me that she was afraid of a second marriage because her first had been disastrous. I knew she was just stalling and that she had no intention of marrying me. I was pleasant to have around and then shut the door on when she grew tired of me."

"That's not true. Mother was not like that—" But it no longer mattered. All that was important about the past was that my mother had probably been spared some terrible tragedy that would have occurred had she married Elliot.

And this was *now*; and Rorke was dead. Not even Catherine and the whole tangled business of relationships were of importance any longer. The dark, doubting weeks were over—but a limbo stretched ahead.

"I didn't mean to kill him, Leonie. You must believe that. It wasn't the plan—"

"*What—plan—*?" As I spoke I moved toward the empty frame where a window had once been, and before Elliot had a chance to answer me, I leaned out and screamed a name. "*Filiberto!*"

"He can't hear you, we're too far away. Leonie, please—" He was pleading with me, his voice querulous. "You must let me explain."

Playing for time might do no good. Filiberto wouldn't even wonder at my long absence; he would think that I had met Rorke, that we were together and there was nothing for him to do but wait for us. All the same, there was a faint chance that Filiberto might get out of the boat to stretch his legs and wander across the island. I had to keep Elliot talking.

"Why did . . . *he* . . . hate you?" I found I couldn't say Rorke's name; it had to be an anonymous man who lay dead in the lagoon.

"He knew what I had done."

"What—?"

"The Melarper specification pages about a miniature computer—the marvelous mind machine. Ten thousand pounds I was being paid for that." His tongue rolled softly round the figure, his voice very English, very different from the harsh broken accent he had used on me on the previous occasions in Venice when we had met. "A fortune for something that would quarter the price of the bloody things."

The truth leapt at me. "Industrial espionage!"

"Exactly. It was my first attempt and I brought it off." His laughter was only a sound; his eyes were hard, his mouth tight across small, nicotine-stained teeth. "They thought I hadn't the brain for a well-paid job, that I only was hired in the first place because of Berenice. 'General dogsbody'—that was me! And in the end, I fooled them; I broke their blasted security as easily as snapping a twig." He paused and waited. "Don't you want to know how I did it?"

"No," I said, knowing that he intended to tell me.

"I had been given a miniature camera for the job. It was fixed into the inside of my coat. When high security things were wanted from the safe, two men were sent for them. I was usually one of them. As Berenice's brother, they trusted me. Do you get it? Years of poor pay and high trust! So, when I was approached by a foreign company, I took on the job. One day another man and I went to the vaults and I stumbled against some files—careless of me, wasn't it? While the other poor fool was picking them up from the floor, I found the specifications, lifted my coat and photographed them. Snap . . . snap . . . And then it was over. For that, my girl, I was to get ten thousand beautiful pounds."

"You said—*was.*" As if I cared!

"Was . . . *was.* That's right. You see, I never even handled the money, although I saw it—all of it. That was my moment of hell." He paused. "Well, are you interested?"

"Horribly," I said, and meant it exactly that way.

"I was to pretend to take my holiday, drive to the continent, pick a man up and drive him over the border into Spain, where he had another job to do. We took the route through the High Pyrenees, and he made me stop at a desolate place and took the money from his briefcase. After he had waved the bills at me, he put them back. 'They're paying you all this for two photographs? You haven't really earned it, have you? I'll take half.' We had a fight and I knocked him out. There was a can of petrol in the trunk. I threw it over the car and set fire to it. As I did so, there was a movement in the bushes and I thought someone was watching. I panicked and grabbed the briefcase and ran. When I was safely away, I saw that what had frightened me was a damned rabbit. So, I sat down and pulled myself together. Then I looked into the briefcase. You know what I'd done? *Do* you? I'd snatched my own case from the car; the other was now in ashes—I felt I could smell the money burning from a distance."

"You killed a man in that . . . terrible way . . ."

"And all for nothing. So, I did the only thing I could. I made a dash for Venice and Berenice."

"But witnesses . . . to the burning car . . ."

"In certain parts of the High Pyrenees, there are not witnesses to anything—just one narrow, wild way through mountains. I told Berenice that there'd been a car accident. I said that Rorke was gunning for me on some trumped-up charge which he had taken very cunning care could be laid against me. I told her I was innocent; I swore it solemnly. I said when the car had caught fire I had tried to save some strange man I had picked up hitch-hiking. I told her that was when I decided, since it was my car, to let everyone believe that it was I who died in the blaze. I pleaded with her to hide me."

"And she believed you?"

"Of course. In some ways she's more gullible than a child. Then you and Rorke came to Venice. I could so easily have panicked, but this time, I didn't. Quite suddenly, an idea came to me to remove the threat of Rorke once and for all. Catherine Mallory's visit made it possible. It became easy, then, to plant the idea that Rorke was trying to get rid of you. Your death would end his pursuit of me and would also eliminate him as Berenice's heir. I knew the scheme had to be worked out very carefully and so I made all preparations. First, I bought a boat because, you see, Eryxa was going to be very important. It nearly broke me—that boat and paying the sneaking little bastard, Willy."

"Paying—Willy?"

"To keep watch on you and report every movement you and Rorke made here in Venice."

Willy, listening, peering, gentle—and hellbent on my destruction! I edged forward, but I had about as much chance of escape as an ant under a gardener's heel.

"Willy will die, of course," he said with satisfaction.

Sense and reason left me. I leapt at Elliot, but he caught me and held me in his arms. It was horrible. His breath was soft on my face and he was smiling as if he were my demon lover.

"It's over, Leonie. And when you and Rorke are found here, the verdict will be that he killed you because he had to have Catherine Mallory."

"*Don't say his name. . . . Don't dare say his name . . .*"

"Rorke. Rorke. Rorke." He breathed at me softly and deliberately. "You get the story that will be accepted by the courts, don't you? Rorke had to have Catherine *and* Berenice's fortune; but she would never accept divorce in the family. That's why you had to die—supposedly in an accident. But tongues were wagging in Venice, rumors were rampant about Catherine and Rorke and he knew it. He knew he was trapped—and so he killed himself, too."

Death stood so close that it tapped me on the shoulder, yet I found I could still speak, my fear numbed by a now useless curiosity. "But you saved my life at the Accademia."

"I had to make it seem like that. Someone saw me push you."

And, on the morning when I went to the church near the Zattere, Rorke had been, as he said, just walking the streets waiting for the architect and the surveyor. As for Riomeyla, Willy, of course, had heard about our plans to meet there. The message asking me to meet Rorke in the glade had come from Elliot. To Cèsara, all foreign accents were the same.

"When I dropped my purse at the Accademia, you slipped a note inside."

"I copied Rorke's handwriting rather well, I thought. But I had to be careful with the wording to have it really incriminate him because Rorke isn't the sentimental kind. And, before you could show it to him, Willy got the note back and destroyed it."

"You're supposed to be *dead*," I cried. "So now what? How can you legally establish a claim on Berenice's possessions?"

"Oh, that's easy. I'll explain to her that it must never be known that I'm her brother. I'll be a 'waif' that she has found, like Willy . . . he'll be dead, anyway. I'll take his place in the house and, as she will, by the time she dies, be an old woman without any known relatives—"

"Money!" My voice was loud with bravado. "The oldest reason in the world for crime."

"Oh no, that's where you're wrong. All that I've planned was for one thing—one fundamental thing. *To prevent loneliness.* The loneliness of an aging impoverished man. With money, I can have friendship."

"You mean, you can buy it."

"What does it matter so long as I have it? Drinks, conversation, conviviality."

"Berenice would never have let you be poor."

"Huh! And what about my working for a low-paid clerk's wage while she lived here in luxury? I know how her mind works. 'Dear Elliot! Not very bright, but I've got him a nice, safe little job with Melarper's.' " He spat out the words. "I was her brother, but Rorke was her darling, her child when he became orphaned."

"She has looked after you . . . hidden you here . . ."

"Because she believed my story. 'It must be some terrible

misunderstanding,' she kept telling me. But she was afraid to dig too deep . . . she dreads trouble. And now it's all over. And my final act in this pretty drama is to talk her into realizing that I can't suddenly turn up as her brother. I'll scare her by telling her that she agreed to my presumed death and so dare not now admit that I'm alive."

"You're mad! It can't work."

"No, I'm not mad. I know my sister only too well. She has to love someone, and there will be only me left in the world. It will all be quite legal—Berenice is British and there are no other relatives to fight the will she'll leave in my favor. Nor any twists and turns of foreign law."

"Rorke has probably already told her the truth about you."

"Until we met last night, Rorke had no real proof that I was alive. And since then he has been busy chasing me. He hasn't been near Berenice."

I said in a whisper, "About Catherine . . . and Rorke . . . It wasn't true. *You* started those rumors . . . you . . ."

"Oh, no. Without a foundation to work on, how could I? They met and in the end Rorke would have left you for Catherine. It was only a matter of time, but you know that, don't you?"

"*No.*" I shouted at him in a voice vibrating with rage and fear. My mind boiled so that I couldn't think clearly, but some instinct for my own safety made me turn and race into the second room.

In the corner was a pile of loosened stones. I reached them, picked up the nearest—too large, too heavy for a long flight —and flung it at Elliot as he came toward me. I, who called for Rorke to come and remove a spider from a room but not to kill it, was prepared to kill a man.

For a moment after the rock had left my hand, I went blind. Then I heard Elliot laugh. Unharmed, he strode toward me and took hold of me. I clawed at his fingers which were at my throat; my feet kicked out and back at him. We moved, fought and stumbled over the ragged pile of rocks just under a gap which must have once been a window; I clung to the ledge and dug my feet into the mound of rocks with such force that they tilted and scattered. Elliot gave a shout of pain as the jagged pieces hit his ankles; his grasping hands released their hold on me.

"Filiberto . . ." I screamed through the opening. "Help me . . . *Filiberto.*"

The pile of rocks gave way under me and I lost my balance and fell back into the room. I heard a wild scream that must have been mine.

XXXI

Everything spun around, changed color, became black. I heard the scream again. Mine? Death no longer just tapped me on the shoulder, it put its arm around me. I believe I said, "Damn you in hell, Elliot Jerome!" Or someone said it, and there was no one else there. Then I passed out.

Seconds, minutes, an hour later—time was nothing; time was gone—I opened my eyes. To see what? Myself after death? Myself in essence? Leonie Thorburn stripped bare and facing eternity . . . ?

I saw Rorke.

He was dripping wet, his eyes blazed and his hair was plastered with mud and a green slime.

"You are all right, Leonie?"

It was almost funny; as if we were both alive. As if . . . I began to laugh and then I burst into wild tears because I knew I really was alive. I struggled up and fell back. Rorke's wet arm went round me. "Are you hurt?"

"I don't know . . ." I moved my limbs slowly, one by one, still dazed. "Everything works," I said, "except my brain. I . . ."

"Don't talk. Just try to get up." Rorke helped me off the pile of stones and, legs scraped, sandals torn, a gash at my elbow, I cried with hystericial flippancy, "I'll live! Oh, darling, I'll live!" and began to shake.

"Can you walk as far as the boat and get Filiberto?"

"Filiberto?" I said the name as if I had never heard it before.

Rorke took my face between his hands, and his intensely blue eyes, alive and splendid in his streaming wet face, brought me to my senses.

"Yes. . . . Yes, I'll get Filiberto."

"That's better," he said. "Just walk, darling, or crawl—go any way you like, but yell for him and make certain that he hears you. Don't waste time going all the way to the boat. Shout and make him answer you. Time is precious."

I saw Rorke's eyes glance to the ground. Elliot lay twisted and unmoving.

"Is he dead?"

"No, but he will be unless we get help quickly. And I don't want him dead. Go *on*; find enough strength, Leonie, because I've got to watch him in case he recovers enough to be dangerous again. Desperate men sometimes manage to dredge up sudden abnormal power. Go, darling. Hurry . . . Hurry . . ."

I fled on shaking legs, weaving as if I were drunk. I called loudly, "Filiberto." And then again, "Filiberto."

He leapt onto the bank, sensing the urgency of my voice.

"Come quickly and help. There's an unconscious man—"

"The signore!"

"No, but we must hurry. I can't, because I've hurt my leg, but you go on. Follow this path and you'll come to a villa."

"But first I must help you into the boat."

"I'm all right. Just get on. Delay could be dangerous."

He sprinted ahead of me, a mahogany-colored man, big yet lithe, straw hat perched on the back of his head, following the overgrown path.

The sprint to fetch Filiberto had drained what little energy I had managed to find, and I limped so slowly toward the villa that by the time I reached it, Filiberto was carrying Elliot like a sack over his shoulders. Rorke followed. Halfway to the boat, he took over and Elliot was hoisted, almost affectionately and completely unconscious, over Rorke's wet shoulder, hands flapping, head lolling like a huge, dead bird.

They laid him on the seat in the cabin and I leaned over him, reaching out to feel his pulse.

"He is not dead," Rorke said. "Leave him."

The mist had lifted sufficiently for *Scaramouche* to go full blast. The engine roared and the wash behind the boat was a valley of foam. Filiberto kept giving us backward glances and I guessed that Rorke had told him very little of what had actually happened. There was enough, though, for some whispered tale to run along the grapevine of Venice; something that would be gossiped over, expanded and then forgotten when some other tidbit emerged to command attention.

The overwhelming joy at finding Rorke alive crashed up against the terror in the villa, and the result was a kind of stupor. I sat limply in the small open space aft of the cabin and watched the waters of the lagoon collect the enriching sunlight.

Rorke had found a towel in a locker and had dried himself as best he could. When he came and sat by my side, I put out my hand to him and he drew away. "You'd better not touch me any more until I have cleaned up. The water around Eryxa is foul."

I ignored the warning and laid my hand against his face. "Elliot said you were dead. He said he had left you lying face down in the water."

"He did. But one of the things I learned during my short spell in the East was how to control my breathing. I played dead until he was out of sight—and thank God for the fog which quickly hid us from one another. Then I got to the bank. I thought he had gone to his boat; I never dreamed, until I heard voices—*your* voice—that you were at Eryxa."

"You told Filiberto to fetch me this morning."

"I can't think, even by the wildest stretch of imagination, how he heard me mention your name." He paused, frowned, and added, "But I think I may know the answer. Let me find out." He left me and went and sat by the wheel, talking to Filiberto.

When he returned, Rorke said, "I told him to come and fetch *me* in the morning. He understood that. But it was some time before he left—I suspect he stretched out and had a short sleep. Then, when he was casting off, he heard a voice quite near him in the darkness call to him to bring you out as early as possible in the morning. One foreigner's voice speaking English is very like another's, and Filiberto had no reason to think there was anyone else on the island."

"Elliot."

"You forgot my warning, didn't you? Remember? We agreed that you would ignore any message that supposedly came from me that didn't contain our signal word, 'Sorrel.'"

I gasped. I had completely forgotten the code—had gone off like a fool, the thought of Rorke and Catherine blocking all sense from my mind.

Rorke did not dwell on my stupidity, but seemed absorbed in reviewing his pursuit of Elliot.

"It took me weeks to track him down and, although he was my relative, God help me, I had to."

I said, "You came to Venice knowing that it was Elliot you had to find?"

"No. I was sent for because there had been an attempted break-in at Ferris Caretta. Someone had tried to scale a high fence and failed. He left a torn glove and a fingerprint on a rough piece of wood. There was a faint chance that there was some connection with the theft of the plans at Melarper's—we can't afford to overlook any possibility. I sent to England for fingerprints of certain of Melarper's employees—past and present. The fingerprints in Milan tallied with Elliot's."

"But he was so well disguised—"

"Which made a long search. Berenice, my poor, naïve little aunt, provided the clue. I went to speak to her in her sitting room one day and the secret drawer in her desk was open. She was too slow in closing it and I saw the ring Elliot had always worn. Her agitation did the rest. I searched that drawer twice, and in the end I found an address scribbled on a piece of paper. It could have been nothing important except that in Berenice's special drawer everything is important. I went to the address and it turned out to be a very pleasant house owned by a woman who let rooms. One was to an Englishman. He was mysterious, she said, came and went without ever telling any-one anything about his life. The woman's brother had a water-taxi and he had seen her English lodger on occasion going across the lagoon in a boat he owned. He said he always went in the same direction, past Burano toward Eryxa."

"So, he was in that house for you to arrest?"

"No. He found out that I had been there and he didn't go back for a while. Instead, he camped on Eryxa. Heaven knows why he chose a place where he must have realized from Bere-nice I would be going."

"I . . . know . . . why. And it's horrible. Rorke, he was

waiting for a day when he would find us both there—one at a time—so that he wouldn't have to take us both on at once. He wanted to . . ." The words stuck in my throat as if horror were still a blanket choking me. I veered away from it and said, "Go on. You found Elliot in the end . . ."

"I called at his house last night. His landlady told me a strange thing. She said, 'I went to his room—I thought he was out and I wanted to clean. He hadn't locked the door and he stood there. But he was fair and his eyes were different. Then I knew that when he went out, he wore a disguise.' She told me this because she was worried, she didn't want trouble with the police. I made her describe the man in detail, clothes—and everything. And then I watched the house. That was last evening. I saw him come out and followed him. I had a feeling he might be going to see Berenice. Instead, he disappeared through a doorway of the Villa Vastomoli. Before I could get in and find him, all hell broke loose there, a tremendous fire, with people running in every direction. We came face to face in the chaos in the street outside and then I lost him. I made a dash for the *rio* where his boat was kept, but it was still there. So, on the premise that you don't look for an escaping man right under your nose, I went to the Ca' di Linas and I arrived before Berenice could hide him."

"I don't understand Berenice," I said. "Why didn't she find out the truth about what she believed was your hatred of Elliot?"

"Because she's one of the many people who have a great capacity for shutting out the unpleasant. I had to jolt her into knowing that someone had searched her desk. I wanted her to contact Elliot and warn him. That was why I came back sometimes on Friday nights, unknown to you, and watched from my old room in the wing. Either Elliot called on her when everyone else in the house was in bed, or she went out to meet him. What I didn't know about was that door on the stairs. He could have come into the house at night that way."

"But you didn't believe, did you, that someone was trying to harm me? You thought I was exaggerating and making small near-accidents into big drama. It was he who almost pushed me into the Canal and who tipped over the candelabra at the church, and lured me to Riomeyla. I was at the Villa Vastomoli, too. Elliot was waiting there for me . . . he started the fire. Rorke, it was *for me*! All those incidents were attempts to kill me and to see that you were blamed." I saw the fury darken his face. Rorke swore. Then, he said gently, "Oh, God save me, how blind I've been! I should have protected you better. But that's something you will have to forgive me for. How could I link those odd things that had occurred to you with a man who had loved your mother? I could not possibly believe Elliot was that bad—or that mad!"

"Berenice adored her brother," I said. "It will break her heart."

"Oh, no it won't. People are tougher than you think. While he is in prison she will write to him and I suspect she will always believe that he was bullied by someone into doing what he did and was too loyal to betray the man. She will pity Elliot, and love him. But she will never dare trust him again. So, all her energies will go into the development of Eryxa."

"The ring," I said. "Elliot's ring. You were looking at it the night I found you in Berenice's sitting room."

"It was reported that nothing had been found in the wreckage of the burning car, no watch, no ring. But the one Berenice had, which I recognized, bore no traces of ever having been in a fire."

And the telephone call Cèsara thought had come from Rorke, mentioning Eryxa, had obviously been from Elliot, perhaps telling Berenice that he was going there—telling her some innocent story about Rorke being on his tracks . . . and paving the way for our destruction.

The boat was drawing near Venice. I saw the towers and spires rise out of the last trails of mist like some pale golden palace in the clouds. I remembered the old name, La Serenissima—the Venetians' love-word for their city.

XXXII

 There was still Catherine, but that was something I had no reserve either of energy or courage to contend with at the moment.

Cèsara opened the water-doors to Rorke's imperious ringing and gave a little scream as Elliot was carried into the house.

"*Dio mio!*" She put her gnarled hands to her face. "Who is he? Is he dead?"

Rorke walked past her with his burden over his shoulder, climbed the stairs to the *salone* and put Elliot on the sofa.

"Go and bathe and change," I said.

"Not yet." He went out of the room and I heard him on the telephone.

Cèsara, who had followed us, said, "It is the man who nearly knocked me over last night, rushing out of here. *Euh!*"

"I think you had better go, Cèsara, and keep the Signora

from coming in here for a while. Please—" I urged as she hung about the room, overwhelmed with curiosity, "the Signora . . ."

Rorke returned while I was speaking and waved Cèsara unceremoniously out of the room. "The ambulance is on its way," he said to me, "and also a doctor. I now have to contact Milan and the police."

I looked down at the gray-faced man. "If he dies—"

"He won't. He will find a long companionship in an English prison."

"*What have you done?*" Berenice uttered small, staccato screams from the doorway and rushed to Elliot's side. "You've killed him. You have, haven't you?"

Rorke said tiredly, "I keep telling everyone that he will live."

"But he is badly hurt and it was you. Rorke, he is your uncle . . ."

"Among other things, he tried to kill Leonie and planned that I should take the blame."

"That is outrageous!" She knelt by Elliot's side, and turned and flashed anger at Rorke. "You were hounding him, out of some private hatred of your own."

Rorke went over and lifted her, protesting, to her feet. "Go away and leave us, Berenice. The ambulance is on its way."

"First Willy—and now Elliot."

Rorke asked with interest, "What did you really think he was doing in Venice?"

"Hiding from you! You were going to get him into trouble on some bogus charge."

"Why?"

"He refused to tell me the whole story. He said I loved you and it would be kinder that I didn't know the whole truth."

"And you never tried to find out?"

She said piteously, "I loved you both. Can't you understand,

Rorke? You were my family, just you two. I could never have taken sides—"

"Oh yes, you could have, had you known the full story. Even you, with all your affection for Elliot, would not have condoned murder."

"Dear God in heaven . . ."

"Oh, Berenice." Rorke's voice softened. "Your duck wasn't a swan, my dear, he was a bloody criminal."

I edged to the door and escaped. This was the moment when Rorke must tell her the whole truth, and I could not bear to be present to see Berenice's anguish. I crept into the little telephone room and felt only half alive, hearing the siren warning of the ambulance launch and then footsteps up and down the stairs. I seemed to remain motionless for an interminable time, waiting for someone to come, for someone to shake me into life again.

"Leonie . . ."

Berenice entered and immediately I went to her and put my arms around her. She was trembling. "It is true, then. Those near-accidents were attempts on your life—to implicate Rorke."

"Yes."

She covered her eyes and made a tremendous visible effort to control herself. She seemed to see for the first time that my arms and legs had been bleeding. "You are hurt. My dear, you must put dressings on those cuts, or let Cèsara—"

"They're only scratches. Come and sit down."

She pulled away from me. "Leave me, please."

"Don't be alone—not just yet. Let me stay."

But she wouldn't and I kissed her dry, cold cheek—she was too shocked for tears—and went to find Cèsara.

Cèsara was coming up the staircase, slowly, her face twisted. "You have heard? Signor Willy is dead." Now that he would never come back, she wept for him.

And Berenice, in her new shock, had forgotten to tell me. I thought, as I went limping to the bedroom, how small a place Willy had had in anyone's life—a poor little mortal taking money to spy on me, making it easy for Elliot—my shadow, Charon—to follow me. Yet in the end, Willy was unable to come face to face with what he was doing, and by saving my life at the Villa Vastomoli, lost his own. Cheating, spying, listening at doors, reporting—and atoning.

I entered the bedroom. Rorke was stripping off his clothes and flinging them in a heap in a corner.

"We've got to talk," I said.

He turned from me. "When I'm clean. Though I'm not sure I won't die of some strange disease after lying in that putrid water."

"If you die, I'll die with you."

"Oh, darling, if you did, who would I haunt?" He laughed with a new lightness, like a man shedding a weight. He turned the bath taps full on, and I saw him reach for my bath essence. "I'm going to smell like an English garden."

"Take the lot," I said and heard his glad cry as he sank into the scented water.

I leaned against the door and watched him through the steam. "You'll boil."

He ducked his head under the water. When he came up again, I said, "Catherine—"

He lay still, looking at his toes. "What about her?"

"The note," I said, "that I found in my purse. Elliot wrote it, but you didn't deny that it was yours."

"Until you could produce it, how could I? I had often written notes to Catherine. She was a great singer. In Milan, I sent her flowers and sometimes, after a performance, I joined the crowd in her dressing room. Whatever had once been between us was quite unconnected with those visits. I was paying a tribute to a great artist."

"That's—all?"

"That's all," he said, still not looking at me. "Obsessions have no depth, though they burn fiercely while they last. And when one has felt strongly about someone—even though the fire has gone out—a certain loyalty remains."

"But Catherine didn't feel like that. She still loved—*loves* —you."

He kicked the water. "All right. Do I have to be frank? Catherine doesn't love, she desires. We had one rather brutal scene in Milan, and I thought that would end the matter. But she came here. She wants the things that are hard to get—in this case, impossible. She even came to the house one day. Fortunately, I was in the garden and I marched her out. Then she telephoned me pleading that she was worried about Isobel. I knew she was perfectly capable of looking after her own daughter in her way, and I didn't fall for that, either. But she was weeping, and I can't bear to hear women cry. I said I'd meet her, but on my terms—to advise, if that was really what she wanted."

Rorke seemed to be playing the piano with his toes. I watched fascinated. It was a strange conversation to be having in a steam-filled bathroom with a naked man.

"Willy is dead," I said.

"Perhaps that is the kindest thing that could happen to him."

Pink-faced, bland, padding about the great house . . . *Who are his relatives? . . . He has none . . . Who are his friends? . . . We, who were, in reality, his chosen enemies . . .*

Rorke made a great final splash and heaved himself up. He turned on the cold shower and yelled at me as the water sprayed him. "Get out of that dress. I never want to see it again."

"You could have told me that Catherine no longer mattered."

"Words! Oh, Leonie, didn't my actions speak?"

I shook my head. "Venice was so full of rumors about you. Surely you knew—?"

"I'm here so seldom, and the victim of that kind of tale is always the last to hear anything."

The matter was ended, like a dark path that opens into a light country. I dragged off my dress and threw it into a corner of the room. Then I put on a housecoat and went onto the balcony. Minutes later Rorke came to me and drew me to him. I said: "You're a very private person, darling. There's so much of you that's closed to me."

He knew immediately what I meant. "I failed you so many times, didn't I? I know my faults only too well."

I closed my eyes. Had Catherine, too, reproached him for being withdrawn, for his unknown-ness? Had it intrigued her? It no longer mattered.

He said softly, "Help me, will you? There should be an understanding, in marriage, of the other's needs."

"Perhaps we ask too much—women, I mean—wanting words."

"Then teach me to please you that way."

"I only wanted them when I was uncertain of you. Now, it's different."

"Is it? I wonder. Perhaps love should be talked about on occasions; perhaps words are part of the joy of it. And women know that." He looked up at the sky. "The sun is very bright."

"Shall we go in?"

"And close the shutters."

Afterwards, there would be Berenice to comfort. But, for a while, the morning had to be ours.

About the Author

Anne Maybury is the author of such successful books as *The Minerva Stone, The Moonlit Door, I Am Gabriella, The Terracotta Palace,* and many others. Though she now lives in "a flat above the trees of Kensington Gardens," she was inspired to write atmosphere novels by a 1640 house which she inhabited for many years.